HAMMETT

"Not since Hammett and Chandler has anyone written quite as well as Joe Gores. He will probably be regarded as one of the masters in years to come." —Ross Thomas

"Exciting and skillfully plotted mayhem that swirls with boot-leggers, white slavers and other villains." —*Publishers Weekly*

"An intriguing mixture of fact and fiction in which ex-gumshoe Dashiell Hammett solves a murder in San Francisco, circa 1928." —*Los Angeles Times*

Francis Ford Coppola Presents

HAMMETT

STARRING

Frederic Forrest   Peter Boyle   Marilu Henner

CO-STARRING

Roy Kinnear   Lydia Lei   Elisha Cook   R. G. Armstrong
Richard Bradford   Michael Chow

MUSIC BY

John Barry

PRODUCTION DESIGNERS

Dean Tavoularis   Eugene Lee

EXECUTIVE PRODUCER

Francis Coppola

SCREENPLAY BY

Ross Thomas and Dennis O'Flaherty

ADAPTATION BY

Thomas Pope

BASED ON THE BOOK BY

Joe Gores

PRODUCED BY

Fred Roos, Ronald Colby and Don Guest

DIRECTED BY

Wim Wenders

From Zoetrope Studios

An Orion Pictures/Warner Bros. Release
thru Warner Bros. A Warner Communications Company

HAMMETT

A Novel by
JOE GORES

PERENNIAL LIBRARY
Harper & Row, Publishers
New York, Cambridge, Philadelphia, San Francisco
London, Mexico City, São Paulo, Sydney

For the Op

for the great H.M.

agent provocateur

and for the ladies, bless 'em
Ev
Milli
Pearl
Dorth
flappers all

The lines from the song "Ja-Da" are used by permission: W/M: Bob Carleton. Revised Lyric and Arrangement: Nan Wynn, Ken Lane. Copyright 1918, renewed 1946, Leo Feist Inc., New York, N.Y.

A hardcover edition of this book was published by G. P. Putnam's Sons. It is here reprinted by arrangement.

First PERENNIAL LIBRARY edition published 1982.

ISBN: 0-06-080631-1 (previously SBN: 399-11600-1)

82 83 84 85 10 9 8 7 6 5 4 3 2

A good many things go around in the dark besides Santa Claus.

—HERBERT HOOVER

One

SAMUEL DASHIELL HAMMETT guided Goodie Osborne out of Loew's ornate Warfield through the jostling midweek crowds.

"Oh, Sam!" she exclaimed. "I just *love* Billy Dove!" She had watched the whole of *Yellow Lily* enthusiastically, her baby-blue eyes even wider than usual.

Hammett grinned. He wore a maroon worsted Shaker coat over a wool shirt, an ideal outfit for the chilly San Francisco May evening. "You hungry?"

"I'm always hungry."

She tucked her arm in his. They made quite a pair: Hammett a lean six feet two, Goodie a petite blonde who came just to his shoulder. They crossed the foot of Powell Street, past gripmen and passengers heaving one of the rattly little cable cars around on the turntable for its next trip up Nob Hill.

Hammett's thoughts were a long way from food. He was thinking about a one-time carnival showman named Felix Weber and his run-down rooming house. Weber was the trouble, all right. Weber and his damned Primrose Hotel.

Goodie was looking wistfully across Powell at the all-night Pig'n Whistle when Hammett said, "You ever been to Coffee Dan's?"

"Oh, Sam!" She danced almost sideways for a few quick steps, skipping to keep up with his forgetfully long strides. Her eyes were alight with excitement. "*Could* we?"

"Coffee Dan's it is."

"Do gamblers really hang around there, and does the man on the piano really sing dirty—"

11

"Just hymns," Hammett assured her seriously.

They went uphill on Powell under the marquee of the sprawling all-night Owl Drug Store. Across the street, Bernstein's jammed itself out over the sidewalk like the prow of a fifteenth-century Spanish treasure galleon.

"Can I ride the chute?"

"Ladies don't. Too much stocking shows."

Pure flapper, Goodie Osborne, from her cheap green felt cloche hat to the hem of her green jersey sports skirt a daring half-inch above her knees.

"Then *you* ride the chute," she persisted.

"I'm too old. Pieces tend to fall off when you get—"

"Thirty-three isn't old."

"Thirty-four on Sunday."

Her face fell. "Three days from now? Sam, you didn't tell me! I don't have a present. . . ."

"Just get me a rocking chair."

Hammett turned in at a narrow basement stairwell on the corner of O'Farrell.

"Sedately, sweetheart," he warned the glint in her eyes.

She made a moue with her small soft carmined mouth. "In Coffee Dan's, who'd care?"

But she didn't try to jump on the shiny chute that flanked the stairs to curve down out of sight below street level. Despite her short skirt and bobbed hair and rolled silk stockings, she was still really just a twenty-year-old small-town girl from Crockett who earned twenty-three dollars a week as receptionist for a credit doctor on Market Street.

The din, mingled with smoke and the odors of good food and bad booze, rose around them like cloudy water as they descended the narrow wooden stairs. A rinky-tink piano was bashing out "Ja-Da" in time with a heavy baritone almost lost in the thunder of mallets on wooden tabletops.

> That's a funny little bit of melody—
> It's so soothing and appealing to me,
> It goes Ja-Da, Ja-Da,
> Ja-Da, Ja-Da, Jing, Jing, Jing.

At the foot of the stairs, Goodie unconsciously posed for the room's male eyes as she looked about. How fast they learned to use it, Hammett thought with open delight—even the Goodies of this world.

He leaned down to shout over the babble of voices and rattle of crockery, "They don't seat you at Coffee Dan's, angel."

"*What?*"

The sleeve-gartered, derby-hatted man at the piano, who was champing a dead cigar despite his singing, finished in a shower of tinkling notes. The mallets thundered out applause.

Hammett leaned close. "They don't seat you, you're lucky if someone doesn't knock you down trying to beat you to a—*there's one!*"

He grabbed Goodie's hand and dragged her across the sawdust-strewn floor. They plopped down facing each other across a plank table, a relic of the wooden wharves of pre-quake days. It was deeply carved with intertwined initials, names, dates, and nicknames.

Goodie tried to pick out gamblers and bootleggers from the crowd. There'd sure never been anything like this back in Crockett, a little sugar town under the new Carquinez Strait bridge up by Vallejo.

Or, she thought, looking across the table, anyone like Hammett. She had met him three weeks before, when she'd been moving into the apartment next to his on Post Street after leaving the rooming house on Geary and Gough where she'd lived while attending the St. Francis Technical School for Girls.

The writer had removed his snap-brim gray Wilton; his fine, prematurely gray hair contrasted sharply with his trim black mustache and expressive black brows. His eyes were penetrating and direct and clear. He weighed only one hundred and forty-five pounds, but there was a stubborn whipcord strength to this man.

Goodie leaned across the table to shout, "Is it always like this?"

"Sometimes it's busy," he yelled back.

13

A heavyset, sweating waiter appeared, wearing old-fashioned spats and a food-stained black cutaway over his dingy apron. He balanced a tray of thick white ceramic mugs on one hand with practiced ease. The piano was working on "Where'd You Get Those Eyes?" Two steaming mugs thudded down to slop java across the planks. The waiter beamed fondly at Hammett from an ugly, battered face.

"So?"

"Ham and eggs?" When Goodie nodded, Hammett added, "Looking at us."

"Punk and plaster?"

"You bet."

The waiter picked up his tray and was gone.

"What's punk and plaster?"

"Bread and butter. Con talk. He pulled a little time at Q once because of me."

A wild-haired youth wearing a loud check suit and a pair of the new square-toed sport oxfords came down the chute to whoosh out across the floor. His arms flailed wildly as his feet went out from under him and he lit on the seat of his pants in the sawdust. The mallets thundered their appreciation.

"See what would have happened if you'd come down the chute?"

He shook a Camel partway from his pack, and extended it.

After a quick glance around to see that other women were smoking, Goodie took it. Hammett lit them both up and waved out the match.

"Sam, why don't the police. . . ."

"Coffee Dan's pays plenty for protection."

She watched his hard, angular, mobile countenance as he drifted smoke into the general haze. He could sometimes seem as insubstantial as smoke himself.

"Penny?" she asked almost timidly.

He merely shook his head. The tough-faced waiter arrived with their ham and eggs. Hammett ate halfway through his before losing interest and fishing out another of his cigarettes.

14

"Writing problem I don't know how to solve," he said unexpectedly. He checked his watch. "When Frankie Shaw's tight enough, he gives out lyrics that'd turn 'em toes-up in Crockett."

Goodie raised shapely arms above her head in an uninhibited stretch. She wanted it all. Fun. Excitement. Experience. She said: "What's a Crockett?"

"Where little girls come from."

She leaned toward him and consciously wet her lips. "I know I'm a virgin, but I'm a big girl now, Sam. I know what I—"

"You're a brat." He jerked his head at a far corner of the room. "You were asking about gamblers. Here comes Fingers LeGrand."

"Why do they call him Fingers?"

"Everything but the national anthem on a deck of cards."

LeGrand was a cadaverous man who moved as if on rubber joints; his dolorous face, with dark-rimmed eyes, was thrust forward on a thin stalk of neck. He wore a very natty double-breasted diamond weave and a hand-tailored silk tie with a wicked purple stripe.

"Miss Goodie Owens. Mr. Harrison LeGrand."

"Charmed, ma'am." He turned back to Hammett. "Haven't seen you around lately, Dash."

"I'm on the hog."

He nodded. "When you get healthy, I'm banking a little game at twenty Prescott Court—upstairs above the wop speak."

He bowed slightly and drifted away.

Hammett measured the piano player critically. Shaw looked drunk enough to start his special lyrics. Hammett put down their sixty cents with a dime tip, and stood up. On the wall behind his head was a sign reading:

1000 BEANS
BREAD, BUTTER
AND COFFEE
15¢

15

Goodie began, "Why—"

"I promised your mother I'd look after you."

"You've never met my mother!"

"That's why," said Hammett.

They caught a rattling little dinky up Powell to Sutter, transferred to a Number 1 Owl, and left that to walk down-hill on Hyde.

"Q is San Quentin, isn't it?" said Goodie abruptly. Hammett, busy with his keys as they crossed deserted Post Street, didn't answer. She demanded, "Sam, what *did* you do before you were a writer?"

"Lived in sin with a three-legged dwarf lady who liked to—"

"Sam!"

Like so many postquake buildings, 891 Post had a lobby suggesting a Greek temple rather than an apartment house, with a huge square pane of mirror beside the elevator to reflect the faces and figures of anyone mounting the steps from the foyer. Hammett depressed the elevator lever.

"I was a Pink," he said abruptly. He pulled open the door, slid back the inner iron grillwork. "A sleuth. A detective for the Pinkerton Agency. That waiter was a steward aboard the *Sonoma* when a hundred twenty-five thousand in gold specie disappeared from her strong room *en route* from Sydney back in twenty-one. I turned up most of the gold in a drain-pipe aboard ship, but he got caught changing two missing sovereigns into paper money and did a little trick at Quentin."

The elevator groaned its way toward the third floor. Goodie said thoughtfully, "I can never be sure I'm getting a straight answer out of you."

"You wouldn't know a straight answer if it bit you on the nose."

"Bite me on the nose, Sam."

Her face was cold against his lips, shiny with the night mist. He could feel the heat of her small firm body through her coat.

"I guess you're healthy."

She giggled. "A cold nose only counts with dogs."

"A dog you ain't, lady."

Goodie reached around the doorframe to flip on the light. "Come in for a while, Sam? Please?"

The door opened directly into the living room, with the oversized closet that hid the wall bed just to the left.

Goodie dropped her coat on a sagging easy chair and headed for the kitchen. "Some dago red?"

"Good."

Hammett waited in front of the couch, which was backed up against a davenport table with a Boston fern on it. Goodie came out of the kitchen carrying two water glasses half-filled with cheap Italian wine. The dim light aureoled her blond hair. She handed the writer a glass and sat down on the couch.

"What do private detectives *really* do?"

"Get enough on somebody down at City Hall to keep their clients out of jail."

"You're a cynical man, Sam."

"Not in this town, lady. In this town I'm a realist."

Goodie made a vague gesture. "I don't know anything about politics."

"When I was a kid, my old man—who was a tobacco farmer then—switched from Democrat to Republican to get the cash to run for Congress. Instead, they just about ran him out of St. Mary's County, Maryland, on a rail. Just for changing party affiliation. But *here*. . . ."

He put one foot on the cushion beside her and leaned forward so an elbow rested on the raised knee. He gestured with his free hand, his voice taking on a surprising intensity.

"Every illegal activity in the book is going on right now in San Francisco—gambling, bookmaking, prostitution, protection. And without mob control. Why?" He leaned closer to laugh unpleasantly. "Because your local government got here first. While our Mayor of All the People stumbles around with his eyes shut, City Hall, the cops, and the district

17

attorney's office own this town. And are owned in turn. Any-thing—*anything*—is for sale here. And anybody."

Goodie's small sure voice spoke to the bitterness in his words. "*You* wouldn't be, Sam."

He set down his empty glass. The light had died from his eyes and the slight, almost consumptive flush had faded from his cheeks.

"Don't make book on it. Thanks for the wine, brat."

"Sam. . . . " Her voice was soft. She laid an inviting hand on the couch beside her. Under his steady gaze, she started to blush, but went on, "Sam, you don't have to . . . I mean, you can. . . ."

He tilted up her face with a lean sinewy hand, brushed her lips with his, and straightened up again.

"I could have a wife and a couple of kids stashed some-where."

"I'd . . . take my chances, Sam."

"Long odds, sister."

He stopped outside her door for a moment before using his key on the one directly adjacent. He slapped an open palm lightly against the varnished wood. He wondered just how big a fool he was.

"Too big a one to change now," he muttered aloud.

Two

AS Hammett's typewriter clacked hesitantly in a vain attempt to do something about Felix Weber and the Primrose Hotel, a muscular Morris-Cowley bullnose was going by the dark empty oval of Kezar Stadium. Egan Tokzek leaned closer to the split windshield through which ocean air poked cold fingers. Sand hissed against the bonnet, almost overwhelming the bulbous headlamps as the stolen car ran west toward the ocean along the southern edge of Golden Gate Park.

"Jesus Jesus," the big man chanted, as if making incantations over the terrible bundle on the back seat of the big saloon car. There was sickness in the white rim around his lips and in the frightened flash of his eyes.

Better not until he'd dumped it. But he had to. Better not. Well, Jesus, he *had* to.

He wrestled the big car over to the shoulder. He'd stolen it only half an hour before and still wasn't used to the right-hand drive.

He fumbled in a pocket as the swirling fog paled the wide-spaced gas lamps. He used his coat sleeve to wipe sweat from his forehead, then thumbed open his snuffbox and snorted a generous pinch of the white C-and-M crystal. His face contorted as the potent mixture of cocaine and morphine bit into the tortured flesh of his inner nose.

Tokzek glanced over his shoulder at the bundle on the rear seat. The rough wool of the horse blanket was soaked through. With an angry curse, he stamped on the clutch and rammed the rigid central lever into low. The jerk slammed him back against the seat.

To his right, Ninth Avenue curved into the park. Tokzek imagined a gleam of nickel and polished steel deep in the shadows under the eucalyptus trees.

No. Nothing.

He burst into triumphant laughter. The fog was thinner, a retreating wall. To his right the black empty reaches of the park, to his left scattered dwellings with empty sand between, the dunes tufted with coarse sea grass and spurges and beds of low succulents.

His eyes whipped wide open. Lights had entered the small round rearview mirror.

The police! Who else would be crouched, waiting to pounce, along this lonely stretch of midnight road?

He tried to urge more speed from his car. Once he had lost his pursuer . . . now!

His breath whistled through stained, gappy teeth as Egan

19

Tokzek wrenched over the wheel to send the heavy machine skidding into Thirty-seventh Avenue.

Holy Mother of Christ, there it was, the big foreign car with the steering wheel on the wrong side, just as the phone call had warned.

Chief of Inspectors Daniel J. "Preacher" Laverty eased his black Reo Wolverine from under the shadows and out into Lincoln Way. It was his own car, not a police vehicle; the call had reached him at home with the family.

Far ahead, through a gap in the roiling fog, was a wink of red taillight. The wind hissed sand against his windshield. All the way to the ocean? Or would the car thief sense pursuit and try to lose him in the avenues running south from. . . .

Another gap. Taillight . . . ah! South it was.

"Two can play at that game, laddie," muttered the plain-clothesman through his teeth. He was a grizzled Irishman with a sad, judging face under a thatch of once-carroty hair now ash-gray. His accent was Mission District, more like Canarsie or Baum's Rush a continent away than a stage Mick's brogue. Only his eyes suggested the copper.

Laverty dragged his steering wheel over and switched off the headlights just as the turn was completed. The mist had tattered enough so he could use the lights of the car ahead as a guide. While trying to coax more speed from the Reo, he removed a long-barreled Police Positive from his mackinaw pocket and laid it on the seat against his thigh.

Fear rode with Egan Tokzek like some obscene Siamese twin. The lights had disappeared from his mirror, but he still had the bundle to dispose of.

Why'd the little bitch have to die, anyway? None of the others had, down through the years. He snuffled painfully. They'd survived, been shipped back east, and that had been the end of them, every one.

Until tonight.

Far enough south to dump her? Had to be at least two miles from the park. The houses that had crowded the first two blocks were gone. He eased off the accelerator. Lug it out into the dunes and dump it. Days, maybe weeks before nosy brats would find whatever the animals had left.

There'd be no more after tonight. Coasting, he pulled toward the shoulder of the road. No more. One dead was one too many. He glanced in the mirror as he reached for the brake.

Egan Tokzek screamed. Filling his mirror was a huge black auto, thundering down upon him.

He slammed the car back into gear, tried to shove his foot through the floorboards, and wrenched over the wheel in the vain hope of cutting the other off. Fenders crumpled. He swung away. The pursuer's radiator was at his rear door, creeping up. Sudden lights flooded the mirror to claw at his drug-sensitized eyes. His hands jumped and shook on the wheel as if electricity were pouring through them.

Dan Laverty's hands were rocks. The cars were shoulder to shoulder. He wanted to do it the easy way if he could. One big hand left the wheel to make violent motions as he pulled up on the left of Tokzek's car.

"POLICE!" he bellowed over the roar of powerful engines and the scream of wind. "PULL OVER!"

But Egan Tokzek was already scrabbling for the scarred walnut butt of his huge old Colt .44 rim-fire.

His first shot passed in front of Laverty's windshield. The policeman's teeth gleamed in a wolfish grin. This was what he lived for, this was when he felt really alive.

The gun roared again. This time Laverty's window shattered. He felt the warm trickle of blood down his cheek from a hurled splinter of glass. More shots. Still no hits. And still Laverty's gun remained on the seat beside his thigh.

Then his lips pursed and his eyes narrowed. A hundred yards ahead the road ended at Yorba Street, without going through to Sloat. The grizzled policeman leaned all the way across his seat to rest the fleshy heel of his gun hand on the door frame where Tokzek's bullets had taken out the glass. He pumped two rounds into the side of the bullnose.

21

Tokzek heard the first shot. A terrible fist struck his shoulder with the second. He fought the wheel. Jesus. Left arm dead. And the road was gone. Jesus Jesus!

The Morris-Cowley rammed headlong into the sand, reared like a stallion, slewed, sheered off two stubby pines while losing a fender and a door. The car canted, almost rolled, butted sideways into a sandhill, and rocked to a halt.

Tokzek was hurled across the seat by the impact. He lay still, panting, hearing without comprehension the moaning wind and a liquid trickling noise. His gun was still in his hand; directly ahead gaped escape where the door was gone.

He slithered forward, jackknifed down over the running board. A push with cautious boots, a twist, and he was out.

On his usable elbow and his knees, he crawled a dozen yards to a lip of dune and sought shelter behind a tussock of coarse fringing sea grass. He bit through his lip to keep from crying out; the wet cold had begun worrying at his bullet-torn shoulder. His lips writhed back from his bloodied teeth. His hand took a fresh grip on the smeary pistol butt. He waited.

Dan Laverty was out of his Reo and shielded behind an open door with the .38 in his hand. Nothing moved in the stark glare his headlights laid on the other car. There was no sound except the high whine of escaping steam. The visible, right-hand door was closed. Laverty moved out past his own car.

Now he could smell gasoline from a ruptured tank. One shot fired . . . .

The Lord is my Shepherd, I shall not want.

The Psalm chanted through his mind, unsought but oddly comforting. He doubted if the man could have survived the crash. Why had he risked his life over a mere car theft?

He placed each step deliberately, so no water-filled succulents would crunch underfoot. Through the window he could see that the far door was gone. Three or four more paces, and he could see something blanket-wrapped in back. Even as this registered, his eyes were finding the awkward

22

turtle-trail scrabbled away from the car. Digging knees and elbows, which meant. . . .

He was spinning and dropping into his firing crouch, but Tokzek had already come up from behind the dune a dozen feet away with the big .44 revolver speaking at Laverty's chest. Its voice was merely a series of clicks. The hammer was falling on empty chambers.

With a groan of terror, Tokzek fled into darkness. He made two paces before Dan Laverty shot him in the spine. He went down in a sudden heap, writhing and screaming, as Laverty turned back toward the car and the hastily glimpsed bundle. He shone his flashlight in through the unbroken rear window. Flung up against the glass as if in entreaty was a delicately boned hand. He recoiled savagely.

"Blessed Virgin, protect us," he breathed.

The sprawled girl had been pitched from her blanket shroud by the crash. Even in the flashlight's wavering rays her nude body was the delicate amber of old ivory. The ebony hair was in wild disarray, the Oriental features contorted with pain and fear. On the flesh were the mottled bruises of a systematic beating.

The policeman went around the car to the other rear window. He could feel the black Irish rage rising, threatening to engulf him again like that other time. When his light again flooded the interior, bile choked his throat.

Blood was streaked across the girl's lower belly and on the insides of her thighs. The flesh there was roughened and empurpled.

She could not have been over twelve years old.

Dan Laverty turned from the car with his face terrible and his eyes feverish. He trudged back to Tokzek with a sleep-walker's step.

"Want me to ease your pain, laddie?" he asked in his soft Irish tenor.

Grunting with effort, he drove the toe of his boot up into Tokzek's testicles. Tokzek screamed, bucked with the impact like a man gripped by a naked high-tension line. Again. Again. As if to successive jolts of electric current. Finally, shattered ends of bone severed his spinal column and ended it.

Laverty's eyes gradually unglazed. When he realized what he had done, he crossed himself and vomited a few yards from the corpse.

Three

WITH sudden impatience, Dashiell Hammett thrust aside the December, 1927, issue of *Black Mask*. He needed more complication, another scene showing the Op stirring things up in Poisonville, for the four published novelettes to work as a novel. And with the book version, titled *Red Harvest*, already scheduled for publication, he had to do any insert scenes damned quick.

He began pacing the narrow cramped living room. How about a . . . no, that wouldn't work. But. . . .

Yeah. Maybe a fight scene. Good. Set in a fairgrounds casino or something, out on the edge of town. Now, how to make the Op the catalyst in it. . . .

Hammett paused in his pacing to look at his strap watch. Still time to get out to Steiner Street and catch the Friday night fight card at Winterland. Just opened, he hadn't even seen the inside of the place yet. So why not? He'd be bound to get an idea or two he could work into *Red Harvest* during his stint at the typewriter that night.

As Hammett emerged into Post Street he almost cannoned into Goodie Osborne, just coming home from work. He caught her by the shoulders.

"Can you live without food for a few more hours?"

"Of course, but what—"

"C'mon." He guided her across Post Street without notic-

24

ing the very big man who was supporting the corner building while relighting his cigar stub. "I'm on my way out to Winterland for the fights. Want to come along?"

Goodie's eyes were sparkling. "Try to stop me."

The big man straightened, tossed aside the newly lit stub, and crossed Post toward their apartment building. His name was Victor Atkinson, and he was a man not easily forgotten: six feet three, two hundred and fifteen pounds, huge restless hands, and a bony icebreaker jaw.

With his work cords and heavy wool lumberjack, he looked like a logger down from Seattle—which is what he wanted to look like.

Atkinson went down the narrow dim hallway beside the elevator to tattoo the manager's door with heavy knuckles. The bleary-eyed woman who opened it and squinted up at him wore her hair in a wispy bun and had about half a bun on herself; he could smell the bathtub gin from three feet away.

"Ain't got no rooms." Her face brightened. She added with a simper, "Big boy."

"Yeah." He crowded her back into the littered, close-smelling apartment without seeming to. "I want a line on one of your tenants."

"That's privi . . . " She hiccuped. "Privileged infor—"

"Hammett. Third floor front, far end. Was up there. Nobody home."

"I told you—"

"Habits. Who he sees. What's he do for a living. Things like that."

"I don't—"

"Ain't got all night, lady." His heavily boned face was brutal in its lack of expression. The boredom in his voice somehow had a menace beyond mere bluster. "I gotta catch the fight card out to Winterland."

Hammett and Goodie paused in front of the row Victorians across Steiner from the huge amphitheater.

25

"Quite a place," he commented.

"And so many people." The blond girl was clinging to his arm with excitement.

Winterland was a massive white stucco structure, four stories high, with spotlights to illuminate the American flags on the poles jutting up past the coping of the red-tiled roof. They let themselves be carried across the street to the open doors under the unadorned sidewalk-width marquee.

"Who do you like in the main event, Mr. Hammett?"

The fresh-faced urchin in knickers, drab moleskin coat, and golfing cap was peddling newspapers and boxing magazines. Hammett bought a *Knockout*.

"The Canadian in the fifth or sixth."

"I dunno," said the boy dubiously. "I seen Campbell in a couple a' workouts and he looked awful strong to me."

"So's a bull, but it can't match a mastiff," said Hammett. "The Frenchie'll cut him to pieces."

The ticket windows, flanked by ornamental green shutters, were set under little roofed cottagelike façades at either end of the foyer. Hammett got two in the third row ringside, which cleaned him out except for cigarette money.

"Who was that boy, Sam?"

"Just a kid hangs around on fight nights. He's got an uncle makes book out of the candy store at Fillmore and McAllister."

"Sam, a *candy* store?"

"Next best place to a smokeshop," he said piously.

They surrendered their tickets and passed through a thick-walled archway beside the narrow balcony stairway. Open side doors, guarded by uniformed ticket-takers, let in the noise of the Post Street evening traffic that inched through the sporting crowd. Over the heads of seated fight fans they could see the square canvas ring that had been set up on the main arena floor.

"Sure beats Dreamland," said Hammett.

But not, he thought, as a place for him to stage Poisonville's fights. Until a couple of years before, this had been the

26

site of the Dreamland roller-skating rink where Hammett had seen a lot of Friday-night fights and Tuesday-night wrestling matches. The old echoing wooden building, with its narrow second-floor balconies extending out toward the ring, fitted Poisonville's grubby atmosphere better than this fancy new place. Unless he picked up something usable from the bouts themselves, he'd wasted his evening.

They took their seats on the vast main floor of the arena, which could be flooded to make ice but was now covered with row upon row of wooden folding chairs linked in pairs for easy setting up and removal.

Goodie craned up at the ceiling. It was very high, arched and vaulted, pierced by glassed-over skylights and with a square frame of spotlights centered above the ring. Around three sides were balconies, their steep rows of permanent seating finally lost in the blue haze of tobacco smoke.

"Evening, ma'am."

The man who owned the breathy voice beside her was very fat and wore a heavy tan coat with an astrakhan collar. His shoe-button eyes had an unusual intensity which frightened Goodie. She turned quickly to Hammett.

"Sam. . . ."

But the fat man was leaning past her, not toward her.

"Dash, I hear you tell the kid outside you take Boulanger in the fifth?"

"Not picking a round, two-to-three he does it by the sixth."

"Thirty says you're wrong."

Hammett nodded. The fat man began talking with great animation to a dapper slick-haired individual with a slightly lopsided face and a carnation in his lapel.

Goodie whispered, "Sam, who is he?"

"Another of those gamblers you're so anxious to meet." The spotlights went on above the ring. "Freddy the Glut. I saw him lose a grand to Benny the Gent in Bones Remmer's Menlo Club on Eddy Street one night, and walk away laughing. Fellow with him is Carnation Willie. Local lads, not in a class with Eddy Sahati or the Rothsteins."

27

The announcer interrupted with the information that Al Flores was going to engage in "four rounds of boxing" with Dancing Frankie Whitehead in the curtain-raiser.

"Keep your eye on the Portagee," said Hammett.

But Dancing Frankie opened fast: Halfway into the round he put the Portuguese boy on the canvas for a six count with a roundhouse right that wasn't fooling. Goodie was on her feet, shouting. She sat down shamefaced when Hammett tugged at her coat sleeve.

"I'm sorry, Sam, I just got so excited—"

"Heck, yell all you want, kid. I just think you ought to know you're backing the wrong boy. Whitehead won't last."

"I'll bet you supper he wins," said Goodie recklessly.

In the second round, Flores put the badly winded Dancing Frankie down with a flurry of punches that kept him down.

"That takes care of supper," said Hammett.

"Quit smirking!" exclaimed Goodie furiously.

The second prelim was a slam-bang affair between KO Eddie Roberts and a colored lad named Battling Barnes, who took the decision. In the third preliminary bout, Roundhouse Revani TKO'd his Filipino opponent after flooring him in the second, closing his eye in the third, and using his gut as a workout bag in the fourth. Freddy the Glut spoke around Goodie again.

"I've got twenty at four-to-seven that says the semifinal is a draw."

Goodie was sure he was offering Hammett a bet of some kind, and was excited. "Go ahead, Sam," she urged. "Take him up on it."

"You're faded," said Hammett to the gambler.

He spent the six-round roommate act that followed explaining to Goodie the difference between a jab, an uppercut, and a cross; why working on an opponent's gut to take away his legs and wind was better than head-hunting; and how a fighter could win by opening an opponent's eyebrow with his glove-laces if the ref was lax.

"Of course nothing like that's going on here," he said. "This is just a dancing lesson."

28

The referee called it a draw. Hammett returned to the obese gambler.

"Freddy, want to double your dough on the Pride of Glen Park?"

Freddy raised an eloquent shoulder under the rich coat. He had it draped around his shoulders like a cape.

Hammett grinned at Goodie. "See what you got me into?"

"I don't understand. I don't understand any of this."

"We had a twenty-buck bet, two-to-three odds. Twenty to me if I won, thirty to him if I lost. Now that's doubled. If I lose I owe him forty—and I don't have forty. Plus, I already owe him thirty-five from the last fight."

"I'm sorry, Sam." Her voice was contrite. "I thought—"

He chuckled. "Don't worry, kiddo. I don't have the thirty-five, either."

By the end of the first round, it was apparent that Campbell was outclassed. By the end of the second, Goodie had become aware of stamping feet and a growing chorus of boos, shouts, and catcalls.

"Hey, Frenchie, why don't you kiss 'im?"

"Me an' my old lady tangle more than that!"

Hammett, watching Boulanger left-jab Campbell across the ring with light stinging blows without real beef behind them, had a calculating expression on his face.

"He's keeping Campbell awake, trying to choose his round. He must have some money down himself. It'll work for *Red Harvest*, right enough."

Goodie looked at him curiously, but he ignored her. Boulanger, dark, lean, intense, a good fighter, trying desperately to keep Campbell from tripping over his own shoelaces and KOing himself on a ring-post. And Campbell, blond, slow, stupid in the ring, throwing roundhouses at whatever got between him and the light. Good.

Only in the novel, the Boulanger character wouldn't be trying to pick his round—he'd be trying to throw the fight. And . . . sure, the Op wouldn't let him. Why? Some criminal charge from back east that the Op had found out about, and. . . .

29

Boulanger was boring in. The catcalls had died under the thud of leather on flesh. Sweat flew as the Canadian pummeled away.

"He'll put him away in the next round," said Hammett.

The fifth started with Boulanger going around the bewildered local fighter, jabbing him at will like a cooper nailing up a barrel. Whenever Campbell would clinch, Boulanger would go inside, working on his belly with solid blows and on his jaw with sizzling uppercuts. The ref stopped it after the round's fourth knockdown.

The lights came up. The ref raised the Canadian's right hand above his head in the victory signal. And just *here*, Hammett thought, would come the flash of silver as a black-handled knife would be thrown from one of the balconies to kill the fighter in his moment of victory.

Freddy the Glut handed Hammett a twenty and a five. "I think our local boy should find some other line of work."

"Unless he wants to end up in Napa cutting out paper dolls."

The lean writer and the petite blonde inched their way toward the Post Street exit. Tonight's stint at the typewriter would just about wrap up *Red Harvest*.

"What was that about cutting out paper dolls in Napa, Sam?"

"A few more beatings like that, and Campbell will be ready for a room in the state hospital for the insane at Napa. Let's go down to Fillmore Street and take on a stack of wheats and bacon."

"Oh, yes! I'm famished!"

"On you. Remember?"

Goodie pouted her way out of the amphitheater.

The very big man wearing the checked lumberjack was bent over to smear out his cigar butt against the sole of one new elk-hide workshoe as they passed him. He came erect against the frame of a deep-set double door to Post Street through which the last of fight fans were exiting. The bare

30

low-wattage bulb caged in the archway over his head cast harsh shadows down across his features.

Atkinson unwrapped a fresh cigar, spat the end in the gutter, and lit up. He seemed to be watching for someone. Overhead, the wet-laden ocean wind creaked the ornamental iron fire escape held in place by pulley and counterweight.

His eyes gleamed. The boy who had sold Hammett the *Knockout* had emerged from the entrance. Atkinson caught his arm in an ungentle grip. The boy's face contorted. The big man asked questions. At the end of them, the boy palmed half a dollar and went his way, whistling.

Atkinson grinned as he departed himself, in the direction of the all-night lunchroom on Fillmore Street where he'd be able to pick up his surveillance again.

Four

IT was Saturday morning. Hammett faked a leap of terror when the grinning youth behind the wheel of the Fialer Limo hire-car goosed him with the electric horn. Still chuckling, Hammett entered the long narrow red brick building at 880 Post that housed Dorris Auto Repair. He unhooked the receiver of the block's only public pay phone, dropped his nickel, and gave the operator a TUxedo exchange number.

An accented voice said, "Verain's Smoke Shop. Make me blink."

"Henri? Dash."

"But of course it is. Who do you like today?"

"Louisville Lou in the second; Easter Stockings in the fifth; Khublai Khan in the seventh."

"All on the nose?"

31

"Where else? And don't tell me."

One of them had better come home, Hammett thought as he hung up, or he wouldn't be paying the rent on the first. No word from Cap Shaw at *Black Mask* about the two Op stories he had sandwiched between segments of *The Dain Curse* for eating money. Unless he could rustle up a few bucks to sit in on one of Fingers' games, he'd have to depend on the monthly disability check from the government, which was about enough to keep him in cigarettes. . . .

"Hey, Hammett."

"How's it going, Lou?"

Lou Dorris fluttered a grease-blackened hand, palm-down.

"The kid's got a fever driving my wife nuts, at least it keeps her from driving me nuts, listen, you oughtta know. Big bird was around early this morning asking what time you're usually in to place your bet, where you go to breakfast, like that."

"What else you have on him?" Sounded like a cop, but Hammett couldn't think why either public or private tin would be stepping on his shadow.

"Big as a moose and dressed in work clothes, a wool lumberjack, heavy work shoes—"

"The shoes new?"

Dorris momentarily checked his spate of words for thought. "As a matter of fact, yeah." Behind him, a wrench clattered on the grease-stained concrete under the Minerva Landaulet up on blocks at the rear of the garage. "Anyway, thought I'd better tell you, an' lissen, who d'ya like in the fourth at Aurora?"

"Thrace, but not well enough to put any money down."

"I figgered having that wop kid up might make the difference—"

"Not at Aurora on a muddy track."

"Yeah, sure not."

Hammett walked rapidly in-town on Post, hands thrust into the pockets of his mackinaw; the temperature was still below sixty, and the wind nipped here in the open street. It would be another three hours before the high fog burned away. His eyes were unconsciously busy on pedestrians and autos, a habit ingrained from the Pinkerton years. Textures. Details. Knuckles and ears and the napes of necks.

Who? And why? Tricky enough to buy shoes for the role, but not tricky enough to remember that *new* shoes gave him away. Hammett's detective years were far behind, his gambling debts were fairly current, and he wasn't playing around with anybody's wife, so why. . . .

Maybe Goodie had a secret husband stashed away up in Crockett. A smile flickered across his lean features as he waved to the counter girl at Russell's Cake and Pie Shop. Goodie. Last night he'd come damned close to not walking away from that crazy little kid. Life got complicated: Somehow the easy time to tell her about Josie and the girls had passed.

At the short-order grill just inside the front window of the Fern Café, a bulky woman with white hair and several chins was frying eggs hard enough to bend the fork. The metal hood over the grill was brown with the grease of dead breakfasts.

Hammett shot a casually searching look around as he slid onto a wooden-backed swivel stool halfway down the counter. A couple of other solitary regulars, nobody at the three tables in the rear, although a half-smoked stogie smoldered in the ashtray on one of them.

"The usual, Moms."

Vile black cigar. . . .

Hell with it. But he realized, with a little shock of recognition, that his wariness about the big man in the plaid wool lumberjack and too-new work shoes was mildly pleasurable.

Moms slammed down the morning's newspaper on the linoleum countertop by Hammett's elbow, slid a cup of coffee at him, and snagged an ashtray for his chain-smoked butts.

"Why are you too damned cheap to buy a newspaper, Hammett?"

"That would deprive me of your warmth, your cheery smile. . . ."

She cursed him while waddling back to the grill. He

checked the Friday morning city news. A Broadway Street tunnel under Russian Hill had been proposed at a million-and-a-half price tag. The Millionaire Kid, with whom he'd played lowball in North Beach a few times, had been indicted as a fence by the grand jury. Parnassus Heights' residents were charging bribery in the attempt to rezone part of Judah Street commercial. An unidentified man in a stolen car had been killed by Chief of Inspectors Daniel J. Laverty in a running gun battle south of Golden Gate Park. . . .

Plaid movement danced in the polished metal front of the pie case beyond the counter. Something hard and blunt was rammed into the small of Hammett's back. The cigar! The goddamned cigar!

"Hands on the table, bo!" barked the heavy remembered voice. "Or this thing goes off."

"Oh." Hammett turned casually. "Hi, Vic."

Victor Atkinson took his forefinger out of the writer's back.

"Hell. I knew that damned cigar would tip you."

Atkinson had come directly to the Fern Café from Dorris' garage because he'd wanted to catch Hammett unaware, look him over. But he'd left his cigar smoldering in the ashtray while he'd hidden himself in the rest room.

"Not soon enough," said Hammett.

"Well, it's been close to seven years, Dash." He led the way back to his table. The two men measured each other as they sat down. "I quit the Pinks just before the Arbuckle investigation."

Hammett made a face. "What the newspapers did to that poor bastard."

They'd had some times together, Hammett thought. At Pinkerton's, Vic had always led the bust-in parties on the theory that anything thrown at that jaw of his would just bounce off.

"I heard you got into the writing game after you quit sleuthing."

"Doing ad copy for old man Samuels," Hammett admitted.

34

"Yeah. Jeweler on Market down near Fifth."

"How about you, Vic?" He asked it casually, pretty sure it was a cop asking him questions. Atkinson confirmed it.

"I bounced around a little, ended up starting my own agency in Los Angeles. The movie studios generate plenty of our kind of business—"

"*Your* kind. I'm out of the game."

"Maybe a good thing, the way I walked up behind you—"

"On your brand-new shoes."

When the implications sank in, Atkinson's laughter cannonballed cigar ash halfway across the table. "If you had a goddamn phone, I wouldn't have to gumshoe around."

"You've got knuckles."

"And a proposition for you."

"Sleuthing?" Hammett extracted his last cigarette and crumpled the empty pack. "Not interested, Vic."

"Sure not." Atkinson hitched his chair closer. "You remember a month, six weeks ago, the Bay Area collector of Internal Revenue made a couple of wisecracks at the Rotary Club about a local madam deducting her protection payoffs as a legitimate business expense?"

"Sure. And the papers made it an open secret that the madam was Molly Farr, just down the street from my apartment. The guy also said that quite a few of San Francisco's finest were going to start paying income tax as a result." Hammett lifted a lip in a faint sneer. "It sold a lot of newspapers, but I didn't see any mass resignations down at City Hall as a result of it. I imagine. . ." He snapped his fingers and pointed at Atkinson across the table. "Don't tell me. A reform committee."

"That's it. A citizens' group was formed to get financial pledges lined up so an outside investigator could be hired."

Hammett looked up sharply. "Meaning you?"

"Maybe. The committee meets Monday night to hear my proposals. If they like them. . . ." He shrugged. "Dan Laverty put my name in, we worked together a couple of times when I was a Pink and he was a detective-sergeant. He wants the department cleaned up—"

"Throw out the chief with the dirty bathwater and take over his job?"

"Something like that. But the Preacher's as straight as they come."

"Good luck with it, Vic." Hammett tore cellophane from a new pack of Camels. "But I don't see you getting anywhere no matter *who* recommends you."

"That's why I want you in this with me, Dash. I'll have damned good people coming up from LA, but only one of them knows the city. And none of them can analyze a situation the way you can."

Hammett shook his head with genuine regret. "It would be like old times, but it's no dice. Even if I *was* interested, your reform committee's going to need the mayor and the DA and the chief of police behind them, and where's their leverage? McKenna knows damned well the people of this burg elected him mayor so they'd have it wide open, and wide open is what he gives 'em. You'd better just hope that something happens before Monday night to give the reform committee more ammunition than they have right now."

"Something might," said Atkinson with stubborn optimism.

Five

THREE BOYS FOUND
IN VICE RESORT;
MOLLY FARR JAILED

Police Trail Scions of S.F. Families
to Hyde Street House After
Mothers Request Action

In a vice raid conducted at the request of mothers who suspected all was not right with their sons, police early yesterday struck to protect the morals of boys of high school age.

They trailed a group of three boys—members of well-known families—to the house of prostitution operated by the notorious Molly Farr at 555 Hyde Street. There, while scantily attired men and girls scurried in confusion, the raiders confronted the white-faced youngsters—they ranged in age from 15 to 17—and rounded up and jailed the inmates of the lavishly furnished two-story vice-den.

Their parents, Captain of Inspectors Daniel J. Laverty said, requested that their names not be released to

Continued on Page 5, Col. 3

Hammett threw aside the bloated Sunday paper to sit up. He swung his feet over the edge of the bed and got his head into his hands in one practiced motion. Ohh-h-h. He explored the inside of his mouth with the dead mouse someone had given him in place of a tongue.

Goddamn all birthdays.

He tottered, bare-footed and bare-butted, into the bathroom. At least, this morning, he was thirty-four. He'd beat Christ.

Just after he'd tottered back into the living room, a terrible agony shot through his head.

The doorbell.

He found his bathrobe wadded under the bed and went down the hall pulling it on. He opened the front door with his head militarily erect so he wouldn't upchuck.

"Wipe off that silly smile," he said. "Good men are dying all around you."

Goodie looked radiant and fresh in street clothes, a hat shading her dancing golden ringlets.

"I've just come back from church. *Some* people stop after their second drink. You've got a phone call."

Hammett padded after her on bare feet to pick up the receiver from her davenport table.

37

"*Sweet Christ!*" screamed Hammett. "*Whisper,* man, whisper."

"Okay," said Vic Atkinson in a softer voice. "You see in the newspapers about the raid on Molly Farr's?"

"I saw."

"It's the wedge we need! This, on top of all the publicity she got out of that tax guy's remark, makes her damned vulnerable. We lean on Molly, she tells us who pays who and why, in return for a promise of immunity. Then we—"

"Not *we,* goddammit! I told you. . . . Besides, you haven't even been hired yet."

"Molly doesn't know that. Her place. Half an hour. From the way you sound, it'll take you that long to get there."

Every Sunday morning Molly Farr, dressed to somber perfection, made the two-block pilgrimage to the weathered old stone building at 611 O'Farrell Street. She figured she owed it. Eleven years before, Molly—along with three hundred other ladies of the night—had descended on this same Central Methodist Church at her gaudiest, her cheap scent reeking and her ostrich plumes nodding, to protest the campaign against vice being waged by Reverend Pastor Paul Smith. She had been twenty-three at the time.

Reverend Smith had persisted in his crusade. The Barbary Coast had been shut down, the parlor houses, cribs, brothels, and bagnios had disappeared for the moment, and a thousand prostitutes had been thrown out of work. Molly had gone south still a whore; but she returned a few years later to become a madam.

Thus, every Sunday she went in somber splendor to the Central Methodist services, because here she had first been shown the true way: Become a businesswoman because there is no security in being a whore. Unfortunately, she'd never been able to thank Reverend Smith in person; during the intervening years he had renounced the cloth to become a used car salesman.

Molly, perspiring slightly from the walk, let herself into 555 Hyde Street, which had been discreetly shuttered since

38

the Friday-night raid. She was a handsome woman, sternly beautiful rather than pretty: a face with the clarity of a cameo.

She passed under the foyer's crystal chandelier, noted that the elevator brass needed polishing, and went upstairs to her small private landing, which overlooked the front entrance. She stopped. The door of her apartment was a foot open and two tall men were talking with her maid in the crowded sitting room.

One of them was very lean, the other built like a bull. Her maid, Crystal Tam, was a tiny Chinese girl who came barely to their chests. She had a breathtakingly lovely face framed in lustrous blue-black hair that flowed down across her shoulders to the middle of her back.

To break it up, Molly said, "Sorry, gents, we're closed."

"Your maid was just telling us," said the heavyset one. "But we were asking her. . . ."

Molly collapsed in the big flowered wing chair that dominated the cluttered room. She set aside her wide-bordered silk parasol, and fanned herself with one hand.

"Get me a beer, that's a darling."

"Of course, Miss Farr."

Crystal wore a fancifully brocaded silk kimono; her arms were crossed on her breast so she could thrust her hands into the opposing scoop sleeves. Her steps were mincing, as if her feet had been bound in infancy. She was only fifteen, but was already much more than a maid to Molly. She was *confidante,* even adviser. It was Crystal who had suggested taking off the police graft as a business expense. It had been a swell idea until that stupid bastard with Internal Revenue had made the joke about it at the Rotary luncheon.

"All right, gents, what were you asking her?"

"How to cure a ten-year-old dog," said Atkinson.

"What'd she tell you?"

"To pee in a shallow dish and dip my thing in it before it got cold. Three times a day for a week."

Molly threw back her head and laughed, a full-bodied laugh that engaged her whole frankly voluptuous body. "If you really tried to cure a dose that way, you'd be in trouble."

39

Crystal returned with a big German mug with a hinged pewter lid. She set it on the red lacquer telephone stand at Molly's elbow. Molly drank deeply.

"*I'm* not in trouble," the bull-like one told her. "*You* are."

Molly wiped away her foam mustache and waited until Crystal had departed.

"You'd better drift, boys, before I use the telephone."

"That's what we're interested in, Molly. I'm Victor Atkinson, this is my associate Dashiell Hammett. We want to know just who you *do* call when you get into trouble. Also, who you pay. . . ."

Molly laughed again. "You must be out of your mind."

"Not really." Hammett spoke for the first time. "The DA's got you where your pants hang loose."

Molly allowed herself a slight sneer. "Keeping a Disorderly House?" She shook her head. "C'mon, boys, what's that— even if he could make it stick? A fine and—"

"How about Contributing to the Delinquency of a Minor?" said Hammett. "Three felony counts?"

Contributing. Jesus! That carried a heavy jolt! Molly buried her nose in her tankard again, then said, "One of those kids, I knew his goddamn *grand*father, can you believe that? I was just a kid myself then, in the old Parisian Mansion on Commercial Street. . . ."

"Quit stalling, Molly." Atkinson loomed over her chair. "We need some names. Who do you juice in the police department? How are the payoffs made? You play ball with us, Molly, and—"

"Sorry, boys. Like I told you, we're closed today."

"We'll be around," said Atkinson. Hammett followed him to the door, then paused and tipped his hat.

"Charmed," said the lean writer.

The door had barely closed behind them when the phone rang. She swung open the phone stand and removed the receiver from the hooks. "This is Molly."

"This is your old sweetheart," said Boyd Mulligan's nasal tones.

40

"Yeah? Which one?"

"How many sweethearts you got, for Chrissake?"

"Oh, *Boyd* darling. I haven't heard your voice in so long I didn't recognize it."

After she had opened the house five years before, Boyd Mulligan had been around twice a week to get a piece of Molly as well as of the action. He was a mean son of a bitch with a woman, so she'd been happy when he'd finally started just sending a messenger for the Mulligan Bros. Bailbond Company share.

"I've been busy, but I've been keeping tabs on you just the same. Tommy Dunne called to say a gumshoes out of LA named Victor Atkinson was around to your place."

"I was just going to call you about that."

"What did they want?"

"Names. Figures. . . ."

"Just what I thought." There were vicious undertones in the nasal voice. "I've been sitting here thinking, what if Molly decides to spill her guts to these birds? What if they promise she can cop a plea or get immunity if she does? What if—"

"Don't lean on me, Boydie-baby!" she snapped. "I've had Chicago amnesia in the past, and will again if it comes to that. But *don't lean on me*."

"Aw, look, sweetheart, I didn't mean it that way. I tell you what, tomorrow morning you go see Brass Mouth Epstein. Tell him we're picking up his fee and that we don't want you to be tried for Contributing. How he gets you off is his concern."

"What if he says disappear?"

"Then disappear—only make sure *we* know where you are. And I'll tell you what: If you have to dump that thousand bucks bail you put up Friday night, we'll swallow it."

She found warmth for her voice. "What can I say except thanks?"

"As long as that's *all* you say, sweetheart." He gave his nasal chuckle. "You let me know what Epstein says tomorrow, okay? I'll be at the shop."

After she'd hung up, Molly sat staring at the thick Oriental

41

carpet. Why was Mulligan paying for Phineas Epstein as her attorney? He would cost plenty and was dead straight besides. He was at no man's command. That meant DA Matt Brady *did* plan to forget his friends and go for Contributing. Fifteen goddamn years, maybe—while on the strength of it Brady leapfrogged into the mayor's seat.

Crystal came into the room lugging her cardboard suitcase. It looked heavy. She had on street clothes and a coat.

"Hey! Where the hell are you—"

"I must leave now, Miss Farr."

"Those detectives? They can't—"

"Not them." Despair glinted in the tilted eyes. "Just . . ."

"For God's sake, kid, what is it? You look like you've seen a ghost."

"I have seen my death." She moved a hand to indicate her newspaper, crumpled open to the news page.

"Is it the trouble from back east?"

"Yes."

Molly wished she knew what the trouble back east really was. "Here? In San Francisco?"

The girl did not respond.

"Okay, kid," said Molly, "tomorrow you go see Brass Mouth Epstein with me. If he tells you to disappear, we'll drop out of sight together where *no*body'll find us. Now, you go in and pack Molly's things like a good girl, just in case."

Crystal hesitated, then disappeared to the rear of the apartment with her cheap cardboard suitcase and a fatalistic shrug.

Molly paced up and down. Hell, she was in as much trouble as her goddamn maid. She knew where the goddamn bodies were buried. If some of them were dug up because of her arrest, the Mulligans would want another in their place.

Hers.

Six

HAMMETT entered his apartment carrying the Tuesday morning *Chronicle*, his meager mail, and a long loaf of French bread. At the far end of the hall he gave the loaf a left-handed toss around the doorframe into the tiny kitchen. He stopped dead at sight of the massive figure sprawled in the living room's only upholstered chair.

"You've got a lousy lock, Hammett." Atkinson made bluish swirls of smoke with his stogie. "Ought to get a rim latch with a dead bolt. I blew this one open with a breath."

Hammett dropped his newspaper and mail on the unmade wall bed and sat down.

"It's not your breath, it's those goddamn cigars."

Atkinson lit another of the nickel monstrosities from the ruins of the old. "You thought over my proposition any more since we had all that good clean fun shoving Molly around the other day?"

"Still not interested. How'd it go with the reform committee last night?"

"I'm hired. Given the green light by His Honor personally."

Hammett's voice showed surprise. "Brendan Brian McKenna himself? What the hell was he doing there? Slumming?"

"Acting as chairman. He showed up unexpectedly, and they—"

Hammett slapped his hands together and crowed, "They form a committee to clean up San Francisco, and as chairman they take the man who's been running it as an open town for sixteen years." He lit a cigarette, and feathered smoke through distended nostrils. "He'll hamstring you, son."

"Maybe. But I was damned careful to get that personal secretary of his, Owen Lynch, to spell out what I was being hired to do—which I'll grant you ain't exactly a moral cru-

43

sade. *Atkinson Investigations* is to probe alleged graft within the police department. Period. But within that framework, no limitations. Lynch is damned enthusiastic."

Hammett was thoughtful. "Your charter makes sense."

"Yeah. And McKenna suggested my closing report go to the grand jury, not just the committee. In case there might be criminal indictments."

Hammett paced the narrow littered room with quick, light strides as if it were a cage. When he wasn't drinking, like now, he found the litter distasteful.

"Too damned *much* sense to be coming from McKenna."

"You don't really think he's behind the police department corruption, do you, Dash?"

"'Plain Bren McKenna from the Mission,'" mused Hammett. "That's what he called himself when he ran against 'Pinhead' McCarthy in 1913. He makes five hundred a month as mayor, and must spend twice that a month on hootch and harlots in that Caucasian geisha house he maintains for visiting politicos out on Sanchez and Twentieth. I guess it's worth it to him to wear Eskimo parkas and Indian feather bonnets and motormen's caps. Corrupt?" He shook his head. "But when it comes to actually running this burg— to handling or delegating power—he can't find his backside with both hands. If you want to know who's behind police corruption in San Francisco, just look a block out Kearny Street from the Hall of Justice."

"Mulligan Bros. Bailbonds. But how the hell do you prove it?"

Hammett chuckled. "I met old Farrell Mulligan a couple of times before he died." His voice took on a nasal quality and a brogue. "'Son, when they crap in this town, they wipe with Mulligan paper.' Which isn't much in the way of proof. When he went, his kid brother Griff took over. Now I hear that Griff just counts the take while Farrell's pup Boyd does the heavy work."

"Well, I ain't got a mandate to go after the Mulligans. Vice, gambling, and the rackets *only* as they relate to police department graft. All I gotta do is find somebody who'll sing. Somebody like Molly who—"

44

"Yeah, look how *she* cooperated."

Atkinson grinned sourly. "Preacher Laverty and Lynch believe the committee's already put the fear of God into the mayor and the DA and the police. Molly may not be singing yet, but they sure closed her up. . . ."

"Vic, the only reason there was a raid at all is that three high school kids went there to celebrate somebody's sixteenth birthday. If the ma of one of them hadn't heard them setting it up by phone, and if her husband hadn't happened to know the DA personally, Brady wouldn't have pushed the cops into making a raid."

"This ain't ever gonna make the papers, but the mother who overheard the kids on the phone was Evelyn Brewster."

"The shipping Brewsters?"

"That's her. *And* she's the prime mover on the reform committee."

Hammett sat down on the bed again, chuckling. "No wonder McKenna showed up at that meeting last night. I'll bet old lady Brewster's the one who pushed Brady into arraigning Molly and all her girls—even that Chinese maid—in municipal court yesterday."

"Yeah. Goddammit." Atkinson slammed a suddenly angry fist on the arm of his chair, hard enough so an inch of gray ash rolled down the front of his shirt. "They came down on Molly at just the wrong goddamn time. If I could have kept working on her—"

"You mean you can't anymore?"

"Don't you ever read them newspapers you carry around? Neither Molly nor the maid showed up for their arraignment." He brightened. "Maybe I can work a deal with Epstein, her attorney, to get at Molly. She talks to me instead of the DA—"

"If Molly was your client, would *you* turn her up? With the Mulligans owning half the cops in town as a private police force?"

"I'd furnish her protection," said Atkinson airily.

"Sure you would."

The big man was on his feet. "Anyway, my people will be in from LA the first of the week. I ain't much of a detective if

45

I can't turn up Molly before then. I told the reform committee I was going back down south today, but I think I'll stick around for a day and try to dig her out. Maybe make a round of the speaks tonight, see what I can get on which cops are being paid off. Want a pub-crawl?"

"I said to count me out, Vic."

Hammett brushed Vic's cigar ash off the frayed tasseling of the venerable Coxwell he had inherited with the apartment, and sat down. He had a whole night at the typewriter ahead of him. He stood up again, went to stare out between dingy lace curtains at the stucco fascia across Post Street.

Dammit, Vic was going at it all wrong. Advertising his presence by going around to the speaks when he should be waiting until he had taps on the Mulligan Bros. phones, and on the bookie joints, speaks and taxi houses with the solidest protection. Because the better the protection, the closer to the pipeline through which money moved up and favors moved down. . . .

Hell with that. He hadn't even checked the mail he'd grabbed off the hall table on the first floor. He ought to be getting the check from Cap Shaw for those two stories. . . .

Hammett felt the blood rush to his face. He was staring down, not at a check, but at a 9 x 12 manila envelope from *Black Mask* that could only contain his Continental Op stories. Rejected. He sat down on the wooden chair he used as a typing chair, and held the stories loosely in his lap.

Rejected! The goddamn magazine hadn't rejected anything of his in four years, not since. . . .

Phrases jumped out at him from the cover letter: *not up to usual standard . . . Op says in "The Gutting of Couffignal" that he's a detective because he enjoys the work . . . not sure you enjoyed writing . . . stories . . . much as you looked forward to cashing check. . . .*

He wanted to be sore. He wanted to boil with rage, tear up the letter, go off on a toot. But. . . .

But goddammit, Cap was right. He was on his feet again, pacing again, still holding the manuscripts in his hand. Finally he dropped them aside, unnoticed. Hell, admit it, Hammett: You wrote them only because you were worried about the landlord. You used the Op as a meal ticket, and he deserved better.

He stopped dead in his tracks at the typing table. There was another envelope he hadn't seen. From Alfred A. Knopf, the New York publisher who would be doing his first book in February. Just telling him when he could expect the *Red Harvest* galley proofs? He picked it up and gutted it with a hooked forefinger that tremored slightly.

But it was from Harry Bloch. About *The Dain Curse,* which *Black Mask* would be running as four separate novelettes in a few months. Harry was . . . God, was enthusiastic!

Biggest problem Harry and Mrs. Knopf saw was Gabrielle's slight physical deformities, which surprised Hammett. Didn't she need them to explain her mental kinks? Also, he wanted her to be slightly . . . what? *Distasteful* at first, so the reader could be *lured* into sympathy with her, a step at a time, almost against his will.

Also, Harry saw the story as overly episodic for novel form, but hell, Hammett knew *that.*

He was pacing again. Felix Weber and his damned Primrose Hotel, that was the trouble. Felix had to go. But who—or what—would replace him, fill his function in the story? Hey! Translate him into someone entirely new, maybe. An ex-con like Tokzek wasn't essential to. . . .

He stopped in the middle of the little room to burst out laughing. Not Egan Tokzek! Felix Weber. Why had the rapist shot dead by Preacher Laverty leaped to mind when he was thinking of the fictional Weber? Was Tokzek maybe an ex-con Hammett had helped send up? Why did that name have a tantalizing familiarity?

Rumrunner, according to This Reporter on the *Chronicle.* Suggest that Vic find out which bootlegger he'd been running rum for, lean on the 'legger a bit? But why, exactly? Tokzek had nothing to do with. . . .

Hammett grimaced angrily. He didn't want to dig out connections, form hypotheses, remember details about real felons like Egan Tokzek anymore. Only about fictional ones like Felix Weber.

And nothing Vic Atkinson or anyone else could do was going to change that.

Seven

"THIS burg is full of rotgut whiskey," said Vic Atkinson.

The cabbie pulled up in front of darkened Pier Fourteen with a shrug. "Nobody makes you drink it."

"Why didn't I think of that?"

Atkinson stood on rubbery legs beside the Yellow's open window, muttering to himself as he handed over a single and waved away the change.

"There any action around here, cabbie? Girls? Booze? A little game—"

"This here's a Yellow, mister, not a White Top."

Atkinson peered blearily after the retreating taillight. A few feet away, below the edge of the heavy timber dock, dark water lapped around iron-bound pilings. He could smell clean salt air. Beyond the dark blot of Goat Island were the scattered pinpricks marking Point Richmond. It was well after midnight and such a still night he could hear the purl of water against the prow of a brightly lit late boat nosing into the Ferry Building slips from Oakland.

Pronzini. That was the word he'd picked up at the Chapeau Rouge on Powell and Francisco. Somewhere here at the foot of Mission Street was supposed to be a speakie run by Dom Pronzini, who had a lock on the illicit booze making its way down from British Columbia.

He crossed The Embarcadero to the cigar store next to the Hotel Commodore. His steps became exaggerated, his eyelids fractionally drooped, a button of his shirt had come open. His shoulder struck the door frame, so he had to grab the edge of the glass countertop to keep from falling on the floor.

"Gimme some Van Camps."

"'A taste of its own,'" quoted the clench-faced old man getting out the cigars.

"Like my boots." He lit up, blew smoke across the counter, and leaned close. "'M in from Seattle, lookin' for a little drinkie."

"'Gainst the law, mister."

"So's spitting on the sidewalk."

The old man gave a long-suffering sigh.

"Next block over, Steuart Street. One thirteen. Back side of the d'Audiffred Building on the corner. Only building left standing on this side of East Street during—"

"Pay phone," said Atkinson to stem the spate of words.

"Down to the Army-Navy YMCA."

Atkinson paused in the doorway. "Who sent me?"

"It's Maxie this week."

The Army-Navy YMCA a short block away was a square gray granite building, eight stories high. Atkinson entered the ornate high-ceilinged lobby, his heavy workman boots slapping echoes from the terrazzo floor. A pimple-faced youth behind the registration desk pointed out the pay phone.

It rang a great many times before a girl's sleep-tousled voice answered.

"I want to talk with Dashiell Hammett," said Atkinson.

"You"—she broke it with a huge yawn—"you know . . . what time it. . . ."

Atkinson put on his tough voice to growl around his cigar, "Hammett, sister. It's important."

Hammett's voice was short and irritated.

"Yeah?"

"Dash!" he exclaimed loudly. "How are you this bee-oo-tee-ful-morning?"

"Christ, I might have known. You bastard, I'm writing."

49

"And I'm walking the midnight streets, alone, drinking in cheap gin mills, alone, ogling pretty girls, alo—"

"Goddammit, Vic, I'm writing!"

"I'm at. . . ." He paused to read off the phone number in the dim light, wondering for the first time whether maybe he wasn't a little bit drunk, after all. "DAvenport seven-seven-eight-nine, and. . . ." He got his mouth close to the receiver. "I'm in *danger*, Dash! Strange men. . . ."

"I hope they beat your goddamn head in!"

Atkinson rubbed his ringing ear thoughtfully, twitched his nose, wiggled his eyebrows, and checked his railroad watch. Going on one. He decided maybe it was a little thick, at that.

One thirteen Steuart Street was a bare white wooden door without any lettering on it, not even a knob. But when Atkinson pushed, it opened inward to a flight of wide stairs going straight back. He reached the second floor winded. Too damn many cheap cigars. A hallway took him back toward The Embarcadero; he checked each door for a peep-slot.

Two-thirds of the way along the hall he thumped a fist on a heavy hardwood panel that turned out to be sheet steel. After a moment the peep-slot slid open and an eye gleamed at him.

"You'll wake the baby."

"Maxie sent me over with the kid's milk." Atkinson laid a five-dollar bill, folded longways, on the edge of the slot.

It disappeared. The door was opened by a man in a dark suit and shirt with a wide white tie. He was a head shorter than Atkinson, but fully as wide. He had dirty fingernails. He gestured.

"Sorry, bo. House rules."

"You got a chill off?" sneered Atkinson.

But he stood patiently for the frisk. It was for show, to impress high-rollers from uptown out for a night of slumming; it wouldn't have turned up anything smaller than a cannon.

"Through the door, bo," said the bouncer.

Atkinson stuffed the cigar back into his face and sauntered away. As his fingers touched the knob, the door opened with a short angry buzz. Interesting. If . . . Yeah. Three feet beyond it, a second door. Yep, hinges on the opposite side. Buzzed through. And beyond that the third, hinges again reversed.

No scrubbed-out stains, no scars in the wood. Again, just for show.

The third door admitted him to a blast of light and noise, and to a carbon copy of the man on the outside, except his chin was a little bluer and his fingernails a little cleaner. Or maybe it was just that the light was better.

"Welcome to Dom's Dump." His grin was as manufactured as his Brooklyn accent.

Atkinson jerked his thumb at the three-door arrangement. "I thought Big Al had a lock on those."

"Where'd you say you was from?"

"I didn't."

Atkinson sauntered on. Dom's Dump was a huge echoing high-ceilinged place with heavy plum curtains around all the walls to mask the windows and sop up the noise. The ornate hardwood bar ran the length of the right-hand wall; it had retained its old-fashioned brass rail, but the spittoons were gone. Too many ladies came to the speakies these days. The center of the room was open, the hardwood floor waxed but well-scuffed, ready for dancers. Tables were crowded around the dance floor, and the long wall across from the bar was lined with dark-varnished wooden booths with high backs.

Atkinson put his back to the bar. He hooked his elbows over it, and one heel over the brass rail. He puffed blue smoke. Few people here this time of night on a Tuesday. Thursday through Monday would be their big play. Suspended over the dance floor was a giant ball covered with hundreds of bits of mirror. It was motionless, but on busy nights it would revolve and the colored spots trained on it from the corners of the high ceiling would cast shifting patterns of light and color across the dancers.

"What'll it be, sir?" Atkinson looked back over his shoulder at the barkeep.

51

"Antiquary, if it wasn't cooked up this morning."

Midforties. Black curly hair shot with gray, a pasta figure under his white apron. Too old by fifteen years for Pronzini, and he didn't have the Capone air they all cultivated these days. The eternal hired hand.

"Here you are, sir."

Atkinson dropped the shot in a lump, shook his head, wheezed, and wiped his eyes on the sleeve of his lumberjack.

"If that's twenty years old, it's been dead for nineteen. Lemme talk to the Ghee with the brass nuts."

"Dom?"

"I don't mean Lindy, sweetheart."

Atkinson sipped his second Scotch and started the slow cremation of another cigar. He figured he wouldn't have to wait long for Pronzini.

"'So who's asking?" demanded a voice at his elbow.

Pronzini was a heavy, darkly handsome man with thick black hair, heavy black brows, and heavy sideburns to the bottoms of his ears. He wore a tight chalk-stripe double-breasted suit tailored for a Pronzini twenty pounds younger.

Atkinson jerked a head at the front door.

"Last time I saw one of those was in a cathouse on the south side of Cicero, out near the Hawthorne racetrack. Button-operated. You get your man between doors, then lock all three electrically. The man on this side pumps a few rounds into the door, maybe chest-high."

There was a sneer in Pronzini's voice. "You John Law?"

"Two weeks after the place opened up, the inside door looked like Swiss cheese. Between doors looked like a slaughterhouse. Hymie Weiss and his boys burned it to the ground for a thousand bucks from a committee of reform. Now Hymie Weiss is dead." He added tonelessly, "No, I ain't John Law."

Pronzini gave a meaningless grunt and jerked his head.

"Let's barber."

They took the end booth, next to a split in the drapes behind which Atkinson assumed would be a rear exit. Three tables away a very young man with a shock of blond wavy hair

52

was talking with a petite girl in a bright red satin cocktail dress. The young man looked drunk and intense, the girl sober and bored.

Pronzini snapped his fingers at the bartender. To Atkinson, he said, "What's your grift? The eastern mobs don't send nobody around ever since a couple of their boys went home in the baggage car."

Atkinson relit his stogie.

"How about one man with money to spend, and willing to play by the house rules?"

"He might find some action," Pronzini admitted.

The bartender appeared at the table. Pronzini looked at Atkinson.

"It was supposed to be Antiquary."

"Yeah. Tony, bring my friend here some of the real stuff. The *real* stuff, you got that?" The bartender went away. Atkinson flicked ash on the floor. The darkly handsome bootlegger leaned forward confidingly.

"Wait till you taste this Scotch. Smooth as a baby's butt."

"Word I pick up around the speakies is that you gotta juice the cops in this town if you want to make connections."

Pronzini chuckled complacently. "I ain't saying you're wrong."

"Anyone special who—"

Tony set down Pronzini's beer and Atkinson's Scotch. Prewar, right enough, rich smoky taste with an edge of bitterness that woke up the throat and nose. Pronzini was watching with delighted eyes.

"Didn't I tell you?"

"I wouldn't mind a couple of bottles to take—"

The golden-haired youth was on his feet, shouting at the girl in the red dress. As he shouted, he jerked greenbacks from his wallet and threw them on the floor.

"Go ahead, take it, take the money!" he cried, tears running down his face. "That's all you're after, isn't it? Isn't it? That's all you're after."

"Jesus Christ," grumbled Pronzini. The bartender and the bouncer were already converging on the table. "Ya gotta let him in, his daddy's on the Board of Supes, but I tell ya, he gives the place a bad name. Can't hold his liquor and can't hold his dames."

The girl was down on both knees like a washerwoman, scrabbling after the money. The boy threw the empty wallet at her head. The bouncer grabbed his arm from behind. The boy spun gracefully, yelling, and threw a right-hand lead at the blued jaws. The bouncer kneed him in the crotch. He fell on the floor. The girl was on her feet, backing away, her face composed and sullen.

Pronzini stood up, shaking his head sourly. "C'mon, we can't talk in all this racket."

Atkinson, carrying the bottle casually by the neck, followed him through the break in the drapes. He was glad to get out of the suddenly stuffy barroom.

Beyond the door was a long narrow room stacked floor to ceiling with wooden crates of liquor. Over his shoulder, Pronzini said, "We got a private room back here we won't be disturbed."

The door at the far end led to another room, this one small and square with a bed and table and dresser and chairs. Three other doors: bathroom, closet, and one probably opening on stairs down to the dark narrow alley he could see from the window. Pronzini sat down at the table and gestured Atkinson to a seat across from him.

"Okay, bo, you tell me what sort of financing you've got, I'll tell you whether there's any chance we can deal."

"Maybe you could lay out your setup for me a little first."

He treated himself to Scotch as Pronzini talked about payoffs and which cops had to be juiced on a regular basis. Atkinson drank and listened and reminded himself to go easy on the hootch; he had a long night ahead, and a lot of details to remember, and he was already getting a heat on.

Only it wasn't a heat. He started clumsily to his feet as he realized what was happening to him. The bitter edge to the Scotch! He cursed the heavy, grinning, distorted face. He reached across the table for it. Tear it off its fat neck. But the floor moved sideways under his feet to spill him over so his chin struck the edge of the table.

Through waves of nausea, Vic Atkinson could hear a voice that sounded vaguely familiar. Then he placed it. Dominic Pronzini. It came back to him. Like a rube from the sticks. The real stuff, Tony. The *real* stuff.

". . . he used to hang around North Beach in the old days when I was a kid. . . . Huh?"

Atkinson realized Pronzini was on the phone. "Naw, I don't know his grift, nothing in his poke but a few bucks. . . . Yeah. No. Sure. He ain't going nowhere. . . ."

Atkinson tried to move his head, but the waves of nausea swept over him again. Chloral hydrate. Probably would have knocked him out for hours if he'd been a smaller man. As it was, hitting his chin had knocked him out. The Mickey Finn had him drifting . . . paralyzed. . . .

He came back again, maybe a little stronger. Pronzini was back on the phone with the same guy and a different conversation.

"Who you sending to—no, check that, I don't want to know. The alley door'll be open for him. But what difference does it make *who* this guy is? My boys can make sure he gets the message. He wakes up in an alley somewhere with his teeth in his pocket. . . ."

Away again, drifting. Try to move the head, so he'd know if he was . . . gently. *Gently*, goddamn you! Ohh-h-h. . . .

Sound of door opening. Footsteps approaching. He realized he didn't even know if he was lying on his back or his face. No feeling. But better now, even so. Not going away and coming back.

Above him, a grunt of surprise. On his back then. The newcomer seeing his face and recognizing him. Had to get eyes open, see who it was had come in from the downstairs alley door Pronzini had left open. *Had* to. It could be the man. *The* man. Crack his case before he even got started on it.

55

Now!

With a supreme effort, Vic Atkinson forced his eyelids open. He was flat on his back, staring straight up. Up, high as the moon, at the elongated, distorted image his eyes gave his foggy brain.

The man, all right. But opening his eyes had been a mistake.

"Yes, well, that's it, isn't it?" said the man looking down at him. Turned away, regret in his eyes, Atkinson could see him go to the door, open it six inches, call Pronzini and shut it again.

He was standing at the window, overcoat collar turned up, hat pulled low on his head, when Pronzini came in.

"Yeah?"

"He opened his eyes. He saw my face."

Goddamn chloral hydrate. If only Dash had come with him, none of this would have. . . .

"I'll need . . . something . . . to—"

"In the closet," said Pronzini quickly. "I don't want to know about it."

"Just so you get rid of it later," said the deliberately muffled voice.

Pronzini's footsteps, going away. Door closing. Other footsteps to same door, key turning in lock, then footsteps to closet. *In the closet.* Coming at him.

Atkinson tried, despairing, to move. Couldn't. God, so sick. Meet it.

With a supreme effort, Vic Atkinson raised his head three inches and opened his eyes.

The bulky man swung the baseball bat. The arc ended with a sickening abruptness on the bridge of the detective's nose. As the home run exploded against Atkinson's eyes and into his brain, his bladder and sphincter let loose. The killer leaped back with a little exclamation to avoid the mess. And the blood. Then he stepped back in to use the bat some more. As long as it had to be done, he might as well enjoy it.

Eight

IT was coming right, now. Felix Weber, the ex-con, was gone. The Primrose Hotel was gone. Hammett's typewriter clacked. The ashtray was overflowing; flecks of tobacco drifted on the top of black coffee long since gone cold.

He stopped, rubbed bloodshot eyes, tugged his mustache, considered. Aaronia Haldorn. Her husband Joseph. And instead of the run-down hotel, their exclusive Pacific Heights place, the Temple of the Holy Grail. Joseph would work as a character where Weber hadn't.

He got up and started to pace. Hell, yes. Joseph would *believe.* That was it. Wield the knife himself. Sure. As for Aaronia. . . .

Aaronia.

Hammett quit pacing to light himself a cigarette. Aaronia. He'd given her the name but not the physical description of his older sister, Reba. Of all his relatives, the only one he still wrote to. He chuckled. Aaronia Rebecca Hammett, as stiff-necked as he was. He'd send her a copy of *The Dain Curse* when Knopf published it. If he ever got the damned thing revised.

But still he stood, gripped by the past. Philadelphia. He'd been . . . what? Two? Three? White house with a little wooden porch and initials carved penknife deep in the railing. Tagging along after Reba to the park to fetch drinking water. Must have been Fairmont Park. And the time the old man took them both—maybe even the baby, Dick, too—to the city dump. There'd been a billy goat with a long white beard and mad eyes, eating tin cans. Or at least the labels off them.

Circle of men around the goat, laughing. Every time one of them would toss a cigarette butt, quick as lightning the goat would piss on it and put it out. Every time. He'd never seen his father laugh so hard.

He became aware that knuckles had been rapping against

the front door for some time. He rubbed a hand over his sandpaper jaw and called, "I'm asleep."

"Sam. It's me. Goodie. You've got another phone call."

Hammett went to the window and jerked at the bottom of the shade. It shot up to slap twice around the roller. Sunshine burst in to squint his eyes. He threw up the bottom half of the double-hung window and sucked in shocking dawn air. Where the hell had the night gone?

Goodie was dressed for work in a checked gingham apron frock with a collarless square neck and a midcalf hem that would turn no sufferer's head in the doctor's waiting room. Following her to her apartment, he talked at her back.

"I'm going to give that damn Atkinson a blast he won't forget, after that trick he pulled last night. . . ."

He knelt on the couch, picked up the phone, clipped the receiver between the side of his neck and a raised shoulder so he could make drinking motions with his left hand to suggest coffee. Goodie nodded and disappeared into the kitchen.

"Yeah, I know, Vic. The cops picked you up and—"

"Dash? Jimmy Wright here."

A well-remembered voice from his Pinkerton past, another operative who'd stayed on when Hammett had left.

"Jimmy, how's the boy, long time no see. You still with the Pinks?"

"Not for a year. I quit to go with Vic down south. Why I called, they found him behind the Southern Pacific station this morning. Worked over with a baseball bat or something, then dumped there."

I'm in danger, *Dash! Strange men. . . . Hope they beat . . . goddamn head in. . . .*

"Dumped?" he asked almost stupidly. The tips of his fingers had turned pale against the phone. "Dead?"

"You never saw one deader."

He was without movement for a full twenty seconds; then a long ripple that might have been a shiver ran through his lean body.

"I'm on my way."

Goodie came from the kitchen with a steaming cup of

58

coffee half-extended. Hammett felt hollow. *Hope they beat . . . goddamn head. . . .*

"Sam, what's wrong? What—"

He was already heading for the door.

Hammett paid off the cab and started across Third toward the bulky colonnaded Mission Revival SP station, built of stucco phonied up like adobe. When he saw the craning knot of loungers at the far end of the long wooden baggage shed, he veered down Townsend instead. At the gate in the iron picket fence, a uniform bull was holding back the crowd. He let Hammett through.

Jimmy Wright, five feet eight and overweight, was at the foot of the wooden ramp leading up into the shedlike baggage building. They shook hands.

"Who found it?" asked Hammett.

"Switchman."

The meat wagon hadn't arrived yet. Another knot of men, all official and dominated by O'Gar's bullet head, was clustered in the five-foot-wide area between the side of the baggage shed and the closest of the tracks. The space was for brakemen servicing the rolling stock. Four of the men staggered toward the timbered loading dock at the foot of the ramp with a sagging Army blanket. When they dropped it near Hammett's feet, one corner flopped back. He had such an acute moment of *déjà vu* that he felt dizzy. Words washed over him.

". . . stink?"

"Shit his pants when he died. . . ."

Baltimore. His first job, at thirteen, right out of Polytechnic Grammar School. The old man had gotten sick and Hammett had tried to pick up the pieces as messenger boy for the B & O line in their Charles and Baltimore Street office. He was late for work as usual, cutting across the tracks, when he'd stumbled on a brakeman who'd been killed by a switching engine.

A head just like Vic's: still whole but oddly misshapen, almost soggy, no more interior structure than a beanbag. Same

59

stink of excrement. A shabby way to die. He flipped the coarse brown wool back up with an apparently casual toe.

"His money was on his hip," said Jimmy Wright. "No wallet." Working undercover, Hammett thought, there wouldn't be. "Clerk from the hotel saw the excitement, came over, and recognized the clothes."

"Sure it wasn't a switching engine?"

"Brakeman was through twenty minutes before. No body. No trains moving on this track last night anyway. You see everything you want here?"

Hammett nodded. They went up Townsend to the side entrance of the depot arcade and walked under arched ceilings past the train gates. In the Depot Café at the far end of the station, they found a table and ordered coffee. Jimmy Wright also ordered ham and eggs. Watching the stocky two-hundred-pound op shovel in hashbrowns, Hammett felt a little ill. He drank scalding black coffee. He fumbled out a cigarette.

"You going to take over the investigation of the police department now that Vic is gone?"

The op's sleepy brown eyes gleamed, then were sleepy again. He was dressed in a brown suit; his collar was soiled and rumpled from an all-night train ride from LA. "I was hoping you would."

"Me? I haven't been a sleuth for over six years."

"And I'm a hired hand." He sopped up the last of the egg yolk with his final bite of toast. "I'm lousy behind a desk, whereas *you*—"

"A writing desk, not a detective's rolltop."

"Mebbe." The op lit a Fatima and feathered smoke at the ceiling. He chuckled. "Remember that check-raising gang you and Vic and I ran down in the old Blackstone Hotel on O'Farrell Street?"

Hammett remembered. Big blond guy with a broken nose that Vic had hung out of a third-story window by an ankle to cool down. He said, "Remember when I got drunk at that hotel on Taylor? The one where all the ex-cons went on Saturday night because they could get together at the weekly

60

dance and plan jobs without being arrested as parole viola-tors? Vic was . . ." He broke off abruptly. "Jimmy, he called me last night. He was on a round of the speaks, wanted me to meet him. If I had . . ."

"Right you are," said the thickset operative meaninglessly.

Hammett leaned forward, elbows on the table.

"Any blood where they found him?"

"No blood. He was dumped."

"Coroner's man make a guess on the time yet?"

"You know them."

"Then here's something you can give O'Gar when you talk to him. Vic was alive just before one o'clock. If he wants to know what Vic was working on, refer him to Preacher Laver-ty. I'd think the fewer cops know about your operation right now, the better."

"Check."

He left the stocky detective getting into a cab for the Hall of Justice, after again refusing Wright's pleas that he join the investigation. He caught a 15 car up Third Street. Dammit, Vic's death really had nothing to do with him. Vic Atkinson had been unwary and had gotten dead. Probably had noth-ing to do with the investigation anyway. As far as anyone on the reform committee knew, Vic had returned to LA to get his crew together.

But at Mission Street, Hammett got off the trolley and walked the two blocks to the Chronicle building. He picked up back issues of the newspaper. When he left the Sutter car at Hyde twenty minutes later, he stopped at the Eagle Mar-ket to get a bottle of rye from the back room.

He had two things neither the police nor Jimmy Wright had. Davenport 7789, from which Vic had called him last night. And the fact they had talked with Molly Farr on Sun-day.

It was easy enough to check out the phone. He detoured to Dorris' garage and dialed the number. It rang seven times before it was picked up.

"Clyde there?"

"Clyde? Look, mister, this is a pay phone."

61

"*Pay* phone?" exclaimed Hammett in a surprised voice. "You sure?"

"'Course I'm sure. In the lobby of the Army-Navy YMCA. . . ."

Hammett hung up. What the hell was there down at the foot of Mission Street to attract Vic at one in the morning? He called the Townsend, where Jimmy Wright had taken over Vic's room, and left a message for the stocky operative. Then he went up to his apartment.

Propped up in bed with the newspapers, the bottle of rye, cigarettes and ashtray, he started rapidly and expertly through the papers. The baseball bat was a mob trademark—which made it easy to copy. Sunday's story on Molly he reread, followed her through. Monday, arraignment due that afternoon. Tuesday, neither she nor Crystal Tam showed up for the arraignment. He also reread the stories on Tokzek's death and his eventual identification as a rumrunner.

He saw his glass was empty again, filled it, and padded over to his typing table and the night's work still laid out. The hell with Atkinson. The hell with Molly Farr and the newspaper dog vomit. He had a book to revise.

But what had seemed so vital a few hours before became shallow and trite against Vic's battered, shapeless head.

He went back to bed. He poured his tumbler half full.

The death didn't make sense. What could Vic have learned in a casual evening of barhopping that was worth his life? As a working hypothesis, nothing. So leave that to the cops and to Jimmy Wright.

Dammit, leave the whole thing to the cops and Jimmy Wright. And where was that damn bottle?

Molly. Atkinson meant to pressure Molly until she broke, but she took a run-out powder. If he'd found her. . . .

Wait a minute, Hammett. Your glass is empty. Hell, bottle empty too. Just as good. Work to do. Writing. Deathless prose.

Deathless death dead, Vic Atkinson, God*damm*it Vic is dead.

62

Molly Farr. Find Molly. Molly's folly.

Instead, Hammett found his shoes and a shirt and the door. When he returned ten minutes later, the empty pint had ballooned to a full quart.

His glass was under the bed and his head hurt when he bent over to get it. Should have had something to eat. Too busy to eat. Busy detecting, Hammett the ferret ferreting through the newspapers, gumshoeing bloodhounding sherlocking

Today's paper. Hadn't checked that yet. And there it was.

MOLLY'S OWN STORY OF BEING ON SPOT

by Harry Warner

In the predawn hours before her grand jury arraignment on vice charges last Monday, a haggard Molly Farr wrestled with her code of life. Four courses, she told this reporter, were open to her.

"I can commit suicide," she told him. "I can squeal. I can fight the case by pleading my innocence in front of a jury. Or I can run away."

As she spoke, her voice was deadly serious.

"I want you to get one thing straight. I have lived my adult life by the code of the underworld. They tell me I may have to go to jail for fifteen years. I won't do that. But I'm not a rat. Sure, I know a lot about police graft. And I know I'm being crucified. I know politics is mixed up in this case somewhere. They're going to feed Molly Farr to the wolves and say they've got the goods on her and that she's a bad woman and they're going to put her away for a long time. But I'm not going to blow the whistle now."

She shuddered.

"I have a code that says, 'Keep your mouth shut.'"

Continued on Page 3, Col. 1

Hammett read it through to the end. A typical Brass

Mouth Epstein maneuver. Take Mulligan Bros. money to defend Molly, then warn them—and the DA and the cops as well—that Molly knew too much for them to expect her to pull fifteen years at Tehachapi. Smear it all over the newspapers through exclusive interviews with feature writers. Make Molly a *cause célèbre*. And then pull the plug, spirit her away, and let everyone sweat a little bit.

And into the midst of all this sweating and careful orchestration, perhaps, had stepped Vic Atkinson. What if he had found a lead to Molly that someone heard about? If someone didn't want him to get to her, there was a motive for murder.

Which, however, only worked if you assumed that Molly knew something worth murder. You'd have to talk to Molly to know for sure.

Hell, he needed a licensed grift, so he could lean on the people who had to be leaned on. That meant convincing the committee he should take Vic's place—just as Jimmy Wright had been urging him. Once he had that. . . .

Who was he kidding? He was a writer now, not a sleuth. He lowered the level in his glass. The cops would turn up some bum or wino who'd ridden the rods up from Stockton or down from Portland, had rolled Vic as a drunk, and had hit too hard. Had carried the body across the street to dump it by the tracks.

Did he really believe that?

"Do you really believe that, Hammett?" he asked aloud.

Goddammit, Vic's death had nothing to do with him, *was* nothing to him. Right? He sat on the edge of the bed, rubbed his hands down over his face. He had a book to revise. So many things. . . .

But all in an orderly progression. First things first.

Where in hell had that bottle gotten to?

64

Nine

AT three A.M. the heavy hardwood door of 891 Post was slammed wide. Hammett came through at an angle so sharp that one tough stringy shoulder hit the wall. This spun him around. To keep his balance, he stepped back on the raised vestibule terrazzo a foot beyond where the terrazzo ended.

He fell heavily on his back on the sidewalk. He lay there motionless, then started coughing. The violence of the spasms curled him to one side. He spat against the concrete and stared intently at it for a few moments.

Then he clambered to his feet. He had not bothered to put on a collar and the bare stud glinted at the back of the neckband.

" 'Rested," he said aloud.

That's what the medicos at the veterans' lung hospital had told him about his consumption. An arrested case. No blood in what he had spat against the sidewalk. No hemorrhaging for over three years, not since he'd twice come around in a pool of his own blood on the floor of Samuels' Jewelers and had quit to go write before it was too late.

And Josie, before she'd left him that first time, *My God, Dash, don't you understand? You're killing yourself with your drinking.* Josie. Nurse and wife and. . . .

"It was the whiskey that stopped the TB," he said stubbornly.

He realized that his right hand still clutched an unbroken quart whiskey bottle. The street was deserted, dark between streetlamps pooling light at the intersections. On Sutter, a block above, an all-night Owl went by with a mournful thinning rattle-rattle and clang-clang-clang. My God, what lonely sounds! He looked at the bottle and chuckled.

"Never spilled a drop," he bragged.

He looked closer. Empty. Must have been empty when he'd left the building. He stepped to the edge of the sidewalk and hurled the bottle, spinning, across the street like a German potato-masher grenade. It just cleared the fabric top of a parked '27 Falcon Knight to burst against the face of Guaranteed Cleaning and Tailoring with a sullen thud.

"Take that, you rotten Hun bastards!" Hammett yelled.

The rotten Hun bastards didn't answer. He had the street to himself. And he was out of booze. *That,* he remembered abruptly, was what he had come downstairs for. A man couldn't prosify if he was out of

Prosify. Word? Hell with it.

Couldn't revenge ol' Vic without lubrication. All the working parts would seize up. Engine so worn the pistons changed valves every other stroke.

How the hell did anyone get along without booze? The old man, never touching a drop of it. Didn't like him drinking, didn't even like him smoking—but Hammett'd always been the family wild one. Still just a kid, ten or eleven, he and Walt Polhaus sneaking down to the corner to buy cigarettes two for a penny. Polhaus always got . . . yeah, Piedmonts, that was it, while he always got Old Mills because they were supposed to be stronger.

Walt Polhaus, where'd he ever get to? Use him in a book sometime. Now, though, where'd his booze go to? All gone. But he'd lobbed that bottle grenade like old Pop Daneri in the trenches at the Somme.

Pop Daneri!

Hell, yes, Pop always had a jar of shine around to get him through the long insomniac hours when the mustard gas he'd whiffed in France seemed to curl through his lungs again.

Hammett started across the intersection. Maybe Pop'd have something a cut above his usual. A tin of turpentine, maybe, or a slug of paint thinner.

Clem Daneri's tousled white thatch was thrust out of the office door so his snapping black eyes could size up any prospective customer coming up the stairs of the Weller Hotel.

"How's it going, Pop?"

"Settin' up and taking nourishment," exclaimed the old man happily. "I thought you was off the sauce."

66

"What makes you think—"

"Don't I know you, Hammett?" He shut the lower half of the Dutch door and belatedly the upper half behind the lean writer. A buzzer beside the door would announce any opening of the downstairs street door. "You only come around when you don't have the price of a jar or can't find anyplace to sell you one."

Hammett sat down all at once in a hardwood arm rocker that had the rockers attached to the posts in the old cleft style. "I fell down," he said. "I hit my head."

"Good it's the head. That's where it can't hurt you none." The thick blue-veined gentle fingers explored the back of the scalp. "I'll get the horse liniment."

The old man went through the connecting door to the other room of the tiny suite that came with his manager's job at the Weller. Hammett sat without moving, his head slightly lowered and his long-fingered narrow hands hanging laxly off the chair arms until Pop bounced back into the room with a dark bottle. Hammett uncorked it to sniff the contents.

"I'd be *afraid* to rub a horse down with this stuff," he said.

"Just apply internally."

Hammett's Adam's apple worked in his lean throat. Pop sank down into a worn mohair rocker.

"Knew a feller killed himself like that."

"Sure you did. See in the papers where a nun choked to death taking communion?" A mulish look on his face, he tipped up the bottle again for a second long slug and lowered it wet-eyed. "Whew! Jesus, that's rotten."

"Just off the boat," said Pop absently.

"Cattle boat."

"Okay, what's chewing at you, Sam?" demanded the old man harshly.

A somber light entered Hammett's eyes. "Vic Atkinson." He lowered his head and started to cry. His sobs had a harsh nighttime sound in the little room. Pop watched him with bright speculative eyes.

"So what makes him being dead your problem?" he asked when Hammett subsided.

Despite all the whiskey, he told it as if he were writing a report, dryly and factually in grammatical, unadorned English. The two men passed the bottle back and forth until Hammett's voice began to slow, soften, slur, lose resonance and direction. His head dipped. He gave a long soft snore.

"Hammett! Sleep on your own time."

His head jerked up. "You old bastard." He'd met Pop in an Army hospital in the desert near San Diego in 1920, where they'd each been sent for damaged lungs. The same hospital where Josie. . . . He demanded blearily, "Where's that bottle?"

"It's empty."

"You've got another."

The old man paused in the open doorway to the other room. "You're goin' after whoever did it, ain't you, Sam?"

"What else can I do?"

Vic was dead because of him, that was the long and short of it. *I hope they beat your goddamn head in.* And here was Hammett piss-ass drunk instead of out finding the bastard that did it. Everything he touched turned to shit. Every living thing.

He started to curse in a low hoarse voice. Pop Daneri came through the doorway with a new bottle. It looked to him like a long night. But all his nights were long, and would be a damned sight longer if it weren't for Hammett. Hammett had gotten him this job back in '21, when Pinkerton's had used the Weller as a place to stash surprise witnesses in court cases. Except for Hammett, he'd have lived at the veterans' hospital until he rotted.

"Drink up, you damned fool."

Hammett drank. The whiskey seemed to revive him. The cursing jag, like the crying jag, had passed. He started to talk about the hospital, and the desert, and the other patients. Everybody but Josie.

". . . time Whitey Kaiser bought the five bottles of patent medicine that was about ninety proof, and drank them all and slugged his doctor?" He didn't wait for a reply. "Remember that bushy-headed guy with half an ear missing that you suckered into betting on the sidewinder against our Gila monster in that boxcar out on the edge of a desert?"

68

"And Josephine A. Dolan," Pop cut in deliberately. "What d'ya hear from Josie these days?"

It stopped Hammett like a wall. She was still his wife, even if. . . . He cleared his throat.

"You know how it is, Pop."

"No, I don't know how it is, Sam. You tell me."

Hammett reached a long arm for the bottle. How did you sum up a love and two lives? Josie. Nurse in his ward. Round face that smiled easily, freckles and the sort of coloring that went with red hair, though hers really wasn't. Slender and wiry, tireless and inventive when aroused.

"Poor Josie," he said aloud.

Married to a lunger and a lush and a writer—all in the same guy. Win, place, or show, and he came in out of the money every time.

After lights-out, they'd sneak out together hand in hand, across the desert to a little ravine where there was a flat place under some trees. You could smell the dry earth and cooked vegetation cooling off after the day's heat, especially the small plants that were crushed under their excited bodies. Athletic and fun and rough-and-tumble, leaving them spent and breathless.

"We used to make a game out of cursing each other, Pop. I always won. She'd put her hands over her ears because I knew more words than she did."

The tenderness was afterward, when they'd stare up through the trees at the big close desert stars while their hearts slowed and the sweat dried on their bodies.

"I think the only really happy times Josie had with me were when I was working for Al Samuels. Steady job, steady paycheck. . . ."

Not fair. It was the drinking that bothered her, not the uncertainties of a beginning writer's life. In the crummy apartment down on Eddy Street. Then after she'd left him once and come back again, out in the nicer place on Hyde, with the old beauty there under the darkness of a thousand waxings of wood-paneled walls. But there it had finally become destructive: the drinking and the cold-faced scenes, and she hadn't covered her ears anymore when the cursing started.

69

"We were going in different directions," he said aloud.

"Where are Josie and the girls now, Sam?"

"Down south. Up in Montana. ¿*Quién sabe?*" He staggered to his feet. "Don't ever need me for anything, Pop."

"Go to hell," said the old man without heat.

"Yeah, sure," said Hammett. "I'll take this with me." He waved the bottle, lurched, straightened. "Vic Atkinson counted on me, and where's he now?"

He weaved to the door, opened it, and rammed his head into the upper half that hadn't opened. He cursed and fumbled at the latch. Pop Daneri could hear him carom off walls to muttered comments on his progress down the hall.

When the sounds had faded, Pop went over and shut the door. From below, faintly, came the careless slam of the front door. He reached in under the scalloped green shade of the floor lamp to pull the chain and plunge the room into darkness.

Pop threw the window up so he could lean on the sill and stick his head out. Hammett was cutting across the deserted intersection, weaving, bottle in hand.

As he slid the window back down, Pop shivered as with a chill. God help whoever had killed Vic Atkinson.

Ten

IT was shortly after nine o'clock on Thursday evening. Hammett, his pace firm, his clean-shaven face pale but his eyes clear of any trace of dissipation, crossed the floor of the echoing rotunda at City Hall. His steps rang on marble so highly polished it gave the illusion of being soft underfoot. As he passed each claw-footed, ridiculously ornate brass light standard, his elongated shadow wheeled across the floor. He skirted the central staircase and moved between pillars supporting the vast domed ceiling five stories above.

In front of a half-ton brass mailbox facing the locked Van Ness Avenue entrance, he shook hands with the larger of two dark waiting shapes. Preacher Laverty hadn't changed much with the years. Same heavy features, same pinkish hair just now beginning to frost with age. They were nearly of a height, although Hammett was seventy pounds lighter.

"So you want to go after the murdering bastards, now that it's too late for Vic." Laverty's soft south-of-Market brogue made it sound very slightly like "murthering."

"Will you back me or not?"

Laverty rasped a heavy hand down over that morning's shave. "Vic thought a lot of you as a detective, and Jimmy here tells me you can't be bought."

"We've already spent the last hour up there arguing for you," said the fat little op.

Hammett went up the marble staircase. As he skirted the mezzanine above the rotunda, his eyes were caught, as always, by the slogan McKenna had caused to be incised above the ornate arch:

SAN FRANCISCO
O GLORIOUS CITY OF OUR HEARTS THAT
HAST BEEN TRIED AND NOT FOUND WANTING.
GO THOU WITH LIKE SPIRIT TO MAKE
THE FUTURE THINE.

He paused for a moment before the darkly varnished door with THE MAYOR chiseled into the granite coping above it, marshaling what Jimmy Wright had told him of the members of the reform committee. Then he pushed on through it.

Evelyn Brewster was a slim handsome woman just shy of forty. Her chestnut hair was short and finger-waved in the latest style. She wore a white sleeveless frock with a tailored collar and a white jacket in heavy crêpe de Chine, the ensemble set off by a bright silk scarf around her slender throat. She smelled pleasantly of eau de cologne.

She cast a covertly furious glance at her husband, Dalton. He was lounged in his chair with one knee braced against the edge of the oak conference table. He'd come to the mayor's office, she was sure, only because *their* son had been one of those apprehended in *that woman's* place, not from any sense of moral urgency.

Which meant it was up to her to make sure that they were represented by an investigator of impeccable personal habits. A moral man. An upright man.

"Even though you come *highly* recommended by Mr. Laverty and Mr. Wright," she said to the lean man standing across the table, "I . . . that is, *we,* feel that a *professional* detective should represent this committee in this trying and delicate investiga—"

"I spent eight years in the profession, ma'am." As an afterthought, Hammett added, "And Vic Atkinson didn't intend to represent you."

Evelyn Brewster's husband stirred for the first time. He was youthfully trim, his hair dark and unthinned by his forty years, the heavy muscles in his jaws giving his face an unexpected craggy appearance. He ran with absolute authority the small coastal shipping empire his grandfather had founded back in gold rush days, and it showed in his voice.

"Then what *did* Atkinson intend to do?"

Jimmy Wright had been mistaken. Get Dalton W. Brewster on your side, and you had his wife no matter how much noise she made ahead of time.

"When you hire a detective, you hire a bloodhound. He uncovers facts and leaves evaluations to the people who hire him."

"I find that unacceptable."

Dr. Gardner Shuman, opening his campaign of opposition. Jimmy had warned Hammett that Shuman was the Mulligans' man, body and soul. He was a bald, stout, middleaged man sitting next to the mayor.

"You aren't hiring my views, you're hiring my expertise." Hammett added, with an indifference that lent it strength, "You hired Vic Atkinson, and I was a better detective than Vic ever thought of being."

"Why aren't you a detective now?"

"I retired. Voluntarily."

Shuman was hurting him; he could see it in the other faces around the table. Especially with Evelyn Brewster.

"We were led to understand that Mr. Atkinson was returning to Los Angeles to organize his staff," she said. "Now he turns up dead in San Francisco." She already had decided that this lean, cool-faced fellow just would not do. Not in the face of Dr. Shuman's opposition. Dr. Shuman was a trustee of the San Francisco Opera Company and a Knight of Columbus. "So I do not feel we can even be sure that Mr. Atkinson's death had anything to do with his planned work for this committee."

"If you really believe that, then you'd better all fold up your tents and quietly steal away."

"Hmph," said Mayor Brendan Brian McKenna from the head of the table.

Eyes turned toward him. He was rotund and balding, with a silvery mustache that lent his face a spurious weight and purpose. A black pearl stickpin gleamed in his gray cravat. A fresh carnation, like those the City Hall wags suggested he wore in his pajama top at night, bloomed in the lapel of his dark cutaway.

"What I mean to say, perhaps Mr. Hammett has an excellent thought there." His own thoughts were with the cut-glass decanter behind a sliding panel in his office. "Perhaps we ought to disband for this evening. Mr. Atkinson's death has been a terrible shock—"

"I want an answer tonight."

Hammett had set his feet, as if the room had begun to rock and he was bracing against it. But he knew he could not carry the fight to Bren McKenna personally. This was the man who, after the 1906 earthquake and fire, had literally direct-

73

ed disaster relief from the back of a prancing white steed; the only mayor in Prohibition America who dared have as his campaign song a ditty titled "Smile with Brandy Bren."

So Hammett said civilly, "Mr. Mayor, Vic Atkinson has been dead for nearly forty-eight hours. Somebody killed him and that somebody's out there right now"—the rough power of his voice held them all momentarily motionless—"trying to make damned sure he's going to get away with it. I want to make damned sure he doesn't. And meanwhile this committee wants to sit around arguing whether I'll be able to use the correct fork for the fish course at their victory dinner."

The silence that followed was broken, not by Shuman as he had expected, but by Dalton Brewster.

"I can understand the temptation to reduce this investigation to a personal vendetta against the men who murdered your friend. But by your own admission what is needed is dispassion, not—"

"I hadn't seen Vic Atkinson in over six years, hadn't written to him or communicated with him in any way. But yes, he was my friend. He was also a husband, a father, a good detective, and an upright man. He died because he wanted to *do* something about a department full of cops who'd become a little *too* corrupt, and a Board of Supervisors a little *too* openly for sale, and a district attorney—"

"As a member of the San Francisco police commission, I resent your remarks about our fine department," interrupted Shuman.

"Vic *believed* in this investigation—and because he had this committee behind him, because he thought his flanks were secure, he got careless. And he died."

Shuman was almost sputtering. "You *dare* to suggest that Victor Atkinson was betrayed by someone in this room?"

"That's *your* suggestion, Doctor, not mine."

"I suggest that Victor Atkinson was struck down by someone from his own highly unsavory past. A man who *drank* and—"

Hammett let his voice go tight and furious, and his eyes be-

74

came coals. He leaned across the polished hardwood table so he could thrust his face close to Shuman's.

"*You* have the gall to call Vic Atkinson unsavory?"

He straightened up. He looked around at the dozen or so uncomfortable faces. McKenna, the Brewsters, Hayden from the City Planning Committee, Walcott, president of the Civil Service Commission, Superior Court Judge Fitzpatrick, Boyle of the Anglo-California Trust, DiReggio of the Bank of Italy, Fremont Older of the *News-Call*, a couple of others he didn't know by sight, Shuman himself.

"Shuman, Gardner, medical doctor." Hammett made it a flat recitation. "Degree from the University of California med school in 1899. Entered general practice, but soon . . ."

Shuman half-rose, face furious. "I'm not going to—"

"*Shut up!*" snapped Hammett.

Shuman's face turned pale, but he sank back in his seat. McKenna's half-raised remonstrative hand gradually lowered. Brewster sat up straighter, with a ghost of a smile on his face. Used to wielding authority himself, he could recognize it in others.

"Member of the Police Commission since 1915, very popular with the department. Carries an Honorary Policeman's badge. We all know that a good deal of the corruption in this city stems from the Mulligan Bros. Bailbonds Company, even if there is no courtroom proof of this fact. Correct?"

He looked from face to face, deliberately. Rapt silence. Shuman was chalk-white.

"Right. Now, Griffith Mulligan holds—*personally* holds—the mortgage on Dr. Shuman's office at the foot of Post Street. He *personally* holds the mortgages on Dr. Shuman's house on the corner of Scott and Pine. He *personally* holds the mortgage on the building at Sutter and Divisadero that houses the general office of Shuman's Prescription Pharmacies and store number one in the Shuman drugstore chain."

Shuman seemed to have shrunk in his clothes. "You have no right . . ."

75

"And Mulligan Bros. Bailbonds holds the mortgages on the other twenty-five Shuman pharmacies scattered around town. What was your word, Doctor? Unsavory?"

Shuman was on his feet, face ashen. He gripped his walking stick like a club. His voice shook. "I do not intend to stay here and listen to any more of this. There are legal remedies. . . ."

He collected his hat and cape. As he stalked out, Hammett was going on exactly as if he had not departed.

"Through his position on the police commission, Dr. Shuman receives all—all, every one—of the department assignments to examine arrested prostitutes for venereal diseases. He also gets as much medical business involving accident, rape, and assault victims as the police department can shove his way without the rest of the doctors squawking too loudly . . ."

"Facts," interrupted Dalton Brewster abruptly. He seemed to have taken a sudden shine to Hammett. He raked the table with his coolly appraising look, then turned back to the lean detective. "But you want a friend's murderer caught. We want a structure of corruption and vice exposed. The two things aren't the same."

"You can't accomplish one without the other, Mr. Brewster. I'm not opposed to your moral crusade. I merely say that the city of San Francisco is the way it is because that's the way its citizens want it. This system has worked so well that the eastern mobs have never been able to get a toehold here. But whoever rubbed Vic Atkinson changed the rules. I want him. I'm going to have him. In getting him, I'll shake enough other bad apples out of the tree to satisfy you people."

"That's as much of a commitment as you can give this committee?" demanded Evelyn Brewster's tight, quiet voice.

"It's as much of a commitment as any honest detective could give you, ma'am. Chopping down the tree is the job of the grand jury and the DA. Yours is making sure they do theirs."

"It isn't enough!" she cried. Her voice quivered. "It has no moral dimension! We are not here merely to *stop* corruption. We are here to root it out; it is that, and only that, which is important, no matter who is hurt or what hardships are worked upon their families. Civic duty takes precedence over personal convenience. The guilty must suffer. Every police-man who has ever taken a bribe, every bookmaker who has ever taken a bet—"

"My dear," said her husband.

"Every speakeasy proprietor who has ever sold an illicit drink—"

"Evelyn."

"Every woman who has ever sold her body to lustful men—"

"*Evelyn!*" His voice was a whipcrack.

"Oh!" she exclaimed. Her voice was breathless, half-smothered, as if her husband had tossed a bucket of cold water over her.

"I've sent plenty of wrong Ghees to the can, and I've never lost any sleep over any of them," said Hammett. "I wouldn't lose any sleep over sending crooked cops up either. But you wouldn't have any police graft if you didn't have prostitu-tion, or gambling, or bootlegging—"

"Exactly! Stop those . . ."

"The trouble is, ma'am, you can't stop those. Statutes that conflict with human nature are ultimately unenforceable and just create disrespect for all law, as we've seen with Prohibi-tion. But if you *legalized* gambling and prostitution, and then licensed and controlled them with the regulating power as-signed to someone other than the police, you'd cut off the sources of police graft and corruption, and—"

"Do you think this committee could ever agree, even in principle, to such immoral, outrageous suggestions?" she de-manded.

"No," said Hammett, "they haven't invented a committee yet that has that much sense. So you still need an investiga-tor. I'll be out in the hall."

Eleven

HAMMETT, on his third cigarette in the corridor outside the mayor's complex of offices, turned quickly when a door opened behind him. The man framed in the opening was about fifty, bulky and powerful, clean-shaven but with thick curly hair, a strong, slightly down-curved nose, and fleshy lips above a stubborn, meaty chin.

"Mr. Hammett. Could you come in, please?"

Hammett went through the door, and realized that he was in McKenna's private office.

"I was eavesdropping from in here," said the man. He gestured at his clothes: patterned plus fours, diamond argyle socks, a V-neck cricket sweater. "I never got home to change after leaving the golf course this afternoon."

Hammett had him then. Owen Lynch, McKenna's executive secretary. Also aide-de-camp, adviser, political guide, speech writer, and—if political opponents could be believed—chief conniver. A man with a private income and no personal political ambition, on whose judgment McKenna relied explicitly.

"Brandy?"

Hammett shook his head. "I'm just coming off a two-day drunk."

"I thought you said that you and Atkinson had drifted apart."

"That doesn't change anything."

"Of course not. Sorry." Lynch slid back a panel to pour himself a generous drink from a Stourbridge decanter. He held it to the light. " 'He who aspires to be a hero must drink brandy.' "

"Sure. But I don't suppose you asked me in to hear you quote Boswell."

"A private detective who reads Boswell. I like that. I pounded that line into Bren's thick head during the twenty-two campaign when the teetotals took to calling him Brandy

78

Bren. It was very effective at rallies. The public likes its heroes slightly flawed."

"I don't follow politics much."

"Meaning you didn't—or wouldn't—vote for Bren? There was a time when I didn't myself."

Hammett knew the story. In 1913, as a feature writer on crusading editor Fremont Older's *Bulletin,* Lynch had been one of the few who opposed McKenna's candidacy for mayor. But despite Lynch's clever and biting attacks, McKenna had won even in the home district of his incumbent opponent, P. H. "Pinhead" McCarthy.

"He's gotten better since then?"

"Or I've gotten less discriminating," said Lynch with an easy smile.

Four years later, embittered by personal tragedy, he had resigned from the newspaper to direct McKenna's drive for reelection. It was successful, for McKenna's personal magnetism had found its perfect complement in Lynch's hardheaded pragmatism.

"Bren is backing you all the way in there with the committee."

Hammett slid down on his spine in a big leather armchair, and said nothing.

After a moment, Lynch chuckled. "You think he'll try to hamstring the investigation?"

"It's his town."

"Which he'll be leaving in two years for the statehouse in Sacramento." He gestured with his empty brandy glass. *"Unless* there's a scandal in his administration that he does nothing about."

"Molly Farr," said Hammett. There was a thoughtful, vaguely approving look in his eyes.

"Molly Farr or some other. Oh, I know he has been elected three times because the citizens *want* a wide-open town. But his popularity extends beyond that. He's America's first lord mayor in the British sense." His eyes were alight with enthusiasm. "When he took office, San Francisco was still a nineteenth-century provincial town; Bren turned it into a

79

twentieth-century metropolis. It was a community with a tradition of political corruption under Abe Reuf, and with a history of mob violence and vigilante violence and labor violence. Bren has brought together employer, employed, and unemployed, and gotten them to—"

"The only thing that won't go away is that political corruption," cut in Hammet in an almost lazy voice.

"And that's exactly why I arranged for Bren to chair this reform committee as soon as I heard about it. That's why I talked Dan Laverty into advising the committee—so they'd get an incorruptible investigator. And when that investigator was killed, I had Dan get us another one equally trustworthy."

"You trust the Preacher's judgment that much?"

"He and Bren and I went through grammar and high school together out in the Mission. We've known each other for better than forty years." He shook his head. "The directions people go! Griff Mulligan was another one in the class. . . ."

McKenna bustled in. One pearl-gray trouser cuff was artfully draped into the top of an oak-tanned cowboy boot. Despite his high heels, he was half a head shorter than the other two men. Through the briefly opened door, Hammett could see the committee members still standing in odd groups around the table.

McKenna beamed, pumping Hammett's hand up and down in both of his. "Congratulations! The reform committee has hired you to investigate graft in the San Francisco police department, and to report to the grand jury all material for criminal indictments against policemen guilty of taking bribes." He crossed to the sliding panel in the Gillow sideboard, which was supported by two magnificently carved wooden eagles. "Brandy?"

"I'm on the wagon." Still wary, Hammett added, "I'll need strong backing in certain areas, Mr. Mayor. . . ."

"Just name them."

"I'll be questioning policemen, everyone from sergeant up, to start—and a lot of them aren't going to want to talk to me."

80

Lynch said, "Dan Laverty will see that anyone your people want, your people get."

"They'll be Vic's people, actually, headed by another ex-Pinkerton named Jimmy Wright. Jimmy's in town now, the rest are due up from Los Angeles next week. They'll start interrogations on Monday, in an office we select ourselves so informants can come and go unobserved for their own protection."

"Anything else?" asked Lynch.

"I'll need some sort of authorization to talk to the phone company to monitor certain lines, with stenographers taking down all incoming and outgoing calls."

"Fair enough." Lynch extended his hand to Hammett; the mayor was working on his second brandy. "I'll get written authorization for you before your men arrive. You'll see that I meant what I said about the total backing of this office." He chuckled. "And you can be as secretive as you wish about your methods and findings, even with us."

"That's right," said Hammett pleasantly.

When the lean detective had departed, McKenna lowered his snifter almost sadly. "That's a man with a grievance, Owen, and you've turned him loose in my city with a meat ax."

Surprising anger suffused the secretary's heavy features. "Goddammit, man, this is your only chance to get out of the mess you've gotten yourself into!"

"Mess?"

Lynch sighed. He plopped his briefcase on a walnut and gilt console table and fished in his watch pocket for the key.

"I didn't plan to spring this on you until tomorrow morning on the Sacramento train, Bren, but . . ." He delved for papers. "You know they've taken to calling you *Randy* Bren around City Hall these days?"

"Haw! That's good, that!" McKenna tossed off half his third brandy with a practiced flip of the wrist. "Randy Bren. I like that."

"I doubt that Colleen would find it very amusing."

"She ain't likely to hear it."

Lynch said nothing. McKenna turned a hard questioning stare on him. Mention of his wife seemed to have troubled him.

"Well, is she?"

Lynch had removed a thin file folder from the briefcase. "Report from a private detective dated Monday, May 21, 1928. Subject of Investigation: BRENDAN BRIAN MCKENNA. Client: COLLEEN DOROTHEA MCKENNA. Quote: 'Subject was observed leaving—'"

"Col . . . you mean that Colly put a *private snoop* on me?"

"What did you expect, Bren? She's no fool and you've been getting more flagrant with it. Quote: 'Nine thirty A.M., subject was called for at City Hall by a blonde . . .' Hmm . . . ah, yes. 'Left Whitcomb Hotel, Market Street, at eleven o'clock A.M. . . .' Ah! Here: 'Twelve ten P.M. ascended to upstairs room above Jack's Restaurant with a brunette' . . . There's a good word, Bren, 'ascended'; it gives a scriptural flavor that I'm sure Colly would find comforting. The investigator points out that there are beds in those upstairs rooms, and . . ."

"You've made your point," said McKenna weakly.

Lynch put the folder back in the briefcase. "And you can ask what mess you've gotten yourself into?"

McKenna said wearily, "Thank God Colly didn't see—"

"Who the devil do you think gave it to me?"

"You . . . can't be serious, Owen!"

"With a note that if this didn't stop, you'd be running for governor as a divorced man."

McKenna went to the ornate rocaille pier glass to nervously center his cravat. The light slanted down cruelly across the puffiness of indulgence around his jowls, the fine veining in his eyes, the first tiny hints of burst capillaries in his nose.

He mumbled, "Colly would go through with it? The divorce?"

"If you force her hand. If you don't, she'll keep it in the family once again. But something that *isn't* going to disappear is that Judah Street rezoning stink. It's all over the papers and liable to—"

82

"I vetoed the damned thing Friday."

"Two weeks too late. It's an open secret that your three handpicked boys on the Board of Supervisors took a thousand apiece to vote for the change from Second residential to commercial."

"I'll have their candy asses if they did," said McKenna with as much anger as he could muster.

"Then there's the rape-murder of that little Chinese girl . . ."

"Dan Laverty shot the murdering bastard dead; the bluenoses ought to be cheering."

"Would they cheer to know that Dan kicked the man's balls up into his belly first?"

"Yes," said McKenna defiantly, "after what he used 'em for."

"Maybe so. But the dead man was a rumrunner for a local 'legger. The teetotals are already saying it wouldn't have happened if you didn't allow the speaks to flourish in San Francisco. And finally is this thing of the Brewster pup and his cronies going off to Molly Farr's place."

McKenna attempted to shrug it off. "So Brady'll have to make a little noise because he plays handball with Dalt Brewster. It'll cool down, Owen. It always does."

"Not this time. Not with Evelyn Brewster on the reform committee. She wants Molly out of business and in jail."

"I'll not see Molly put away for fifteen years." He raised a hand to forestall objections. "I know, Owen, you don't use whores and don't see why anyone else should, but it's more than just that. Last election, Molly had every Mary Magdalene in this city out voting tombstones for us from morning till night. I'll not throw her down." He brightened abruptly. "Besides, nobody knows where she is."

"Epstein does, no matter how much he denies it to the newspapers. If I were Hammett, I'd be trying to make a deal with Brass Mouth for her secret testimony."

"And you wanted him hired!" He burst out suddenly, "Why are we suddenly so worried about the reform element, anyway, Owen? In the old days—"

"The old days are gone. To be governor two years from

83

now, you have to get the clean money in San Francisco behind you now."

"It was the not-so-clean money put me in this office."

"Don't you understand *yet*, Bren? *That* money has nowhere else to go."

They descended the broad marble stairway to the floor of the rotunda, and paused at the head of the granite outer stairs while the chauffeur brought up McKenna's grand yellow and black 1927 Lincoln coaching brougham with its gleaming side-lamps. Then Lynch went up Polk alone to his four-year-old Auburn. His thick shoulders slumped slightly. He was tired. It was all getting so damned complicated.

"Bren, Bren, you damned fool," he said aloud in fond exasperation as he watched the brougham's retreating taillights.

What wouldn't he give to still have a wife to buoy him up, comfort him, inspire him as Colleen McKenna would do for Bren, given the chance? But his wife, Clarissa, had died, childless, in the influenza epidemic of 1918, and he had been alone ever since.

Twelve

HAMMETT went down Prescott Court, a narrow cul-de-sac off Vallejo Street, looking at house numbers. He paused in front of 20/22, an older building with white scrollwork on the roof overhang and around the windows of the lower flat. From somewhere, very faintly, came the tang of fermenting grapes. It was only in the past ten years, since the Italians had begun pushing the Irish out, that the billy goats had disappeared from the lower slopes of Telegraph Hill and the bootleg winepresses had begun to outnumber the whiskey cookers.

Which reminded him that he needed a bottle if he was going to play in Fingers LeGrand's poker game. It was tricky to try to get information about payoffs over the poker table in seemingly casual conversation; but Fingers knew him as a writer, not a detective, and he doubted that news of his hiring by the reform committee would be out on the street yet. He'd left McKenna's office less than an hour before.

And the sooner he found Vic's killer, the sooner he could return to the revision of *The Dain Curse*.

Hammett knocked, then rattled the heavy brass knob of the alley door. He had to stoop to press his nose against the heavy-gauge wire mesh that covered the window. It was gritty with street dirt.

A blocky silhouette moved toward Hammett, a latch was turned, and the window opened inward. A garlicked voice shoved words at him through the mesh. "I don't know you."

"Fingers does."

"Fingers who?"

"For Chrissake, knock-knock."

The door scraped open. The man's gray sweatshirt stank of stale sweat and was stretched taut over a broad hard mound of gut. He led the way to the speakeasy, a square concrete cell, the walls damp-stained and unadorned with either picture or calendar, the ceiling the rough pine joists of the subfloor above. A single light globe hung from an electric flex stapled to one of the rafters.

"Nice little place you've got here," said Hammett politely.

"Yeah, Palm Court at the Palace." He went around behind a two-by-twelve of unplaned wood laid across two upended wooden beer kegs. "What's yours?"

"Rye?"

"Seven-year-old Canadian."

Hammett leaned an elbow on the plank and looked around. There were a few straight-back chairs and two kitchen tables with chipped white enamel tops. One was empty, the other held a bottle and three glasses and six elbows.

The Italians who belonged to the elbows wore their overcoats buttoned and their fedoras precisely centered on their dark heads. None of them was speaking. The light laid down

85

their shadows as thick as tar across the floor and up the walls.

"Flip a lip over that," beamed the barkeep. He had a crooked nose and the eyes of a spaniel.

Hammett laid back the shot. His eyes popped wide open. "What's a pint of this run?"

"For you? Three fifty."

"And for everybody else?"

"Three fifty. Listen, that stuff goes out of here at fifty-six bucks a case. My cousin, see, runs this fishing boat for Dom Pronzini, and part of his cut he takes in—"

"Giusepp'." One of the men with his elbows on the table swung the word at the barkeep like a sock full of sand. To Hammett, he said, "Now you have your bottle, now you get on your way dam' quick."

Hammett laid a five on the stick. The bartender replaced it with a pint. Hammett dropped the bottle into his overcoat pocket, picked up his buck change, and asked how to get to the game.

"I'll show you the way."

Giuseppe led him through a small concrete area past a couple of battered garbage pails to steep exterior stairs. A dozen feet below, the yellowing grass of the hillside fell away to Sansome and Vallejo. Refuse, empty tins, and broken bottles lined the foot of the wall.

"Top flat. Don't bother the girls in the lower, y'know?"

Something in his voice made Hammett ask, "Blisters?"

"Now, nothing like that. Dead swell dames. Ya want some of that I can maybe arrange it, but no just knockin' on the door lemme in, see?"

"Sure."

One of the dead swell dames was outside her open back door. Her body, silhouetted through her filmy negligee, was full and lush and Mediterranean.

"Blisters," she said scornfully to Hammett as she ground out a cigarette beneath the heel of her pastel French mule. "We're no coffee-and hustlers, big boy."

She swayed against him, turning so her breasts were cushioned against his chest and her strong whore's thighs gripped his leg.

86

"That's the best you'll ever get next to."

"Sorry, sister, my weakness is liquor." He clamped power-ful fingers around the hand trying to slip the wallet off his hip. Her unabashed laughter followed him up the stairs.

Fingers' back door opened on a bright kitchen. A short mustached walleyed man came in from the hall as Hammett was taking out his pint.

"Pantry," said the man. He disappeared again.

Hammett could hear voices and chips. Stale smoke hung in the air. In the narrow white pantry he found a glass and opened the old-fashioned zinc-lined cooler. He chipped enough ice from one of the twin hundred-pound cakes for his drink, rammed the pick back into the wooden top of the waist-high cooler, and was dousing the ice with rye when the walleyed man popped back in.

"Dining room," he said.

The dining room was paneled in blond wood; its plate rail held only empty bottles and mail-order junk. The massive oak table bore scores of burns and dozens of pale rings to mark its years of service for poker rather than dining. In the corner behind Fingers' chair stood his loaded ten-gauge goose gun, outfitted with an extra heavy frame and breech.

LeGrand's dolorous face swam up at Hammett through the haze of smoke like a carp surfacing in muddy water.

"Table stakes with a pot limit. I'm the bank." He indicated whites, reds, blues. "Quarters, halves, dollars."

Hammett bought twenty bucks' worth of chips. Fingers started the first-name-only introductions.

"Dash, you met See-See out in the kitchen. . . ."

They nodded to each other. Hammett happened to know that the dapper little man with the reputation for looking in two directions at once was the best "soft-touch" pickpocket in the game. In thirty years as a cannon he'd never taken a fall.

Directly to See-See's left was a tough, handsome, loud-mouthed Irishman named Joey. Auto mechanic by his hands. He said it was his night off.

Finally there was a pudgy, middle-aged German named Dolf, whose last name Hammett knew to be Geltwasser. He peered myopically through spectacles thick as bottle glass

87

and ran a pawnshop and was one of the city's deadliest amateur poker players. He had killed two men that Hammett knew about.

Hammett also knew he was probably wasting his time there that night. There just weren't enough players for the conversation to develop along the lines he needed. But now he was here, he may as well try; and what the hell, maybe he could pick up rent money in the process.

Fingers broke out a new deck, shuffled, and burned the top card. Despite deliberately erratic play, Hammett took two hours to lose the first of two double sawbucks he had gotten from Jimmy Wright as an advance against expenses on the *Atkinson Investigations* fund. He ran a few bluffs as advertising, and two of them took good pots.

By the time he bought his second stack, he'd killed half his pint, and the group had loosened up a bit. All of them were punishing their bottles, especially Dolf Geltwasser. He drank prodigious amounts of whiskey; the eyes magnified by his thick glasses became only more kindly, and his play only more deadly.

Time to start. Hammett said, "Dolf, whatever happened to the Silver Fox?"

"He went east, Oklahoma City, I heard, Joplin, Mo., maybe." The old German shook his head. "That Silver Fox, he would bet his lungs."

"When he was running that gambling hell on Pacific and Montgomery, wasn't his landlord a cop?"

"Sure," said Fingers. "Patrolman Paddy Quinlan. Rents that and the place next door to a couple of 'leggers now. Charges 'em fifty a month rent each, and receipts 'em for thirty."

"How does he get away pocketing the extra twenty?" asked Joey in a belligerent voice.

"Because they're engaged in breaking the law," said Fingers.

"I should have been a cop," said Hammett.

"Heard the latest?" asked See-See. "Tickets to the policeman's ball. Some of the cops sell the same tickets over and over, and don't turn in any of it. They arrest somebody, he gets off if he buys enough tickets."

The talk drifted to a famous poker game that had run for two years at the Kingston Club, a fancy downtown place with liveried waiters and velvet settees and superb French cuisine. Nick the Greek and Titanic Thompson, playing partners, took over nine hundred thousand each out of the game.

"And I heard Titanic went into it broke," said Hammett, shoving in chips. Out of the table talk he'd gotten only one name, Paddy Quinlan, to pass on to Jimmy Wright. "Let's see who's doing what on whom here."

"Whom, yet," said See-See. "You're there when it comes to spreading the salve, Dash."

"I had a deprived youth."

Fingers had two pair. "Mites and lice," he said sadly. "Hammett, I can't do a thing with you."

Joey lurched to his feet. "Deal me out, I gotta tap a kidney."

The evening might have been a bust from the investigation point of view, thought Hammett, but he was coming out of it a heavy winner: He was up something well over a hundred bucks. Joey came back and sat down.

"I hope that was a local phone call," said Fingers.

The burly Irishman looked sheepish. "South City, I didn't think you'd mind. Girl down there, I figured maybe when this broke up. . . ."

"She got a friend?" asked Hammett.

"She's busy herself, dammit."

"Let's play cards," suggested Geltwasser softly. His eyes twinkled at Hammett across the table. "I think I have you figured out now, Mr. Dash."

He did indeed. An hour later the lean detective was broke. Drunk or sober, nothing wrong with the old German's nerve. It had been an education in bluffing. He remembered a story about three drunken patriots during the war who'd decided to show their hatred for the Hun by messing up Geltwasser and his hockshop. One had died, one had fled, and now, ten years later, the third still walked with a limp.

Hammett shook his head at the new stack Fingers had begun to shove across to him. "I'm tapped out." He jingled the change in his pocket. "And I'm already into my bookie. Pleasure, gents."

The outside air was like wine. He buttoned up his overcoat as he went down the terrazzo steps. A fine damp fog was in to soak up the misty gaslight at the alley's mouth.

Hammett stopped dead. Three silhouetted figures were coming through the fog toward him. They were spread across the alley so he would have to pass between them to get out to Vallejo.

Hammett fished out smokes and matches and leaned back against the rough stucco of a housefront as they came abreast of him. The closest one checked his stride.

"Got a match, buddy?"

The one in the middle had stopped directly in front of Hammett, the third a yard beyond. They had him neatly boxed in.

"A match? Sure."

It scraped, flared at the end of Hammett's cigarette. The other man leaned just enough forward, as if to share the flame, so that Hammett would have to take his back from the wall and thus bare the nape of his neck to a rabbit punch.

But Hammett drove off the wall with the toe of his right shoe snapping into the man's left kneecap. Pivoting on his left foot, he rammed his cigarette into the second man's eye while the first was still yelling.

That left the third, coming in hard to cut off his break for the mouth of the alley. Instead, Hammett met his charge. He smashed the top of his head up against the attacker's face and through his mashed fedora felt teeth give inward. He sprinted for the concealing shadow at the far end of the cul-de-sac.

"We've got the bastard!" yelled one of them.

But Hammett had once questioned a witness in Prescott Court and he knew that the blank red brick rear of Broad-

90

way's Washington Irving Grammar School was not completely flush with the final house on either side of the alley. The gaps were closed off with rough plank fences ten feet high. He veered right in the darkness, jumped to catch the top of the fence with his fingers, and swung his lean body to one side so he could hook the back of his shoe over the top also.

Grunting, he heaved again, pulled, rolled belly-down across the top of the planks and let go to fall away into blackness. The twenty-foot drop ended with bone-jarring abruptness on the gravel playground. He limped on stinging feet around the corner of the building and away.

Once on Broadway, he laughed aloud in the deserted three A.M. street. It was the first time anybody had tried to roll him when he'd *lost* at poker. He drew his overcoat tighter against the chill seeping up off the bay, and wondered if his hat would have any toothmarks in it.

Fast work. The committee had hired him only a half dozen hours before. Too fast. It gave him somebody obvious to work on. They were making mistakes already.

Thirteen

"JUST a second," Goodie called in answer to the gentle kicks on the bottom of the door. She threw a kimono over her slip, ran a hand through her unruly golden hair, and went to open it.

Hammett came by her bearing a steaming pot of coffee in one hand and a cheap tin tray in the other with both of his cups and saucers on it, both of his spoons, sugar and cream, and two buttered sweet rolls hot from the oven.

"Look, ma, no hands."

91

He continued into the kitchen where he deposited his treasures on the table. He was dressed in a business suit, a dress shirt, and a patterned tie with a large loose knot. He busied himself laying out his peace offering.

"I have a vague recollection of trying to bust down your door the other night."

Goodie blushed. "I . . . wouldn't let you in, Sam. A little later I saw you going over to the Weller."

He looked at her with keen dark eyes. His mouth quirked beneath the trim mustache. "I was hootched up like a bat, sweetheart."

"I'm . . . sorry about your friend." In a small voice, she added, "The newspapers say it was a gangland slaying, but you said . . ."

"Don't let it get cold." He waved at the table and sat down himself. Around bites of sweet roll, he outlined what had happened since Atkinson's death, ending with the attack a few hours previously. "I really red-lighted Shuman, and this must have been his idea of a smart way to get back at me. It was actually stupid, because it's given me a place to start."

"A member of the *police commission* ordering you beat up?" Goodie sounded rather dazed. "I bet you were followed to the poker game, and—"

"Uhuh. Spotting a tail is like riding a bicycle, darling—you never forget how."

She turned Hammett's wrist to check his watch, then was on her feet and flying for the bathroom. "It's after seven thirty—I've got to comb my hair and get to work!"

"I'll just use your phone. . . ."

She stuck her blond head back around the doorframe from the big wall bed closet beyond which was the minuscule bathroom. "Is *that* why you're being so sweet this morning, Sam?"

"What sort of bum do you take me for?" he demanded virtuously.

He could hear her laughter as he sat on the sofa, set the telephone on his knee, and told the operator that he wanted DAvenport 20. When a voice said, "Police," Hammett said,

"Central Station," waited some more, then asked for Sergeant Manion.

"Jack, Dash Hammett here. I'm trying to get a line on a Chinese girl named Crystal Tam, who . . . huh? Right, that's the one, Molly Farr's maid. . . . Mmm-hmm. No, I'm not even sure she's local, but I thought . . . yeah. Right. That fast? Okay, many thanks, Jack."

He broke the connection, released the hooks, gave the operator a SUtter exchange number, got no answer, and was hanging up when Goodie emerged from the bathroom fully dressed and pulling on her coat.

"Will you shut the door when you leave, Sam?"

He blew her a kiss, returned to the phone and got DAvenport 8398 and asked for Jimmy Wright. When the fat little detective came on the line, his voice was still full of sleep.

"What have the cops turned up on Vic?" Hammett asked him.

"Last solid thing is him leaving the Chapeau Rouge at the foot of Powell sometime after midnight, under his own power. They thought he was a timber beast out of Seattle. The Homicide boys are checking cabs now."

"All right, I want you to ask around the Army-Navy Y, the Lawrence Hotel, the Commodore—places like that near Mission and The Embarcadero."

"Will do," said the cop, without asking where the lead had come from.

Hammett tried the SUtter number again, and this time was told that Phineas Epstein would be in court until four thirty. Hammett identified himself as a reporter named Hawkins from a Los Angeles paper, and made an appointment to see Epstein at six P.M.

His last call was to the business office of the phone company.

"My name is Harrison LeGrand, I have TUxedo eight-two-seven-three. I'd like to check my toll calls for the past week. . . ."

He got the information, thanked the girl, and hung up. He carefully pulled Goodie's door shut behind him, tried it to

93

make sure it was locked, and went next door for his overcoat and his now-battered gray Wilton fedora. He went out into Post Street.

Hammett hadn't known Chinatown before the fire, when Grant Avenue had been Dupont Gai, Street of a Thousand Lanterns, and the climb up from Bush had been lined with clattering shooting galleries. Where now were restaurants and bazaars and import shops and warehouses, then had been houses whose half-open shutters revealed scantily clad, foulmouthed Caucasian whores.

He passed Old St. Mary's Church on the corner of California. Even that had been gutted to the walls by the fire following the quake. Catty-corner across the intersection was the new, beautifully oriental Sing Fat Trading Company, with tilt-edged pagoda roofs and narrow balconies with delicate filigree railings.

Mostly gone, too, were the trousered women and silk-jacketed shopkeepers, the lily-footed wives of rich merchants, and the highbinders swarming around the gambling clubs even at noon. Some of the hatchet men were still around, but the last tong killing had been in 1922, a year after Jack Manion had taken over as sergeant of the Chinatown Squad. Manion, who had earned the fear and hatred of the Six Companies and the name of *Mau Yee*. The Cat. Because he seemed to have eyes that could look behind him.

Hammett stopped with one foot in the gutter to keep from running into a blue-denimed waiter hurrying someone's hot lunch from the Shanghai Low. Half a block beyond, an aged man with the beard of a billy goat and the timeless Oriental eyes of Confucius was wielding a gleaming cleaver in a white tiled butcher shop, sectioning up a whole pig, smoking hot and roasted to a deep mahogany color. A dozen smoked ducks hung by their necks behind him.

Hammett doubted that Manion would have anything for him on Crystal Tam. It was only three hours since he had called. Still, Jack could do some incredible things in Chinatown.

The heavy warring odors of ginger, hot grease, and herbs drifted from an import shop as he stepped around a big wet wooden tub half-filled with sea snails; next to it was a wooden crate of dried South Seas *bêches-de-mer* used in making soup.

He bought a Mandarin orange from a sidewalk stand, and pushed toward the thickset, unruly-haired Caucasian who seemed to be reading the calligraphy posted outside one of the Chinese-language newspaper offices.

Hammett dropped peels on the sidewalk. He shoved a juicy segment of orange into his mouth. To Manion's back, he said, "What's the news?"

The Irishman turned and grinned. There was a cleared space around him. In these narrow streets, The Cat bore invincibility like a physical aura.

"The price of opium is going up."

"They put that in the papers?"

When they were clear of the throng and crossing narrow Grant Ave to the far sidewalk, Manion said, "Hell, you know I can read only about six words of Cantonese. Psychology, Dash—just psychology."

"You have anything for me, Dr. Freud?"

Manion grinned again. He was craggy-browed and square-jawed, and moved with the easy grace of a man who never hesitated to drop through a skylight in pursuit of a hatchet man. "Have I ever failed you?"

"How about lunch at Yee Chum's while you tell me about it?"

"Lead on, Oh Father of Detectives."

Hammett stopped dead on the Washington Street sidewalk. "Don't tell me you save old *Black Masks*. 'Dead Yellow Women' appeared three years ago—"

"*Black Mask* is better than corncobs in the bathroom," Manion assured him seriously. "You can read 'em before you use 'em."

On the corner of Waverly Place, narrow worn stairs led down to the basement, a spotty inset mirror giving them back their reflections. At the bottom were heavy wooden double doors that they shoved wide as they entered the noisy, steamy, clattering, low-roofed room. The round-topped tables were crowded with Chinese shoveling in rice with chopsticks while the singsong of high-pitched conversation went on unabated. They were the only Caucasians.

"Hello, Daddy!" cried the little girl standing on the cashier's stool behind the glass-topped counter to the right of the door.

"Hello, Sweet Flower," said Manion. "Still studying your lessons?"

"Study very hard, Daddy!" the moon-faced child shouted with delight.

The girl's mother came from the rear of the restaurant, wiping her hands on a limp dish towel. "*Min Bok*, we are honored."

To the noncriminal citizens of Chinatown, Manion was *Min Bok*—Old Uncle. The woman led them across the white tile floor and between close-set tables to a curtained enclosed booth. A skinny waiter with a seamed yellow face and bad teeth brought the tea and two small heavy white handleless cups with green and gold dragons painted around their sides.

"Who was the little girl?"

"One of my godchildren. I can't keep track of them anymore."

The waiter returned with their order: chicken clear soup, pork fried rice, green *chow yuk*, sweet-and-sour pork, almond duck. They ate with chopsticks, with Manion doing most of the talking.

"You wanted to know about Crystal Tam. Christened Lillian Tam Fong by her folks, educated at the Sunday school of the Methodist Chinese Mission. She was an excellent student, especially at English—"

"How old is she?"

"Fifteen. Why?"

"She looks twelve and talks forty. Are we sure we've got the same girl? This one didn't strike me as having only a mission-school background."

96

Manion was dipping startlingly green *chow yuk* into hot sauce. He chewed thoughtfully. "It's the same girl, all right. She visits her folks on Sunday afternoons. Told them she was a domestic for a well-to-do family up in Marin County, and leaves them in time to catch the Sausalito ferry back before supper. Really, I suppose, going back to Molly's in time for the Sunday-night trade."

Hammett pushed away his barely touched plate and fished for cigarettes. "She visit them last Sunday?"

"*And* told 'em she was going away on a trip with the people she works for, and would be in touch when she got back. Apparently planning to skip out even then. Now they're damned worried."

"Because you came around?"

Manion poured green tea into both cups. The waiter appeared to set a fresh pot in place of the old.

"No. Because four years ago, when Lillian was eleven, she answered a newspaper ad for her first domestic position. She didn't come back from the interview."

Hammett hitched his chair closer to the table with a sudden glint of interest in his eyes. "That sounds familiar."

"Yeah, doesn't it? Next day her folks went to the cops." He shrugged. "You know how much that got 'em—a yellow girl. . . ."

Hammett nodded.

"A month later, a letter came, postmarked Chicago, to one of her mission-school chums who could read English. Her folks can't, of course. The letter was in Lillian's handwriting, asking her to tell the folks that Lillian had a job as servant to a rich man and was well and happy. . . ."

"Yeah," said Hammett. "Everything fits the white slavery racket except the letter actually being in the kid's handwriting. Usually the ones they grab can't read or write. Anyway, how do we get Lillian Tam Fong back from Chicago as Crystal Tam?"

"You want me to do *all* your work for you?" grumbled Manion. "One Sunday afternoon about nine months ago, Lillian walks in, spins the tale about her job in Marin, and starts showing up every Sunday since. She even finds a few bucks for the folks now and again."

"And nary a word about the years in between? Not even to the girlfriend?"

"Nup. Chicago, that's it. And apparently the girlfriend dislikes Lillian's current Chinatown pals so much that they aren't friends any longer."

Hammett was silent, frowning, his forearms crossed on the table. The cigarette between his lips spiraled a thin line of smoke up toward the grease-darkened ceiling.

"What's the address over in Marin?"

"It'll just be a blind anyway." Manion was digging out his hip pocket notebook as he argued. "No phone, I checked."

"A blind?" Hammett shook his head. "This Crystal is a very bright kid, she wouldn't just pick an address out of the hat. And it's probably isolated enough to make a hell of a fine hideout for someone on the dodge from the law like Molly Farr is."

"I didn't think of that angle," admitted Manion. He read from the notebook. "Mrs. Heloise Kuhn, the old Borne house on the Bolinas Road."

"Living with all the rest of the rich folks up by Bolinas?"

"Yeah, come to think of it," said Manion in a chagrined voice. "Fishermen and bootleggers and farmers and not a hell of a lot else. All of a sudden I have the feeling you might be saying hello to Molly Farr this afternoon."

"That's the idea," said Hammett.

Fourteen

THE woman bent over the wooden-staved rain barrel was better than six feet tall and weighed three hundred pounds.

- 98

Her back was to Hammett as he came up the weed-grown drive to the white farmhouse; great knuckles of hard fat rode over the buried hipbones under her faded check house-dress.

"Mrs. Heloise Kuhn?"

"Huh?" The huge moon buttocks tensed in unconfined nastiness as she straightened in surprise and swung around to face him. "Who's asking?"

Her face was decorated with a rosebud mouth above too many chins, and mean black raisins stuck behind square-rimmed eyeglasses.

"Hammett. Homemaker's Insurance Agency."

"I ain't buying."

He moved around her to the other side of the rain barrel. She was drowning a kitten. The water boiled briefly around her thick forearms. Pleasure pursed the rosebud lips. One tiny taloned paw spasmed a despairing arc of red parallels across her flesh.

"Bastard!" she burst out softly.

She slammed the small dark head against the side of the barrel. Hammett saw the glint of bone through the wet-plastered fur on the delicate skull as she buried the kitten in the water once more. Four more small bodies, their thinness emphasized by wet clinging fur, lay in the weeds beyond the corner of the house.

"Kittens ain't as much fun 'thout you do their ma with 'em."

The water was quiet around her forearms. Her voice filled as if she were eating pastry.

"Put 'em all in a sack an' th'ow 'em offen a bridge into a river, 'long with a old hunk of scrap iron. One old tabby I seen stayed up near twenty minutes that way, tryin' to save them kits."

"Yeah," said Hammett. He had broken a fingernail on the rim of the barrel.

She clacked ill-fitted dentures together. "Near bust a gut laughin', I can tell you. My brother won hisse'f five bucks off another feller, bettin' how long she'd stay up." With a regretful sigh she abandoned the past. "Insurance, you say. Payin' out a claim?"

"Tracing a witness, Mrs. Kuhn. We think your maid saw a car hit a woman over in the city two Sundays ago, and—"

The fat woman started to laugh. Her whole body participated, like waves bouncing back and forth in a bathtub.

"I look like I got a maid out here, mister?"

"Lillian Tam Fong," said Hammett. "Oriental minor."

"I wouldn't have no chink on the place."

"Miss Fong gave this as her place of employment to the police officer investigating the accident. Mrs. Heloise Kuhn. The old Borne farmhouse on the Bolinas Road." Hammett was reading from the blank back of an envelope he had taken from his suitcoat inner pocket. He returned it. "The driver I hired in Sausalito brought me here. If there's some mistake. . . ."

The fat woman jabbed a still-wet finger against his chest. "You better clear out of here you don't want no trouble. Ain't no chinks on my place, ain't been no chinks on my place, ain't gonna be no chinks on my place."

"Then you won't mind if I glance around."

He went by her up the weathered front steps toward the screen door leading to the front room. The screen sagged in its frame. When he reached the porch, she said behind him, "Don't try it, mister."

He looked down at her, unmoving beside her rain barrel.

"What'll you do? Drown another kitten?"

He swung back toward the door. The woman said, "Andy," in her fat, pleasure-filled voice.

The screen door opened a foot and the muzzle of a double-barrel shotgun—an Eastern Arms hammerless takedown twelve-gauge—came through the opening. The muzzle bored into Hammett's breastbone. He backed down the steps. He felt breathless.

The door was shouldered wider by a towheaded seventeen-year-old with the build of a bull and a snub-nosed freckled face almost idiotic in its vacuity. Sweat stood on his forehead and his cheeks were flushed as if from sustained physi-

100

cal effort. His faded workshirt was buttoned crookedly. It hung outside his trousers. His grin was delighted and quite mad.

"Shud I do him, ma?"

"Let be."

Andy quit advancing. Hammett was three steps below the porch with the twin muzzles angled down against his collarbone.

Hammett made himself take another backward step, then another, and then a third to the ground. He turned stiffly away. Flies were already buzzing around the little heap of dead fur by the corner of the house.

As he went by her, the fat woman said, "Just a minnit, you."

Hammett stopped.

The woman looked at him, the raisins unwinking in their sockets of suet. She took a breath and made a sustained grating noise in her throat. Her rosebud mouth worked. She spat what she had hawked up against Hammett's necktie, just under the knot.

Hammett went wordlessly down the narrow rutted grass track. Behind him, mother and son were making noises he took to be laughter.

As soon as the track dipped and curved to hide him from the house, he stopped and took off his tie. He threw it into the waist-high reed grass that flanked the track. He began to curse in a rising voice, as much madness in his tone as there had been in Andy's laughter. The muscles stood out cleanly along the sides of his jaws as he ground his teeth. His face was fashioned from scraped bone. Somewhere in the trees arched over the narrow ruts a crestless scrub jay began its rusty-hinge of protest at his presence. Hammett could feel the black rage loosening its fingers from his mind.

Without being reckless, he'd never been afraid of dying. He didn't like finding out that now he was.

He started down the track again toward the high-shouldered old Model-T coupe he'd hired in Sausalito. His progress sent a pair of mourning doves careening away, sunlight gleaming off the white feathers edging their pointed gray tails.

"The hell with them," he muttered aloud.

Molly Farr wouldn't be jungled up at a place like this. She wouldn't give anyone like the fat woman that much of a hold over her. A fat woman who, goddammit, seemed familiar.

He came out on the Bolinas Road. His teenage driver was leaning against the fender of the Model-T. The coachwork of the car had been cut away with a blowtorch behind the cab so a pickup bed could be welded on. A devil with a thumb to his nose rode the cap on the flat-sided brass radiator.

Hammett jerked his head back at the house. "Where's her husband?"

"Ain't nobody ever seen him that I know," said the boy. "Guess she was married just long enough to have Andy."

"No man around at all?"

"Just her brother, sometimes. Big, mean-looking guy runs rum for some bootlegger over in the city."

"What's the brother's name?"

"Don't rightly know. Maybe my paw . . ."

"Doesn't matter."

He got in the car. The leather seat was hot from the sun. Hot breeze came through the opened upper half of the windshield as they started off with a jerk. He was reduced to Phineas Epstein after all. Epstein was going to be a damned tough nut to crack.

The fat woman and her son had watched Hammett out of sight around the bend in the twin grassy ruts. The boy stood spraddle-footed on the porch, the shotgun muzzle-down in the crook of his arm.

"He comin' back, maw?"

She turned to look up at him, considering, squinting against the late afternoon sunlight. Finally she shook her head. "We scairt him." She added, "I need them kittens th'owed back up the ravine 'gainst they start stinking."

"Right after I finish, maw. I promise."

"Now."

102

Andy leaned the shotgun against the edge of the porch and went off. While he was gone, the fat woman heard, very faintly, the Model T start up down at the foot of their track.

"You can go finish up now, son."

He went back into the house eagerly, letting the screen door flap shut behind him. He climbed narrow stairs to the second floor two at a time.

The window shades were lowered, making the room dim despite the bright sunshine outside. Andy carefully locked the door behind him before turning toward the bed. His face was already flushed with renewed excitement.

"He ain't gonna be back," he crowed. "Ain't no way he's gonna find out we got you here."

Crystal, nude, was crouched back against the juncture of the walls at the head of the bed, tense as a coiled spring but her face totally without animation, her eyes, too old for her fifteen years, totally fathomless. If her features bore an expression, it was resignation.

"Where was we?" demanded Andy with a clumsy attempt at roguishness. "Oh, sure. . . ."

He started to take off his trousers again.

Fifteen

BRASS MOUTH EPSTEIN didn't run to front. His second-floor office at 35 Powell Street was small, crowded by a big golden oak rolltop and a couple of massive fumed oak chairs with brown Spanish-grained leather upholstery. The three unwindowed walls were outfitted with floor-to-ceiling bookshelves crammed with dark-bound lawbooks in enough disarray to suggest use, not show.

Epstein was on his feet behind the desk, taking in Hammett with shrewd sparrow eyes. He was a small dark man in a brown suit to match his eyes; a gold watch chain glinted across his spare belly. His big nose dominated the other features.

"Take off your coat, Mr. Hawkins. Heat builds up here, afternoons."

Hammett nodded his thanks and draped his overcoat across the back of one of the leather chairs. He sat down in the other. Beside the desk, within reach of both men, was a walnut smoking stand with brass fittings. At its foot was an old-fashioned brass cuspidor. On the wooden coatrack in the corner was the lawyer's melton Chesterfield and fashionable beaver fedora.

"Now, what can I do for the Fourth Estate, Mr. Hawkins?"

Hammett settled back in his chair and got out his Camels. "The name is Hammett. I'm a private sleuth."

Epstein's eyes got sleepy in the same way that Jimmy Wright's got sleepy when he was thinking. He fiddled with a spindle upon which was impaled a fistful of memoranda. "Why the charade this morning? And why tell me now?"

Hammett glanced up at the attorney through fresh cigarette smoke.

"I want Molly Farr. We don't have to fight about it."

Epstein chuckled. Somewhere back in the open mouth a gold-capped tooth glinted. "We *won't* fight about it, Hammett. This office has no information concerning Miss Farr's present whereabouts."

"I've been hired by the reform committee to take Vic Atkinson's place. Forget all that stuff in the papers about a gangland slaying. Vic wanted to talk with Molly about police corruption. Instead, you let her talk with the newspapers and then dust while they built her up into the biggest story since the Gray-Snyder electrocution. That's fine with me. You're doing a great job for her. But if you'd let Vic talk to her before—"

"Mr. Atkinson never contacted this office."

"That's one of the things I wanted to know." A smile twitched the thin lips beneath his mustache. "I knew we didn't have to fight."

104

"I am an officer of the court, Hammett. Molly is a fugitive from justice. If I knew where she was, naturally I would produce her. From what I read in the papers, she's in New York—or Chicago—or Paris. The Mexican border patrol is going to nab her in the next hour or so, and the London bobbies are only waiting. . . ."

"Oh, I know *where* Molly is," said Hammett. "From what you say, I know more than *you* do. And frankly, I have more power than you do to *use* what I know."

Epstein bounced to his feet. He went to the window. Through the Venetian blinds, the dying afternoon made stripes of light and shadow across his body. He turned, still abruptly, to face Hammett. There was an ominous look in his eyes.

"Is that supposed to be a threat?"

"I've been authorized to tap a number of phones around town. I'll be questioning police lieutenants and captains on Monday. I'll be subpoenaing records." He paused to flick ashes. "I'd like to count on *your* cooperation."

Epstein's dark eyes were unwinking, rat-beady. He said: "You're doing the talking."

"I'd like Molly to do some talking. To me, in private. Vic wanted to bring her in, make her testify under oath. That was the wrong approach, I felt. Better to—"

"You can damn well believe it's the wrong approach," Epstein snapped. The blinds clacked dryly as he moved against them.

"What she tells me will be used," Hammett admitted, "but won't be attributed. Her name will never appear . . ."

"I'm sorry, Hammett, but you're wasting your time."

"I'm being paid for it." Hammett looked at his watch and stood up. "I wouldn't want to make you late for supper. As it stands, I'm afraid I'll be talking to Molly without your permission."

"You're bluffing."

He nodded. "Sure, I *didn't* talk with her direct, just with the lady who. . . ."

He bit off his words, stubbed out his cigarette, and retrieved his overcoat. Epstein watched, his eyes beady and unwinking. Hammett went out and pulled the door shut behind him.

After a full sixty seconds, Epstein crossed to the door, opened it and looked around the frame. His secretary's typewriter instantly stopped clacking.

"Jenny, did Mr. Hawkins leave?"

"He went straight through without stopping, Mr. Epstein. If you would like me to try to catch him, sir . . ."

"No, that's fine, Jenny."

He went back inside and sat down at the desk. He frowned at his green blotter, then picked up the phone and dialed the long-distance operator. He leaned forward intently.

"Yes, ma'am, I would like to make a person-to-person call to Mrs. . . ." He broke off abruptly. The tension left his small, tidy body. "Uh . . . cancel that, operator. I nearly made a mistake."

He put the receiver back in the hooks with a grimace, and stood up for a turn around the room. He went to the window. He looked out. He muttered, "Damn him," under his breath. Hammett might have told him about putting listeners on phones just to panic him into doing what he nearly had done—calling before they got around to him. Then Hammett would subpoena his records from the phone company.

Epstein got his hat and coat from the rack and went out. "I'll be back in a few minutes, Jenny, if you don't mind waiting."

"I've got two more revisions to type on the Wilcox brief anyway, Mr. Epstein."

Epstein went down the narrow stairway to emerge into Powell Street with the Pig'n Whistle on his right and the Edison Theatre on his left. His eyes darted and probed. No Hammett. The Turpin Hotel a few doors down, the cigar store next to that? The Pig'n Whistle itself, maybe?

No, all too risky, too exposed.

He turned abruptly up Powell toward Ellis with quick, nervous strides that his small stature made almost strutting. He went by Gene Compton's and the United Cigar store on

106

the corner without pausing, although both had pay phones, and right across Ellis. He'd made up his mind.

On the far corner he darted across Powell and started back down the even-numbered side. No Hammett. The tall, hawk-faced detective would be too conspicuous even in a crowd to be missed.

At Market he ducked abruptly into the Owl Drug's brightly lighted, cavernous interior. Beside the front entrance was a pair of pay phones with green metal trays holding the current directories. Epstein spilled silver across one of the trays, dialed the long-distance operator and asked for a three-digit Marin County number. He completed the call, fed in the required coins, and talked for a scant thirty seconds.

He hung up with a complacent look on his face. "What I thought," he muttered aloud. "Faking it."

Three minutes after he had disappeared across Powell toward his office, Hammett lowered the newspaper that had been shielding him from view at the lunch counter. He hissed out a cigarette in his coffee cup, left a dime for the waitress, and sauntered over to the pay phones.

He thumbed a nickel into the slot of the phone Epstein had used. His face felt flushed. Goddamn, to play the percentages that way and have your number come up! It had just felt *right* that of all the pay phones available on the block, Epstein would choose the crowded, bustling Owl as the place he'd be least conspicuous while calling.

"This is your long-distance operator. May I help you?"

Hammett drawled, "Inspector O'Gar, Homicide, Central Station. Five minutes ago a long-distance call was placed from this number. SUtter eight-seven-three-seven."

"Homicide?" Excitement vibrated in her voice. "What. . . how can I help you, Inspector?"

"Number called. Name of party called. Location of that phone."

"Ah . . . the number is two-three-two Mill Valley, Inspector. That is registered to a Mr. George F. Biltmore on Corte Madera Street—"

"I'll be damned!" exclaimed Hammett.

"I *beg* your pardon!"

107

"Oh. Yeah. Sorry." He got back into his imaginary O'Gar's skin. "Who'd he ask for?"

"Mrs. Biltmore."

Hammett hung up in her ear without thanking her; it was what she would expect from a real cop.

George F. Biltmore!

Who would expect madam Molly Farr to be stashed in the Marin County estate of San Francisco's Commissioner of Shipping? Biltmore was a power on the Street, a wealthy man who had started out as a sea captain and now had one of the city's largest ship brokerage firms. Did Biltmore know *who* he was hiding up there in the redwoods? Or had Epstein lied to him about a secret witness or an endangered client or. . . .

Tomorrow for Biltmore. He thought he had a way to get to him. But meanwhile, he had other things to find out.

He dialed Fingers LeGrand's number, TUxedo 8273, but he got no response. From the operator he got the phone number for 22 Prescott Court, the flat directly below LeGrand's. He was in luck. He recognized the sultry voice that responded.

"This is the man with the blisters," he said.

There was silence for a moment, then a low laugh as the whore remembered their brief encounter on her back porch.

"Hi, big boy."

"My weakness is still liquor, sweetheart, but maybe you can help me. I'm trying to get in touch right away with Fingers. . . ."

Sixteen

ABOVE the pounding shoes, strong ankles swelled into muscular calves. The girl on the table held up her skirts so her petticoats swirled about her plump dimpled knees as she danced. Work-thickened hands clapped time to the accordion, and voices shouted encouragement through the din and smoke.

Hammett and Goodie paused in the open doorway, squinting. Goodie said, in an exhausted voice, "Oh, Sam, it smells so good! Can't we eat now? Please? We've been to six places already—"

"Now we eat," said Hammett. Through the smoke he had glimpsed the dolorous features of Fingers LeGrand at one of the gingham-covered tables in the rear. The whore had said Fingers always ate supper in one of a dozen little family-style Italian cafés around Broadway and upper Grant.

"Hey!" Hammett exclaimed in great surprise. "Fingers!"

"Hello, Dash." The skinny gambler stood up. The table was scattered with fragments of brown Italian crust; a demolished antipasto was shoved to one side. He bowed to the golden-haired girl. "Good evening, ma'am. Out for a night on the town?"

"Just trying to get fed before I collapse of hunger."

Hammett, who had eaten only half a Chinese lunch, realized he too was ravenous. They sat down. The air was rich with the mingled fragrances of tomato and mushroom sauces, pastas, steamed clams, roasting chicken, and veal. A vast woman bustled over to their table and clopped down a bottle of illegal wine.

"The first pint's free," explained Fingers. "After that it's a dime a bottle."

"You eat here a lot?"

"We're trying to fatten him up," shouted the fat Italian lady over the din. She laughed hugely and dug a porcine elbow into Hammett's ribs. Somehow it was not at all like Heloise Kuhn's elbow. "You're even worse than he is, you boys must be undertakers." She roared with laugher and winked at Goodie. "You'll eat?"

The stockings of the girl dancing on the front table fell down and she was helped, suddenly red-faced and embarrassed, to the floor.

As the racket momentarily ebbed, Hammett said, "Soup to start. Ravioli. Salad after. Then we'll order."

Over huge flat bowls of rich brown steaming minestrone, thick with beans and mostaccioli, Hammett asked offhandedly, "Who came out big winner at the game the other night?"

"Who do you think?"

"The fat German."

"Right you are." Fingers started a toothpick toward his mouth, realized that Goodie was watching, and morosely returned the pick to his vest pocket.

"I went down forty," admitted Hammett. "I guess that Irishman was big loser. Funny, I keep thinking I've seen him around, but. . . ."

"Joey Lonergan." Fingers took out a cigar instead. "Came out here from back east a year or so ago. Owns a repair garage in the six-hundred block of Turk Street. Takes the night calls himself, but must be coming up in the world—just bought himself a second tow truck."

"In solid with the cops, then, I guess," said Hammett idly.

"They call him right from the scene of the accident, so he'll beat the other towers to it. He kicks back a percentage, of course. Carries the nickname of Dead Rabbit, I don't know why."

It seemed to have some meaning to Hammett. He raised questioning eyebrows. "Lonergan a tough boy?"

"He says he is."

Goodie sighed and leaned back against the cracked leather seat of the Number 15 streetcar they'd caught at Kearny and Broadway. "You invited me along tonight only because you wanted to find that Fingers LeGrand without him knowing you were looking for him, didn't you?"

They rattled by the Washington Street intersection where lights burned in the windows of Mulligan Bros. Bailbonds. Behind that window a pair of crude Irish power-brokers had planned to grab control of a city—and had succeeded. Where had they learned the subtlety—and gotten the original necessary cash—to play the power game?

To hell with it. For tonight, anyway. He looked down at

110

the golden-haired girl beside him. What he wanted to do was go home and make love to her. The trouble was that he couldn't. It would be like breaking the wing of a songbird.

"What about that man with the funny monicker?"

"*Monicker?* You *had* better quit hanging around with me. Dead Rabbit Lonergan. Way back before the Civil War there was a gang of street toughs who ran the bloody old Fifth Ward in East Lower Manhattan and called themselves the Dead Rabbit gang. Claimed to be dead game for anything. Lonergan's the bimbo set me up last night."

"How can you be sure?" she demanded, wide-eyed.

"Fingers never uses last names at his poker games—few professional gamblers do. . . ."

He broke off as they went out the folding doors to the deserted financial district corner. Hammett watched the double-nose car clack away, then turned back to Goodie.

"During a break in the play, Fingers mentioned my last name. Immediately Lonergan made an excuse to get to the phone. To call a girlfriend in South San Francisco, he said. But the phone company records don't show any toll calls from Fingers' number last night."

"And on that you assume—"

"Men have been hanged on less, sweetheart."

His eyes were caught by the Sutter Hotel, spilling bright light from its ornate lobby across the street. He'd put the hotel in the novel about Sam Spade and the blackbird, the script lying at home in a drawer in rough draft. A block away, on the corner of Montgomery, was the Hunter-Dulin Building where he had put Spade's office.

What the hell was he doing back in the detective business? If he couldn't make love to Goodie, at least he could be writing. He longed for one of his all-night sessions with the typewriter. A session in the fictional San Francisco of fog-bound streets and hard-minded victorious heroes, where he could control the blood and manipulate the men. He had *The Dain Curse* to revise, now that he'd figured out the way to go with that book, and in *The Maltese Falcon* he had a chance to do something that nobody else had ever done before.

But it wasn't to be. Not right now. Because in the *real* San

Francisco men were for sale and his friend had gone to his death with a pulped skull and loosened bowels. The friend whose call he hadn't answered. So Hammett owed him.

As Goodie's door shut, Hammett leaned on the wall beside his own and very gently drifted it open with his fingertips. Dim light came up the interior hallway from the living room. He'd left the room in darkness.

Dammit, he hadn't expected things to happen this fast after the attempted jacking-out last night. He wasn't packing anything more lethal than a penknife. Get to the kitchen for a butcher knife. Best bet.

Hammett eased down the hall to flatten himself beside the open doorway to the living room. He edged an eye around the frame. He stiffened, than gave a snort of disgust and walked into the room.

"I may as well live in the Pickwick Stage Depot," he said.

Short dumpy Jimmy Wright, sprawled in Hammett's sagging overstuffed Coxwell, slid a forefinger between the pages of one of Hammett's *Black Masks*. "You've got a lousy lock." He raised the magazine slightly. "This is good stuff, Dash. I ought to sue."

"Which one is it?"

The op leafed back to the title. "'Dynamite.'"

"Yeah, that'll be part of a novel titled *Red Harvest* in January."

"This is supposed to be Butte, Montana, ain't it?"

"That and Boulder and Anaconda." He sat down on the unmade bed and leaned back on his elbows. "You get anything on Vic?"

"The cops turned up the cabby who took him from the Chapeau Rouge. Dropped him at Pier Fourteen. So I nosed around at the foot of Mission like you told me. Old gent in the Johnson and Larsen Cigar Store next to the Hotel Commodore steered a guy answering Vic's description over to Dom Pronzini's speak a block away on Steuart Street. Even gave Vic the password."

"The cops get any of this?"

"Who the hell ever talks to cops?"

Hammett took a turn around the room. "Dom Pronzini. Old Rinaldo's pup—I sent the old man up to Q on a five-to-twenty back in twenty-one. I hear that Dom brings in most of the real Canadian from the rum fleet these days."

"Through Bolinas and Sausalito," the dumpy little detective nodded sleepily. "He's giving the boys down in Half Moon Bay a run for it."

Hammett stopped pacing. Sure! Goddammit, the connection he'd almost made in Marin County snapped together in his mind.

"That rapist the Preacher shot out by Golden Gate Park—Egan Tokzek. Wasn't he a runner for Pronzini?"

"If you can believe the reporter from the *Chronicle*."

"How's your stock down at Pinkerton's these days?"

"They don't spit on the floor when my name comes up."

"All right. See can you find out if they've got anything in their files on Tokzek." He was frowning, tugging his mustache in thought. He jerked his shoulders in an odd little shrug. "See if he had a sister, too. We're starting to move on this."

Lonergan's Garage at 639 Turk Street was a one-story brick building with a false front. A sign hung on the post between the big double doors: ATTENDANT WILL BE BACK IN 20 MINUTES.

Hammett nodded approvingly at the lock on the double door, and took from his pocket a flat strap of steel six inches long and slightly angled and tapered at one end. Inserting this between door and frame, he applied steady leverage. There was a muted crack.

The dim interior was heavy with petroleum smells. A tow truck was backed up against the wall beyond the vast well leading down to the basement parking area. Hammett leaned over the unshielded edge to stare into the gloom. A concrete ramp led down to a concrete floor a good twenty feet below. It would do.

The littered little office had double windows painted black

113

to well above head-level. Backed against that same wall was a man-high black safe with a big brass handle and a brass dial.

Hammett spun the dial idly. Give him a couple of hours and he could strip the side off her, but none of her secrets would be valuable to him. Lonergan was too far down the ladder to have more than a name or two. He'd settle for that. Or even for a phone number.

He sat down behind the desk and put his feet up and waited. The desk was butted up against the partition between the office and the garage floor, so he could see out into the main area through the waist-level window. The clock over the window said midnight had passed. Clipboards of work orders, aged by greasy fingers to a blackish brown, decorated the doorpost.

Five minutes later, headlights arced across the ceiling. Hammett's eyes brightened, but he did not change position. The lock on the overhead doors rattled on its chain, then the doors creaked up to shoot hot light across the grease-stained concrete. A tow truck, towing nothing, was driven past the office window and stopped with its motor thrumming and the cab out of Hammett's sight.

Dead Rabbit Lonergan sprang suddenly into the doorway, crouched like an ape, a tire iron swinging loosely in one hand. When Hammett made no move, Lonergan came slowly erect. A huge grin split his face when he saw who was there.

"On your feet, bimbo. The boys are gonna be glad to get another crack at you. *Fast,* before I smash both your shoulders with this."

"I don't carry a gun," said Hammett mildly as he was patted down by the big Irishman. He kept his arms wide and raised. Lonergan worked left-handed, keeping the tire iron cocked in his right fist. The tow truck grumbled acrid exhaust fumes.

"I don't know why they want you," said Lonergan. "But I think we'll stick your head in that exhaust while I make a phone call."

"I'll tell you why they want me," said Hammett. "They're

114

afraid of me. That's why they wanted me taken out last night. I represent some of the boys back east. The BIG boys back east. We're moving in, taking over this town. It's just a matter of time. We figure that you're small-fry, but you're a place to start. So why don't you get smart and tell me who you called to get those three gorillas who were supposed to beat me up?"

Lonergan had been staring at him, slightly slack-faced, as he had been speaking. He hesitated for a moment, then crinkled up his rugged, handsome features and laughed out loud. He leaned against the doorpost with the clipboards on it.

"What you been smoking, Hammett? Whoever's behind you, it ain't gonna work. We got the cops behind us in this burg. No outsiders are gonna—"

"Before you left Five Points, you ever hear of a big Irishman named Babe?"

"Should I have?"

"Might have been after you left," Hammett muttered thoughtfully. "The Babe was an expert with a tire iron and made the mistake of trying to use one on a fat little killer out of Baltimore named Garlic."

Lonergan slapped the tire iron against his open left hand. "This ain't Baltimore, bo."

"Garlic blew away both the Babe's kneecaps with a matched pair of .45's. They had to take his legs off just below the hips because he got gangrene from the garlic on the bullets. These days he rides around on a little board with casters on it, selling pencils around Forty-second and Times Square. . . ."

Lonergan chuckled and tightened his grip on the tire iron. "I think you want to get petted with this thing, bim—"

He shot forward across the room to crash headfirst into the far wall. He whirled off it with tire iron upraised and lips drawn back from tobacco-stained teeth.

"I like to burn 'em when they're comin' at me," grated Jimmy Wright. The lumpy .45 automatics in his fists stared at Dead Rabbit with unwinking eyes.

115

The tire iron clattered to the floor. Dead Rabbit's hands shot up, shaking. His face was pinched and tired around the eyes as if he had developed a sudden head cold.

Hammett hadn't moved during the flurry of action. He said: "Garlic, why don't you walk this bird over to the edge of the basement well so he can tell us what he knows? If he don't tell us in thirty seconds, he jumps off. Twenty-nine . . . twenty-eight. . . ."

"Jesus, man, that's twenty feet down!" cried Dead Rabbit. Wetness was mooning out from beneath his arms. "I'll get all busted up."

Hammett watched the big terrified Irishman. "When you can't crawl up the ramp anymore, he puts one .45 in each of your ears and pulls the triggers at the same time."

Hammett and the op walked away from Lonergan's Garage.

"Once he gets his nerve back, he's going to call 'em up and tell 'em we were here," said Jimmy Wright thoughtfully.

"I want him to. I want them to start knowing I'm around. My God, is that crude, Jimmy! A phone call from Shuman after he left the reform committee meeting Thursday night. And that second phone number he gave us—that's Boyd Mulligan's home phone!"

"Crude is right. A direct line to the Mulligans. But I guess they never expected anyone to be around asking questions." Then the operative started laughing. "Without anybody laying a glove on him! They should call him Scared Rabbit."

Seventeen

HAMMETT went up the sloping walk between carefully trimmed privet to the rambling two-story pseudo-Elizabethan in the exclusive Parkside District. When he rang the bell, the inset door was opened by a young pretty colored maid much like his own Minnie Hershey in *The Dain Curse.*

"Mr. Hammett? Come right in, sir."

The living room was two-storied under a cathedral arch, the furniture heavy, leather, of a scale to match the room.

"Right in here, sir."

Two of the solarium walls were floor-to-ceiling glass that framed a staggering sweep of Pacific beyond the rolling miles of dunes.

Evelyn Brewster, seated on the cretonne cushions of the cane sofa, did not rise when Hammett entered. Her eyes were frosty.

"I should have thought I'd made my feelings about you clear on Thursday night."

Hammett bowed wordlessly, then said, "But I'm sure you would wish me to carry out the committee's objectives properly."

An unexpected smile touched her lips and she leaned forward with sudden animation. "I know I must seem inflexible to a man of your . . . background, Mr. Hammett. But the work of the committee is all-important to me. The punishment of the guilty must take precedence over merely personal considerations, so if you have come here to plead special circumstances for some friend whose activities—"

"Quite the contrary, Mrs. Brewster." He fell easily into her stilted cadences. "A prominent San Franciscan to whom I need an introduction might inadvertently have information vital to my investigation."

She looked intrigued. "The name?"

"George F. Biltmore."

"My God!" She was genuinely shocked. "You can't suggest that Captain Biltmore could possibly—"

"Not for a moment, ma'am. But . . ." He lowered his voice confidentially. "A man in Captain Biltmore's position can open doors. . . ."

She nodded wisely. "I'll call him at his office."

As Evelyn Brewster picked up her phone in Parkside,

117

Boyd Mulligan was spinning his swivel chair to answer the phone in his Kearny Street bailbond office.

"Mulligan Bros.," he snapped self-importantly as he unforked the receiver.

It was the muffled voice that over the years he had come to recognize if not know. "Get him."

"Oh . . . uh, yeah, sure."

Mulligan laid the receiver on the desk and went down the narrow room to the doorway of the inner, private office. He was short and strutting, his shoulders were narrow and his posture just slightly swaybacked, so he always walked as if he were about to start tap dancing.

"Uncle Griff, it's . . . uh . . . him."

He returned to his desk and hung up the phone noisily. All three of them knew he wasn't bright enough to know things he wasn't bright enough to know.

Griff Mulligan was a white-haired banty rooster with a lilting Irish tenor as light as a Shannon mist. He wore a faded comfortable flannel shirt and old-fashioned armbands that matched his garters and galluses.

"A pleasant good morning to ye."

"It isn't," grated the no-longer disguised voice.

"And what might the trouble be with it?"

"I just heard about that stupid attempt to scare off Hammett."

"I'd not heard of it meself," said Mulligan with a sideways gleam of his faded blue eyes toward the doorway beyond which his nephew sat. "But I suppose that Boyd thought—"

"That would be a first. Hammett learned it was Joey Lonergan who fingered him for the strong-arms, and last night he and his right bower, Jimmy Wright, paid a visit to Lonergan's Garage. Lonergan opened the bag for them."

Mulligan's voice remained as mild and melodious as before.

"Well, now, faith, it's not that Joey knows the devil of a lot. A couple of phone numbers without any names to—"

"It's given Hammett a connection. He's tough and he's smart. . . ."

118

"So was Atkinson."

"Whoever killed Atkinson did us no favor," snapped the other man quickly. "Remember that." His voice became elaborately casual. "I want Hammett left alone, but I don't want him getting hold of Molly. Where do you have her stashed away?"

"Faith, I don't know meself. I've let Boydie handle that." He lowered the receiver. "Boyd! Where is it that you have Molly holed up then?"

"Ask her little kike attorney. He wouldn't tell me."

To the phone, Mulligan said in an ominously calm voice, "Boyd seems to have lost sight of her for the moment, but Molly won't sing—"

"Tell him to find her. Now."

"Right ye are," said Mulligan in his lilt.

"And be careful on that phone after Monday."

"Right ye are," he lilted again.

He hung up and went down the office, cat-quiet, to stop behind his nephew's chair. With a great deal of relish he swung his right arm to explode his fist against the side of Boyd's head. The younger Mulligan was knocked sprawling out of his chair, the scalp under the oily hair split by his uncle's ring. He sat on the floor with a hand to his head.

"Ye stupid git!" snarled Griff Mulligan. "Who told ye to go after Hammett?"

"But . . . but I thought . . . Shuman said. . . ."

"Now get y'rself out o' here and find where Molly is, before Hammett finds her for us."

The private office was heavy with the smells of leather and saddle soap. It was just across California Street from the new Robert Dollar building. George F. Biltmore stood up behind a huge rolltop with innumerable pigeonholes lined in green felt. His white walrus mustache was ragged and yellowed at the edges from being chewed on; snarled thickets of white brow bristled above his deep-set eyes.

"Going to clean up this town, are you?"

"So they say."

119

"So Evelyn Brewster says."

Hammett matched the power of Biltmore's massive hand with his own wiry strength. Biltmore sat down in his deep leather chair with a surprised look on his face. He had captained his own five-masters around the Horn and in later years had made his fortune from shipping and marine insurance.

"She's a fine woman," he said. "Fine woman. You're a close friend of hers?" When Hammett didn't respond, he added challengingly, "Hey?"

Hammett, remembering everything he'd heard of this tough old man, said, "She hates my guts."

"Then why'd she ask if I'd see you? Hey?"

"She thinks I'm going to smite the wicked."

"But you ain't." He made it a statement.

"I'm going to find a murderer and smite him."

"Murderer, hey? Humph." He drew the tangled white thickets down over piercing blue eyes that had never seen the need for eyeglasses, and burst out, "Clean up San Francisco! I remember when that husband of hers was fifteen, *his* father Derry—God rest his soul!—and I took the boy to Diamond Jessie Hayman's parlor house on Ellis Street to start the lad out right. Then he marries that whey-faced ninny! Reform committee, had the gall to ask *me* to be on it! Why . . ." He jerked his head around toward Hammett. "What do you want from me? Hey?"

"You have a houseguest in Mill Valley—"

"I have a lot of houseguests at various times." He got to his feet and went to the window. There was no fat on his seventy-year-old frame, no sag of age. "I've been a seafaring man, I remember my friends."

"This houseguest is a woman, a client of Phineas Epstein's."

"A gentlewoman from back east," he boomed. "Tragic personal loss—"

"Molly Farr," said Hammett. "The missing madam."

Biltmore returned to his desk to select a cigar from his hu-

120

midor. He raised shaggy eyebrows at Hammett and, when he was rebuffed, clipped the cigar and lit it with a wooden match. He watched Hammett sideways through clouds of aromatic smoke.

"I've got dogs on the estate, son. Hounds, a whole pack of 'em. The sheriff in those parts, I own a good piece of him, too. Not because I've tried to, but because it's the natural order of things, power being what it is. . . ."

"Sure," said Hammett readily. His voice was thin; he hitched his shoulders unconsciously. If he read the old man's temperament wrong, he wouldn't get to Molly. He said: "When I was a Pink, I worked for a lot of men like you, Mr. Biltmore. Men having labor trouble at the mine or the factory who needed somebody to bust heads and put the workers back in line. You're big and old and tough and mean, and you think you're never going to die. So you take what you want and do what you want, and worry about the consequences afterward."

Biltmore seemed unangered by this appraisal. "You've drawn your full ration of gall, son, I'll give you that. But tell me: Why am I supposed to be hiding out this Molly Farr?"

"Because you get a hell of a kick out of it. Or because Epstein has something on you that even your money and influence can't—"

"Nobody's got anything on me, son," he snapped. "I came up rough and I came up hard, but I came up clean. I don't have to look behind me on dark streets. . . ."

"'I've picked up my fun where I found it,'" quoted Hammett. "Only Evelyn Brewster wouldn't call it fun. She takes her sin seriously."

"Mmph. How'd you find out I was hiding Molly?"

"Epstein got so clever he got careless."

The big ex-seaman stared at him from eyes that were blue chips of ice. "What d'ya want her for? Hey?"

"Talk, that's all. The man who got killed talked with her the day before she lammed. I think one reason she lammed was because she didn't want to talk with him again. I don't intend to put her on any witness stand and I don't intend to turn her over to the DA, but I have to know if she has anything that would help me find my friend's killer."

Biltmore brooded a moment more, then slapped the desk in sudden vast delight.

"Yes! All right, goddammit! Tomorrow afternoon. If you know a presentable lady friend, bring her for a social afternoon. Then you just slip away—Molly spends her time in one of the guest cottages, you can go talk to her there and no one else the wiser."

They shook hands. At the door, Hammett paused. "Why *are* you hiding her out? And why are you letting me see her?"

"I like Molly. Within her own limits, she's an honest woman. As for you . . ." Biltmore's expression became that of a gleeful schoolboy. "I've been waiting for years for somebody to come along who could stick a thumb into Brass Mouth Epstein's eye."

Eighteen

CHINATOWN wore a new aspect at night, especially with the sea fog drifting through its narrow alleys and steep side streets. The hurrying pedestrians were mere undetailed forms in the swirling mists. Only the sound of heels on concrete betrayed their passage.

Hammett turned up Jackson past a group of tourists huddled under a streetlamp, ingesting their guide's lies about the labyrinths six and seven stories below the Chinatown streets. Hammett knew you could work your way down the hill from cellar to cellar, but you were never more than one flight below the pavement.

In Ross Alley—known as Old Spanish Alley before the Chinese pushed the Mexicans out—he went down a shallow set of stairs from street level into deep gloom. At the foot of the steps was a small concrete alcove holding a pair of battered stinking garbage pails. Hammett slapped his hand with a measured beat on the flaking red door behind them. Nothing happened. Hammett kept on. Finally a voice inside called something in Chinese. Hammett persisted. The voice repeated its high-pitched exhortation. Hammett continued.

"Go 'way," the voice finally called in English.

Hammett didn't. There were the sounds of a whole series of bolts being drawn. The door opened a bare two inches on a stout length of chain.

"Go 'way."

"Chin Kim Guy," said Hammett.

The door was slammed shut and bolted.

Hammett sat down on the steps and lit a cigarette. He finished it and started a second. Mist wet his face. The bolt ritual began again. He ground the butt against the pale brick wall, dropped the shredded remains at his feet, and was waiting in moody patience, hands in overcoat pockets, when the door opened again.

"You come," said a different voice from the darkness.

A dim unshaded lightbulb at the far end of the twenty-foot hallway showed that his grossly heavy Chinese guide was as tall as he, and wore Occidental clothing. He stopped at a door halfway down the hall and called out in Cantonese. The door was unlocked. They went through into a passage like the one they had just left, only at right angles to it.

Near the far end of this hall they paused before another door, different from the others. Its seasoned oak panels were thickly studded with the square heads of iron carriage bolts.

This door had a buzzer, which the binder pushed in a quick uneven rhythm; no voice could have carried through the two-inch hardwood thickness. Noise and lights and tobacco smoke came out at them—underlaid with incense and the faint sweetish reek of opium. The voices, high-pitched

123

and singsong and excited, all male, mingled with the clack of buttons. Which meant fan-tan, not a *pai gow* parlor or a *do far* lottery.

Blocking Hammett's way was another Oriental, dressed in loose baggy trousers of a coarse material, wearing slippers and a wide-sleeved buttonless jacket cinched at the waist with a two-inch sewn cloth belt. Between the parted edges of the jacket were the shifting planes of his immense hairless chest. He was six-six and two hundred and fifty pounds, none of them fat. His head too was hairless. His features were more Mongol than Chinese.

He stepped back a pace, crossed his arms into the wide sleeves, and bowed deeply from the waist. "We are honored, Prince of Men."

"You been demoted, Qwong?" asked Hammett cheerfully.

"Demoted, oh King of Pursuers?"

"Chin has you on the door."

He bowed again. "Merely awaiting your August Self." He made a graceful gesture. "My Master is impatient for the unutterable joy of your presence."

Hammett bowed himself. "Lead on, O Giant of China."

"That's terrible," said Qwong Lin Get.

Hammett's earlier guide manipulated the heavy swiveled bar on the door back into the cleats that held it in a locked position. The lean detective followed Qwong down the square low-ceilinged basement room. It was crowded with a couple of hundred male Chinese, massed around a dozen four-by-ten fan-tan tables. The din of voices flowed and ebbed as the bottons were drawn down.

Qwong indicated the tables with an almost contemptuous sweep of one steel-muscled arm.

"What your friend *Mau Yee* would give to know of this!"

"You think he doesn't?"

The enormous homosexual bodyguard caressed Hammett with his eyes. "I know that you would not tell him."

Hammett nodded wordlessly. He wouldn't have to. It was from Manion that he had gotten the current location of Chin Kim Guy's fan-tan parlor.

124

He stayed a moment to watch the play.

The table was covered with a mat, in the exact center of which was diagrammed a twelve-inch square divided into quarters. Each corner bore the Chinese character for a number from one to four.

Across from Hammett was the dealer, an Oriental ancient in skullcap and silk jacket. Fastened to the table in front of him was a leather bag filled with small black and white buttons.

"My Master awaits his Peerless Friend."

"Sure," said Hammett.

The venerable dealer dipped into the sack with a colorful lacquer bowl, brought it out full of buttons, and turned it upside down on the table under the avid eyes of the players. As Hammett moved off, he had begun drawing buttons, four at a time, out from under the bowl with a hooked bamboo stick. By placing money on a numbered quarter of the diagram, the players were betting whether one, two, three, or four buttons would be left under the bowl for the final drawdown.

At the rear of the room was a partition of antique Japanese screens, which had been among Guy Kim's most valued possessions. They had partitioned the players from the dealers in one of his *do far* parlors. Now they were his son's.

Inside the carefully guarded little chamber was a hardwood table bearing piles of crumpled bills, a black-beaded abacus, and nothing else.

Chin Kim Guy bounced to his feet behind the table, hand extended. "Hammett!" he exclaimed. "Long time no see. Hear the one about the minister and the little boy he caught swearing? He says, 'Little boy, when you talk like that the chills run up and down my spine.' And the boy says, 'If you'd heard my ma when she caught her tit in the wringer, you'd of froze to death.'" He burst into high-pitched laughter and waved Hammett to a chair across the table. "Rest the dogs."

Hammett sat.

The dapper Chinese was dressed in a gray Glenurquhart plaid and a knitted silk tie with a fancy crocheted weave. He looked like a Chinese pimp, not the king of an illegal gambling empire stretching from San Francisco to the Chinese colonies in Stockton and Sacramento. As long as Hammett had known him he'd been telling terrible jokes and laughing uncontrollably at them.

Now he uttered a short burst of Cantonese at another of the giant bodyguards, who was leaning against the back wall. The man quickly disappeared through an unframed door at his elbow.

"Did your father get the magazine I sent him a few years ago?"

Chin laughed. He had very white buckteeth and wore his black hair parted in the middle and combed tightly to his skull. His utterly black eyes glittered with amusement under delicate brows.

"I read the story to him, he got a hell of a wallop out of Chang Li Ching. He didn't know he impressed you as such a bloodthirsty character. You knew he's *Kam Sam Hock* now?"

"I'd heard he'd gone home from the Golden Mountain," Hammett admitted.

The Golden Mountain was what the old-generation Chinese still called San Francisco. One who had been to the Golden Mountain and had returned home to China, wealthy and respected, for his declining years, was known as a *Kam Sam Hock*. Only Chin Kim Guy's generation had begun to consider America as home.

The bodyguard returned with a delicate china pot and two small handleless bowls set on doughnutlike saucers. The tea was pale amber, clear as spring water, and steaming hot. With it was a dish of four small round sesame seed cakes baked to a pale brown. Hammett nibbled at one and sipped tea.

Chin's laughter bubbled up again; it was said he laughed the same way when his binders hacked an enemy to pieces.

"You hear the one about old Nate? Rebecca is downstairs in the front room with Abie, see, and Nate hears some strange sounds coming from down there, so he goes to the head of the stairs and he calls, 'Becky, are you and Abie

126

fighting?' And Rebecca says, 'No, daddy, we're screwing.' And old Nate says, 'That's nice, children, don't fight.'"

His gales of laughter trailed away in chuckles.

"Anyway, Hammett, you want to see the Honorable Pater you're out of luck—"

"Came to see you," said Hammett.

He jerked a thumb over his shoulder without looking around; he knew the massive bald-headed Qwong would be directly behind his chair with a *snickersnee,* the swordlike Chinese knife that could take out a man's throat with a single slash, strapped hilt-downward to his left forearm beneath the flowing jacket sleeve.

"Remember five years ago your father promised to lend me this character if I ever needed someone's leg broken or eye poked out?"

"I remember."

"That still good, all-ee-same like father like son?"

Chin considered gravely for a moment, then gave a very Occidental shrug. "Sure, why not, he's getting fat and lazy anyway."

"How about all of them?" said Hammett.

Chin cocked an eyebrow. "Leaving me naked before mine enemies?"

"Maybe that's the idea."

Chin laughed out loud and clapped his hands in delight. "Only you could come up with a remark like that, Dash!" He leaned forward in his chair. "You hear the one about the Chinaman asked this fellow, 'You telle me where raillerroad depot?' And the guy says, 'What's the matter, John, you lost?' And the Chinaman says, 'No! Me here, dam' depot lost!'" Before Hammett could make appropriate noises, he demanded, "What are you doing, starting a war?"

"Something like that."

"Other Chinamen?"

"Wops."

"Good!" Chin laughed out loud again. "Too many wops around anyway." He shifted his gaze to the giant Qwong. "I got through four years at Cal without him around, I guess I

127

can . . . besides, he's always been in love with you, this'll give him a chance to work off his Freudian repressions."

Hammett walked home from Chinatown through the fog. Everything was moving. Tomorrow, Molly Farr. He'd open her up and find out what—if anything—she could tell him about Vic's death. He would also ask her Chinese maid about the fat woman over by Bolinas Lagoon.

The fog that lay above the city cut the tops off the hills, and made the taller buildings seem to disappear five stories above the street.

Goddamn he loved this city! There wasn't another like it anywhere, and he'd been in a lot of them since he'd answered that blind box ad in the Baltimore paper back in the summer of '12. He'd gotten bored chalking up stock market transactions from the Poe and Davies ticker tape; because he was big for his eighteen years, he'd been able to lie his way into the job as a Pinkerton operative.

Eight years of manhunting—interrupted by the Ambulance Corps and the government lunger hospitals in Tacoma and San Diego. Christ, the towns he'd been in as a Pink! Pasco and Seattle and Spokane; Stockton and Vallejo; Butte, Denver, Cleveland, Dallas; Gilt-Edge, Montana, and Lewiston, Idaho; El Paso, Jacksonville, Detroit, Boston; Rocky Mount, North Carolina, Louisville, Kentucky, and the Big Apple itself, New York City. Finally, San Francisco. The City That Knows How.

At the south end of the Stockton tunnel he looked up to his right above the top of a billboard. Yeah. Just there were the tops of the railing posts through which he had Miles Archer pitch after being shot in *The Maltese Falcon.*

Hammett looked up at the concrete parapet where Bush Street bridged the tunnel. He'd lived for half a year at the mouth of the alley just across Bush—20 Monroe Street—and when he'd needed a secluded, dramatic spot for Archer to die, dead-end Burritt Street had just naturally come to mind.

He was suddenly in a hurry to get home. The *Falcon* would have to wait for revision until this whole mess was finished, but not so *The Dain Curse*. He'd thought of a way to characterize Minnie Hershey's boyfriend, Rhino Tingley. Let Rhino count out his eleven hundred and seventy dollars, braggingly, bill by bill, in front of the Op's cynical and Minnie's terrified eyes. Hell, he'd created Rhino's name by mating a British slang word for money with the name of a little street off Silver Avenue; so why not let his character be created by the act of counting money?

Hell, yes. He liked that.

Nineteen

ON Christmas Eve, 1910, a quarter of a million people—the greatest crowd in San Francisco's history—had gathered around Lotta's Fountain to hear an impromptu concert by famed opera soprano Luisa Tetrazzini. Today, as the streetcar went rattling by the ugly, ornate, cast-iron monument at Kearny, Geary, and Market, the intersection was Sunday-deserted.

Goodie did not notice the lack of people. She was too elated to notice much of anything.

"Oh, Sam, I'm so excited!"

"Maybe they'll meet us at the door with a shotgun."

She mocked a pout. "You mean I'm just window dressing again?"

"You've got a devious mind, girl."

Goodie leaned back against the shiny leather and looked out at the cable car making the turn up Sacramento. Beside the wedge-shaped corner building were steep steel stairs leading up to the pedestrian crosswalk that bridged The Embarcadero to the Ferry Building.

"I don't care," she said, "George F. Biltmore!"

The afternoon before, Goodie had spent a dollar and her lunch hour at Le Maximilian Coiffeurs to have her blond ringlets water-waved by Georgia. After work, another five dollars and ninety-eight cents had gone on the stylish "tomboy" dress she now wore: a light-green velour blouse with dark-green silk kerchief and swagger tie, and a plaid cashmere skirt and waistband.

Two weeks' lunch money, and then some, but she was going over to Mill Valley for tea with the George F. Biltmores! Wait until she wrote her mother about *that!*

The car made the loop around the fenced grass oblong directly in front of the grand arched central entrance of the Ferry Building. A couple of bums dozed in the noontime sun.

Hammett bought two round-trip tickets to Mill Valley, and they joined the waiting-room throng beyond the gleaming gilt metal grillwork.

Going up the creaking wooden gangway to the side-wheeler *Eureka,* with the salt air keen in their nostrils, Goodie clung to Hammett's arm.

"I've never ridden this before."

"It must have been a long swim from Crockett."

"You know what I mean. *This* ferry. To Sausalito."

The mooring lines clumped solidly on deck as they were heaved clear of their bollards; the boxy white boat shuddered as its enclosed paddle wheels began churning. White water foamed as it slid from its high-sided timber slip and made its way past Goat Island and Alcatraz for the thirty-two-minute trip to Marin County.

"I know," said Hammett in a sympathetic voice.

"You know what?"

"You're hungry."

From the restaurant in the upper deck's enclosed cabin, Goodie got a bowl of Exposition clam chowder and a roast beef sandwich with mashed potatoes and gravy. Hammett had coffee and pungled up the required fifty cents.

"It's an expensive wench," he said sadly.

130

They chose places on one of the curved wooden benches; life jackets were stacked under them in case of disaster. Through salt-rimed windows they could hear the sea gulls demanding scraps from the passengers on the open cabin deck below.

"What's he like?" demanded Goodie, licking a dollop of mustard from the corner of her mouth.

"Who?"

"Biltmore. All that money, all that power . . ."

In perfect imitation of her tone, Hammett went on, "That frail wife, that healthy mistress—"

"Oh, Sam, does he?" Her eyes sparkled with excitement. "A *mistress?*"

"Named Gerty. She won't be there today, although they say he takes her up to their summer place in Napa even when his wife is there."

"I bet Gerty has fun," said Goodie enviously.

Sausalito was a small fishing village nestled along the narrow neck of Richardson Bay across from the rich sparkling villas of Belvedere Island. It was also the railroad terminus for anyone traveling north into Marin or Sonoma or Mendocino. The ferries moored right in the center of town, in three slips formed of massive wooden pilings. A hundred yards away was a pseudomission travelers' hotel.

"Northwestern Pacific runs a spur line up to Mill Valley from Almonte," Hammett said. "The whole trip takes only ten minutes."

The olive-green wooden car, crowded with Sunday excursioners, clacked north along the Sausalito waterfront. To their left, white frame houses dotted the steep wooded hills behind the town, buried in foliage. Flowering shrubs and bushes crowded and climbed and burst in their demand for attention—rhododendrons and azaleas and delicate dangling fuchsias in the shady areas, bristling red bottle brush and gold-clustered Scotch broom in the sun.

To their right, sharp-prowed racing sloops and thick-

131

waisted weekenders flashed dripping flanks at them, mostly from moorings at the San Francisco Yacht Club, which had moved to Sausalito half a century before.

Sausalito was more than a Bohemian fishing village and railhead; it was also a zany blend of seaport, yachting center, tourist attraction, and artist colony—and focal point for rum-runners.

"A lot of the old waterfront warehouses on the south side of town are stacked to the rafters with bootleg booze," Hammett said, and thought, courtesy of Dom Pronzini. "At high tide you can bring a whaleboat of rum right in under the pilings and unload it up through the trapdoors in the floor without any danger of being spotted from the street."

Through the train's open windows came the dense dark odor of drying mud flats. Puddle ducks, darting grebe, and mud hens with red beady eyes skittered away over the draining tidal flat at the train's approach. At Almonte's tile-roofed little station they transferred to the waiting one-car spur train.

"Next stop, Mill Valley," said Hammett.

It was a rustic village buried in the redwoods. Far behind the town, Mount Tamalpais, where legend said the Indian maid Tamelpa had died, laid its softly contoured edges up against the summer sky. The train was jammed with travelers who intended to ride The Crookedest Railroad in the World from the top of Mount Tam down to the center of town.

A freckle-faced kid wearing knickers and a cloth cap and leading a three-legged mongrel directed them to the road that ran along Corte Madera Creek. In a bare twenty yards it had lost itself among the giant redwoods.

It was a russet earth track and even now, two months after the rains had stopped, damp underfoot. The arched vault of foliage overhead kept it cool and moist. The hill to their left was so heavily forested that there was little undergrowth.

"Look!" breathed Goodie.

It was a coast mule deer, its liquid eyes staring at them, its jackass ears twitching, its russet flanks heaving. Then a smaller version of itself appeared from behind the massive dim trunk of a fallen tree. Finally a tiny spotted fawn appeared, delicate as Dresden.

"Not too usual for a yearling to be hanging around with mama after this year's baby is born."

Three pairs of ears twitched to Hammett's low voice, as if to a signal. Suddenly they all were gone, with only the thump of hooves on the damp carpet of needles under the trees to show they had been there at all.

They came to a rough rock gateway, unmortared but beautifully fitted, which supported double redwood gates with hand-beaten iron hinges and massive iron rings to serve as handles.

"We're here," said Hammett.

The meandering packed-earth path, edged with decorative granite chips partially sunk in the ground, made a circle in front of the house. A circle crowded with breathtaking purple-blossomed rhododendrons and clumps of waxy-leaved pyracantha. The house itself was rambling, with red-shingled roofs and redwood shake siding. The broad shallow verandah was partially obscured by straight-trunked young redwoods.

"It's *beautiful,*" breathed Goodie.

Hammett grinned and jerked the bellpull. The windows were flanked with redwood shutters that could be fastened shut during the heavy storms of winter.

The door was opened by a stocky, well-built man with only one eye who wore a chauffeur's uniform. His accent was Australian or South African.

"Dashiell Hammett to see Mr. Bilt—"

"Hammett? Come in, boy, come in," boomed Biltmore's jovial voice from the background.

Goodie, captivated, stared about the living room. Square-cut, rough-hewn redwood supported the ceiling and paneled the walls. The fireplace had a Belgian marble mantel. The furniture was old-fashioned and unabashedly Victorian.

So also was the frail, china doll woman who rose when they entered. She was delicate and exquisitely boned, dressed in the floor-length elegance of a forgotten decade, her skin translucent as alabaster. She was gray-haired and remote, with a badly crippled left hand that she made no attempt to disguise.

"May, this is Dashiell Hammett," boomed Biltmore. "He's an attorney works with Phineas. Mr. Hammett, my wife."

Hammett bowed over the unflawed right hand. "I'm charmed, Mrs. Biltmore. May I present my *fiancée,* Miss Augusta Osborne." He flashed the delightful smile he reserved for special occasions. "Everyone calls her Goodie."

"Goodie it shall be!" cried May Biltmore in sudden animation. She turned to the one-eyed chauffeur. "Harry! Where has Bingo gone?"

"He was in the kitchen trying to bite the cook the last I saw, ma'am," said the one-eyed man gravely.

"Oh, dear, I'd better go find . . ."

A tiny white fuzzy dog burst into the room, yapped once, then threw himself headlong against the leg of May Biltmore's chair.

"You have a wonderful home," said Goodie impulsively.

Biltmore stroked his vast walrus mustache. "We like it, m'dear. Moved over after the fire. Thought it might happen again, y'see? Seems a bit silly now, perhaps, but in those days—"

"Let's have tea!" exclaimed May Biltmore.

The chairs were Chippendale walnut, or Louis Philippe rosewood with Aubusson tapestry coverings. Goodie had never seen anything so elegant. Hammett was more interested in the South Seas tapa cloths and displays of African assegais that covered the walls.

"Loot from my sailing days. The tapas are Marquesan, with one by the western Pacific blackamoors. Made of beaten mulberry bark, dyed with crushed roots and barks and berries." He moved down the wall. "The long spears are Masai from British East; the short ones are Zulu. . . ." He broke off with a chuckle. "Harry could probably tell you more about those than I could."

"I came around the Horn, you know," interrupted his wife with her charming, abstracted smile. She made it sound as if she were another trophy. "What a trip it was, with one's furniture and china!"

An awkward, uniformed girl with close-set eyes interrupted. "Tea, mum."

Tea! Goodie could never have imagined the finest supper in the finest restaurant being half so grand. It was served from a trolley, the tea and coffee poured from chased silver plate.

She had had sandwiches, of course—although not ones made of watercress, or mustard beef, or tongue paste, or roe. But who had ever seen asparagus rolls? Anchovy rolls? And potted cheeses and biscuits, and home-pressed meat, and hot crumpets, and golden brown cream scones crumbly in the mouth. And fresh-baked bread with sweet butter from a moisture-beaded crock. Cornish saffron bread like fruitcake, and Scotch shortbread like butter cookies in disguise.

But there were proper sweets as well: lemon curd tartlets, lemon sponge roll, seed cake, English loaf cake, and something called Lancaster treacle parkin, a ginger-flavored confection that, May Biltmore explained, had been aged for weeks in an airtight container.

"It's all so delicious!" Goodie exclaimed, after a pause because of her mother's oft-repeated warnings about talking with her mouth full.

"I don't know where she puts it," said Hammett ruefully.

Biltmore hitched his chair fractionally closer to Goodie's. "Well, m'dear, it certainly has made you the picture of health. Tell you what . . ."

"So you're an associate of that rascal Phineas," beamed May Biltmore at Hammett. "Perhaps you know dear unfortunate Mrs. Starr . . ."

Biltmore harrumphed from across the tea cart.

"As a matter of fact, darling, it's to interview Mrs. Starr that Mr. Hammett and his charming *fiancée* are here this afternoon."

"It *is* tragic, isn't it?" she asked sorrowfully. "To lose one's entire family in a ghastly train wreck! No wonder she has come west to try and forget . . ."

"Tragic," Hammett echoed. He laid a hand on Goodie's

135

shoulder as she also began to rise. "Stay here and fill up on cakes and sandwiches, sweetheart." He grinned at Biltmore. "Maybe I won't have to feed her tonight."

"How charming!" exclaimed May Biltmore.

As Hammett went out to look for the cottage just beyond the stone bridge past the tennis courts, Biltmore's shining dome was bent solicitously over Goodie's gleaming ringlets, and Mrs. Biltmore was cooing over Bingo, the little white dog.

Twenty

THE three-room cottage was peak-roofed like the main house. Smoke wisped from the stovepipe through one side of the roof. Hammett rapped sharply at the door.

"Hawkins, Mrs. Starr. From Mr. Epstein's office. He sent me out with a few things for you."

"Just a moment."

Just before the door swung open, he checked in his overcoat pockets the reassuring bulges of the weapons he planned to use against her.

"It's about time he sent some—" Fire blazed in the blue eyes as recognition washed across her face. *"You!"*

Hammett pushed by her, tensed for a knee at the groin, but all she did was fall back, yowling.

"That kike son of a bitch sold me out!"

"Hush. You'll wake the neighbors." He kicked the door shut with a heel, leaned against it, hands in his overcoat pockets and a sardonic grin on his face.

Molly had retreated to the center of the small living room. It was furnished with main-house castoffs. On the wall, "The Lone Wolf" competed with "The End of the Trail" in cheap gilt frames.

136

"I thought that pickle-nose Jew bastard was dead straight!"

"Brass Mouth didn't set you up."

"I'd believe you?" she demanded scornfully.

"You can believe this."

His right hand came from the overcoat pocket with a gun-drawing movement. Molly cried out in alarm. Then, when she saw what he was holding, her face unclenched.

"You're kidding me. It's a mirage."

Hammett set the bottle of Old Dougherty on the glass- and cigarette-scored top of the wicker table and dropped his coat on the sofa.

"I figure being a fugitive as dry work."

"Come to mama!" She had the cork out before getting cautious again. She went into the kitchen carrying the bottle, to return with two water glasses that she splashed half-full.

"Let's see you put that down, mister. Then we'll talk."

"Mud in your eye."

Hammett shook his head and reached for the bottle to replenish his glass. He sat down. Molly drank, refilled, sat down across from him with a beatific look. Hammett lit a cigarette and drank rye.

"You make a passable grieving widow."

"I looked in the mirror this morning, I thought I was my goddamn mother." She brooded in silence. "Damn near a week without anyone to talk to, except that dotty old woman out there. She talks to her dog. Her goddamn *dog!*"

"So talk to me."

Her lip curled. "What's a nice girl like me doing in—"

"What do you know about Vic Atkinson's death?"

"Vic Atkinson? The guy you were . . ." It belatedly hit her. "*Death?* You mean he's—"

"Monday night. With a baseball bat." It could be true, she might not have heard. In her role as grief-struck widow, she wouldn't have been able to evince much interest in local news.

"Look, Hammett, I'm sorry about your friend, but you can't expect me to act all broken up. I only met the gentleman the one time." She shrugged. "I heard somewhere that Scarface Al uses a baseball bat to—"

137

"Now you sound like the cops," said Hammett. "Nope, this was local, something Vic was working on." He paused deliberately. "He was going to find you, and he was going to shake you until something fell out. Say you were scared enough to make a phone call after we left your cathouse—"

"Parlorhouse," she interrupted automatically.

"Bullshit."

"All right, I was scared." She wore a black floor-length dress with a cameo brooch at the throat to set it off. "But that's all you're getting from me. I know what you're doing, bringing your bottle to—"

"Have a drink," suggested Hammett.

"Go to hell."

"Have a drink, Hammett." He leaned the other way. "Thanks, I will."

Watching him pour, she said in sudden impatience, "Gimme that bottle. I can match a beanpole like you drink for drink any day."

"You've got more to lose," warned Hammett.

She laughed harshly. "Try it, buster, you'll be walking like a cowboy for a month."

"I meant names," said Hammett. "All those big important names you'd never *dare* talk to me about."

"Damn right. Hoping I'll get drunk . . ."

"I think one of us already is."

A surprising shudder ran through her. "I hadn't ought to be talking to you like this. If certain people—"

"I could always *tell* them you spilled your guts," said Hammett thoughtfully to help her along.

"Jesus H. Christ, you seemed like pretty straight Ghees last week."

"Vic was, see what it got him."

Hammett lurched to his feet, stood waiting for the dizziness to pass. The jug was mortally damaged. Those water glasses could fool a man. He pulled aside the Nottingham lace curtain and looked out. Beyond the path, the stream purled and foamed between its banks. Dusk. And he hadn't learned a damn thing, except that neither he nor Molly was

138

liable to drink the other under the table. He turned back to the room.

"All I've got is that Vic was looking for you, and that he was murdered. Is there a connection? Help me out, for Chrissake! If I was going to snitch you away to the gumshoes, you'd have the sheriff's brogans on the back of your neck instead of me with a bottle of bad hootch. Speaking of which . . ."

He refilled the glasses, sat down again, and cocked his feet on the edge of the table.

"Okay, ask your goddamn questions. I probably won't answer any of them, but you might get lucky."

"Who'd you call after we left last Sunday?"

She shook her head, slowly, her brilliant blue eyes fixed on his face, then grimaced and said, "Oh, what the hell? You were barely out the door when Boyd Mulligan called. He knew you'd been there and he wanted to know why. I told him you were after names. That's all."

Hammett put his feet back on the floor and found his crumpled pack of cigarettes in one pocket. He shook his head.

"Nope. I can't buy the Mulligans as ordering Vic killed because he'd been around asking for names. They'd *know* he'd do that. There had to be some desperation . . ." He interrupted himself. "Who do you pay off in the cops?"

She hesitated. "Hammett, you aren't stringing me along, are you? If you rat to the DA or—"

"You're safe with me, Molly."

"Where'd I hear that before?"

"The rumble seat on your first date."

"Screw you. Okay." She grimaced. "The man on the beat, the sergeant and lieutenant at Bush Street station. They might give the captain a cut, but he's never been around with his hand out. You have to realize that the patrolman is usually more important than the brass in a payoff setup."

Hammett lit a cigarette, nodding, expelling smoke with the words, "Sure. But there's nothing there, Molly. Nothing worth a man's life. Now, if someone thought you'd been will-

139

ing to talk to Vic about some of the things you and your girls hear from *customers* who are on the inside in San Francisco—"

"I never would, and they know it. That would be worth *my* life." She dismissed it with a shrug. "Jesus, am I getting high!"

"We may as well kill the bottle before it spoils."

They drained it equally between the two glasses, taking exaggerated care not to spill a drop. Hammett sighed.

"So it doesn't have anything to do with you, Molly. Then who? And why?"

"You said the police think it was a mob killing. Are you sure they aren't right?"

He drained his glass. "You too? Why does everyone have the mob on the brain?"

"It's that damned Crystal. She told me once she was on the run from somebody in the mob in Chicago." Her eyes and voice brooded. "Never told me who or why. But that Sunday you were there, she saw something on the front page of the newspaper that made her pack up and want to leave. Good kid, 'at Crystal. Been with me a y'r." She had begun slurring words.

"Sure," said Hammett blearily. "First Chinese saint onna Cath'lic calendar."

"Screw you! I doubt you ever spent a whole hell o' lotta time helping old WCTUers 'cross th' street. Tell ya, offered Crys'al chance to be one of a' girls, work th' schoolgirl lay— you know, school uniform, she can pass for ten, twelve, drive the 'ole goats wil'. But : . ." Her hand got up to her face just too late to intercept a ringing belch. "But she jus' wanna be maid! Bright kid. Talks like college grad-you-ate." She added sadly, "Booze all gone."

"Lissen, gotta talk to 'er," said Hammett. "P'rade 'er out. Gotta ask 'er 'bout a fat, bad woman near Bolinas who—"

"But Crys'al isn't *here*." Tears came to Molly's eyes. "Monday mornin', Brass Mouth, he tol' her not come with Molly."

That struck Hammett as strange, even as he realized that Molly was crying. Crying over li'l lost Crystal. Or over empty bottle. He went around the table so he could put a comforting arm around her shoulder. A nice warm shoulder.

"Hammett will find 'er. Hammett, th' eye that never closes, th' ear without wax, th' nose that never drips. . . ."

Molly leaned her head back against his hip. He bent and kissed her. His tongue touched a salt tear that had run down to the corner of her mouth. It was a nice mouth. He left it to get his overcoat from the sofa. He took his hand triumphantly out of the coat pocket. The hand had another bottle in it.

After that, things got hazy. He remembered trying to get back into some items of clothing so they could troop up to the main house for some bright city lights. And he remembered them raising their voices in glorious song together.

> City girls use Kotex,
> Country girls use rags.
> But LuLu is the only girl
> Who uses burlap bags.

Or was that *after* they'd trooped up to the main house?

"It serves you right," said Goodie cruelly.

"Please." Hammett's voice was broken.

"They'll never invite us back again, or . . ."

"Tell me about it tomorrow."

"It *is* tomorrow."

Hammett staggered across to the railing and peered wisely out over the water, crinkling his eyes in the farseeing way of old salts. He could see seven, perhaps eight inches into the roiling fog.

"How d'you *know* it's tomorrow?" he demanded triumphantly when Goodie materialized beside him.

"I have to go to work in just a few hours."

Antiphonal, he thought. Like the two sides of the church choir singing at each other during the Holy Week services at St. Nicholas Church down the road from his granddaddy's tobacco farm. How about *them* apples, kid? Antiphonal, and drunk besides. They'd sung 'em in Latin.

141

"Why don't you talk in Latin?" he suggested. "Very softly."

"Who *was* that terrible woman? That . . . that *song*. And when she got up on the piano in the drawing room and started to shimmy—"

"I don't remember that."

"Do you remember what went on in that cozy little cottage of hers?"

"I detected."

"Mr. Biltmore was *very* upset. He offered to take me to lunch next week to make up for—"

"At Jack's, I'm sure." Hammett felt a little stomach upset coming on. They never should have started that second bottle. Rather, he thought sagely, they shouldn't have *finished* that second bottle.

"What's that supposed to mean?" she demanded stiffly.

"Private rooms with beds upstairs above Jack's."

"Sam, that's a *rotten* thing to say!"

"I feel rotten."

The ferry lurched, then wallowed in a trough of wave. Goodie took his arm. Hammett's stomach lurched.

"Better let go of my arm, Goodie."

"Well!" Goodie exclaimed. "I never . . ."

"Something my sainted mother once told me. Never stand downwind of somebody who's . . . about to be . . . sick. . . ."

Twenty-one

BRASS MOUTH EPSTEIN, ferret-face mobile with delight, reached across the desk to shake the lean detective's hand. Bright morning sunlight streaming through the blinds danced dust motes in the air and made the Persian carpet seem alive. He said maliciously, "Drop around to give me a message from Molly?"

"She said you were a kike son of a bitch and a pickle-nose Jew bastard." Hammett's hours in a Turkish bath had pushed color into his face.

Epstein chuckled. "You damn near convince me you *did* see her."

Hammett leaned forward to drop his match onto the smoking stand ashtray.

"Bingo sends his regards, too."

The laughter faded from Epstein's face. "Bingo who?"

"Bingo Biltmore. Arf, arf." Hammett's eyes sparkled; he was enjoying himself.

"I'll be a son of a bitch," said the dapper little attorney. "I'll even be a kike son of a bitch." He got to his feet and began pacing the carpet between the desk and the window. "You mind telling me how you did it?"

His horse-faced secretary stuck her head in the door. "You're due in Judge Conlan's courtroom in half an hour."

"Thanks, Jenny."

She withdrew. Hammett put his head back against the fine-grained Spanish leather and blew one of the few perfect smoke rings of his life. He brought his eyes down to Epstein's.

"I figured the odds for you using one of the Owl Drug phones to make the call at a probable four to seven. So I was having a cup of coffee at the counter when you came in."

"Set up!" exclaimed Epstein to himself, sadly. He sat down and fixed his eyes on a pencil lying on the desk. "Molly tell you anything helpful?"

"Even negatives are helpful. Who are you hiding her from? Brady? The Mulligans? Or both of them?"

"The DA isn't going to put Molly away for fifteen years," said Epstein obliquely.

"Maybe not. But only because she'll spill her guts once he starts squeezing her."

"Brady isn't going to put any pressure on her."

"You don't know Evelyn Brewster very well. Five bucks says she'll push Brady into going all the way on Molly."

143

Epstein checked his watch. He sighed and rose. "Conlan is a bastard about attorneys being late. I don't think *you* know Mrs. Brewster very well. And I doubt if you know me at all."

Hammett got to his feet. "You figure to save Molly with your brilliant courtroom pyrotechnics?" Epstein grunted wordlessly. "Or maybe Molly's just not going to show up at all."

"In this state there's ninety days before her bail will be declared forfeit. On the eighty-ninth day she's going to show up in court—and I'm going to take your five dollars."

"Don't count on the reform committee folding up or on my brilliant investigation uncovering all the corrupt policemen. Evelyn Brewster wants Molly's hide nailed to her wall no matter *what* else happens." Hammett suddenly remembered his drunken promise to Molly. "By the way, Molly wants to know where you've hidden her maid."

"Crystal isn't with her?"

"She thinks you told Crystal to find her own hole."

A frown creased Epstein's brow. "But I'm not even Crystal's attorney! I was very surprised when she didn't show up for the arraignment."

"Didn't she talk to you about some mysterious trouble she'd had back east? In Chicago? With some mobster or other?"

"No, nothing, not a word."

Hammett hurriedly dropped the subject before the little attorney got intrigued, and they parted with a handshake.

Hammett headed downhill for Market and a streetcar. Crystal Tam. Strictly speaking, not part of his investigation at all. But damned interesting. Maybe even germane. Vic killed in what *could* conceivably have been a mob killing. Crystal on the run from some mobster after seeing something about him—presumably—in the local newspaper.

Maybe, out of curiosity, somewhere along the line he'd drop by the *Chronicle* for a look at the front page for his birthday Sunday, the day before Crystal disappeared.

Jimmy Wright's room at the Townsend was just a buck-and-a-quarter hotel room, anonymous as rolled oats. A room

144

for a reasonable night's sleep, for an hour of hired sex, for a poker game, for a suicide note and a straight razor slippery with arterial blood.

But this Monday it was a business conference. Hammett had looked over the four new men up from LA and liked what he saw. Unmemorable men, the first requisite for a good op.

He lounged against the dresser, ashtray at his elbow.

"We've been hired to investigate corruption in the San Francisco police department, not merely to probe vice in the city. We're not surveying conditions, we're seeking punitive evidence. The cops know this, so we can expect damn-all in the way of cooperation from the department."

"How much authority do we have?" asked a pock-faced man.

"We've got the Chief of Inspectors on our side, and the mayor's office is supposed to be behind us. We've got a reform committee that might or might not have some teeth in it, and we've got power to go to the grand jury."

"Sounds pretty good to me."

"That's all just on paper."

"Somebody said something about phone taps," cut in a cheerfully round-faced operative sitting on the foot of the bed.

"McKenna's right bower, Owen Lynch, is giving us the mayor's written authorization today."

The round-faced man had a notebook open. "Names and numbers."

"Dr. Gardner Shuman. General office number is WEst sixty-seven. Two phones at the drugstore downstairs, WEst six-four-six and six-four-seven. Home phone, WAlnut two-three-two. Two numbers at his office down on Post Street. DOuglas five-eight-eight-five. . . ."

As Hammett continued to rattle off names and numbers without using any notes, Jimmy Wright fired up a Fatima. Hammett had chosen an excellent way to announce himself as a fellow pro.

"Home phones on the Mulligans?" asked the wireman without looking up from his flying pencil.

"Griffith, no. He's too smart to transact business from the house. Boyd, yes. He's a dummy who likes to throw his weight around. You know the drill. Anything in or out that sounds interesting or suspicious."

"My meat," said the rotund man.

Hammett lit a cigarette of his own. "Jimmy, pick out the six top taxi-trade houses—on a par with Molly Farr's—and tap 'em. Ditto on the six biggest speaks in town, and make sure Dom Pronzini's is on the list."

"Got you," said Wright. "How about Brass Mouth Epstein's office?"

"I talked with Molly yesterday."

"Busy weekend," he said admiringly.

"Yeah. Also the six top books in town. Concentrate on those who use wire services from back east."

"We'll need a raft of stenos," warned Wright.

"Hire 'em." He pointed at the swarthy pockmarked man. "Find an office where we can keep records, question witnesses, and record answers. Two telephones. Security. A back entrance that'd be tough for anyone else to keep tabs on." He swung back to Wright. "Jimmy. Make damn sure that nobody gets the phone company to tap *our* phones."

"How many men should Tommy use for interrogations?"

"Two besides himself. Not you." He had turned to the final pair of men. One looked like a drinker, with sad bloodhound eyes, the other like a labor organizer in a loud check suit. Neither of them was either one. "I want you two on prowling assignments."

"Expenses?" The labor organizer hadn't removed his derby hat.

"Within reason, they'll be covered. Get around to the speakies and bookies. Listen. Watch for payoffs. Don't ask questions—that might be what got Vic rubbed. Any uniform bulls on the take, get their shield numbers. Plainclothes, listen for names. If they're driving, get the auto license numbers. If they use a cab, get *his* number so we can try for an ident from the driver later. Questions?"

"You want us to tail anybody?" asked the drinker.

"We're too thin in the field for that until we've got fingers pointing at specific people. Anything else?"

Nobody spoke. Hammett nodded.

"All reports in writing to Jimmy. I want the taps to go on today, the interrogations to start tomorrow. We begin with sergeants on up."

Pockmark grinned for the first time. "I like it already."

"You won't get anything out of them this time around, except somebody gets stupid. I just want them to know we're in business."

Twenty-two

VIC Atkinson had been right, had he but known it: Mondays were busy nights at Dom's Dump. Though it was the shank of the evening, the place was still over three-quarters full, and both barkeeps were sweating as they shoved it out over the stick. The thousand-faceted mirror globe was solemnly revolving, the tinted spotlights sending flecks and dots and streamers of color across the faces of the dancers. Up on the dais, a colored band Imported Direct From Connie's In Harlem At Great Expense was backing a torcher using body English on "Runnin' Wild."

The sweating Negro leader tried one of the soaring cornet solos with which Father Dip was challenging King Oliver in the Windy City, and blew nothing but air. Who cared? There was plenty of booze, plenty of money, and the girls had parked their girdles in the ladies' room so they could do the shimmy and the black bottom and the Charleston with proper abandon.

At just seventeen minutes before two o'clock in the morning, the front door was buzzed open to admit Dashiell Hammett. His gray houndstooth jacket had three buttons and his charcoal slacks had a knife-edge crease. His black wing tips were freshly polished. He leaned slightly on the polished ebony cane in his right hand while telling the blue-chinned bouncer his pleasure.

"That way for the bar, sir."

"Thank you, my good man."

Hammett spoke with the considered enunciation of one whose condition makes of the term "drunkenness" a *non sequitur*. His eyes had a slightly glassy, slightly hooded look, like the eyes of a resting hawk. He laid his stick on the bar and placed his freshly blocked and newly banded Wilton beside it.

The bartender wiped his hands on his apron. "Yessir, what can I . . ."

He broke off as a watchful Dom Pronzini, on the customer's side of the stick, exclaimed, "Bless my soul! Mr. Hammett! Say, this is swell!"

Hammett nodded to him with careful courtliness.

"Dom." His words were barely slurred at all. "I believe I will have a Dunbar's on the—"

"For you, it's on the house, Mr. Hammett!" He gestured up the bartender. "Tony. Dunbar's. Bring the bottle."

The torcher started "Oh Daddy," which Ethel Waters had made so famous. She didn't have the Waters voice or the Waters style, but the half of her that was out of her red-sequined dress apparently made up for it.

Tony brought the drinks. Hammett kept his back to the room.

Pronzini's heavy face was alight with a grin showing big stained teeth. "So, Mr. Hammett, you're back in the sleuthing game. Papa still says you're the best in the business. He got out two years ago, and he's . . . ah . . . . looking forward to running into you again."

"Just working for wages in those days, Dom." He toasted silently with his glass, then tossed it off. "It's a little different now."

Pronzini nodded. He leaned closer, so their shoulders

touched. "You mean that friend of yours. That Atkinson guy. A tough break."

Without looking at the big Italian, Hammett said in his soft drink-slurred voice, "What time was he in that night, Dom?"

"In here? *Here?* That night?" Pronzini reared back as if dismayed. He said humbly, "Well, gee, Mr. Hammett, I guess he could have been. But you see how busy—"

"Like the morgue that night, Dom."

Still hunched over the bar, Hammett poured. It was excellent whiskey.

"Well, Mr. Hammett, even so! I didn't know the man . . ."

"Had a couple of drinks with him, Dom." He held up his shot glass as if displaying it. "Like us, tonight."

The jovial Italian's eyes narrowed slightly. "I'm not sure I like that, Mr. Hammett."

Hammett looked directly at him for the first time. It was four minutes before two o'clock. His voice was softly suggestive.

"Who killed him, Dom?"

"Whew!" Pronzini shook his head in a dazed way, at the same time raising a hand at the bartender. "It ain't right, Mr. Hammett, you coming around trying to jack me off that way. We have one more drink, you'd better leave."

The bartender stood across the stick from them, his hands on the varnished wood. "Yessir, Mr. Pronzini?"

"Mr. Hammett wants one for the road, Tony. Take this piss away and bring us a bottle of the real stuff. The *real* stuff. Okay?"

"Yessir, Mr. Pron—"

"No thanks, Dom." Hammett had stepped back a pace from the bar. His pose matched that of the bartender's, with his right hand a bare inch from the heavy ebony walking stick.

"Tony," said Pronzini in a flat voice.

Tony's hand was six inches away from the bottle of Dunbar's when Hammett moved. No drunk ever moved that fast. His stick smashed down on Tony's hand. Tony screamed and tried to jerk the shattered hand away. Hammett put his

149

weight on the stick, grinding it down against the trapped hand.

"No Mickeys, Dom. No back room. Not me." He lifted the stick and pointed it toward the blue-chinned bouncer, who was reaching under his left arm. "No guns, Dom. Or I smash your skull while he's getting it out."

Pronzini waved off the bouncer. The bartender had crashed backwards against the bottles, clutching his pulped hand. Pronzini swiveled his heavy head past the suddenly silent, staring patrons toward the equally silent band.

"Play, you goddamn boogies!" he yelled.

The piano player started a fast riff of "Cemetery Blues." The drummer and brass caught in raggedly. They settled in behind the vocalist's body English.

"Enjoy yourself, folks!" Pronzini boomed. "Just a little joke."

Faces turned, dulling as curiosity left them. Bodies began swaying to the beat. Somebody laughed. Somebody dropped a glass. On the floor, somebody started dancing. Pronzini turned back to Hammett, his face dangerously suffused with blood.

"How do you think you're getting out of here, wise guy?"

"Not feet-first like Vic, that's a pipe." His smile touched only the muscles around his mouth. "I was outside, in the alley, when they carried him out, Dom. His head looked like a pumpkin."

"Yeah," said Pronzini softly but explosively.

A second bouncer had come from the rear door behind the partition in the drapes. Pronzini looked at Hammett from eyes ugly with triumph. It was a dozen seconds before two o'clock.

"You're going out the back way with me, Hammett, and then—"

The front door came off its hinges with a tearing sound to smash into kindling against the blue-chinned bouncer's back. He hit the floor nose-first, his scalp spraying blood. A woman screamed like a broken calliope pipe.

A massive baldheaded Chinese ran lightly over the fallen gorilla. He wore soft slippers and gray canvas trousers and

150

no shirt. His immense naked torso was splattered with the downed bouncer's blood. In his right hand waved and glittered a lather's hatchet sharpened to a-razor's edge. His eyes were wild; a high keening noise came from between his foam-flecked lips.

He skittered to a stop in the center of the dance floor, as the people jostled back with terror-filled faces. Hammett thought he was doing a beautiful job. His hatchet arced deadly patterns in the air.

But with a muttered curse, the remaining bouncer woke up. His hands darted for his gun. As it did, two more massive highbinders appeared on silent slippered feet from the split in the drapery through which he had come himself. They wore loose cotton shirts sashed at the waist over canvas trousers.

As his gun cleared its holster, they engulfed him from behind. The bouncer hit the floor like a dropped sack of grain, bleeding but alive. The front door belched four more binders. Two cradled tommy guns.

Pandemonium greeted the choppers. Pronzini's hand was frozen halfway under his jacket. The Chinese took positions against the walls. The band was playing "Alabamy Bound" as if there were no tomorrow. The uncrippled bartender kept his hands spread wide on the bar in an attempt to deny ownership of them. The man Hammett had maimed was out cold.

Only Hammett had not turned as the Orientals burst in. He poured a fresh drink from the bottle he hadn't let Tony take away. He spoke to Pronzini without looking at him.

"They're from the Bo Sin Sere tong. They like their killing." He finally looked over. "Who killed Vic?"

"*You* brought these chinks—"

"Who killed Vic?" said Hammett.

From the back room came the sound of breaking wood. Pronzini went white-faced. There was a crash from back there, a loud crash followed by the reek of raw whiskey.

Hammett felt a gentle hand on his shoulder, and he looked up into the expressionless face of Qwong Lin Get.

"Give out a couple of cases to the customers, compliments

151

of Dom," said Hammett. "Smash the rest of it." He turned to Pronzini. "I figured you'd have most of the Canadian stuff cached here."

He had to raise his voice over the wailing of the band, the shouts of the customers. One woman had begun smashing a chair on a table, laughing hysterically. The Chinese lined the walls like statues.

"You can't get away with this," said Pronzini hoarsely.

"Who killed Vic?"

A shout of joy went up from the trapped customers as the free booze began circulating. The good prewar stuff, down from Canada. Another chair was kindled, and another. A table was upended and its legs torn off.

"You . . . you're ruining me!" cried Pronzini.

Hammett sipped his drink. A hurled bottle shattered against the revolving mirrored ball. Pieces of glass and bits of dislodged mirror rained down on the dancers, who ignored them.

"Who killed Vic?"

Pronzini's eyes were getting desperate. "You'll make me a dead man."

"So Vic *did* get it here."

"But you said—"

Over the din of the disintegrating speakeasy, Hammett said, "Don't you know a con when you hear one, Dom? Home in my bed."

Pronzini hurled his glass to the floor in anger. "Goddammit!" he yelped, "you son of—"

A sweeping paw smashed him half over the bar. He twisted off it, ashen-faced with rage, but a glittering hatchet slammed into the wood so close to his head that a lock of severed black hair fell to the floor. Pronzini froze; he didn't even try to jerk his head away. He stared up at the seminude Oriental giant with stark terror.

"Shouldn't make threatening moves, Dom."

The dais on which the band played was being rocked. Hammett was pouring himself another shot. He was getting mellow. They wouldn't have much more time. The din would be reaching the street by now.

"Who'd you call when you recognized him, Dom? Griff or Boyd?"

"Boyd runs errands," Pronzini said with a sigh.

"Who'd Griff call?" Hammett sipped, a tall, lean, erect, very correct figure amid the wild party evolving from the destruction of Pronzini's speakeasy.

"I don't know, that's God's truth. Only Griff knows. All right, I slipped Atkinson a Mickey. And I left the alley door open for the guy to come in. But Atkinson was alive when I seen him last."

Some draperies were afire on the far side of the dance floor. Pronzini looked that way, agonized, just as the dais slowly collapsed. But he shook his head.

"I ain't got nothing else to say to you, Hammett, not even if your boys wreck the place."

"They already have."

The band went off the edge of the dais in a crash of instruments. The upended torcher wore no step-ins under her tight red sequins. Four men were fighting drunkenly in the middle of the floor. Nine more, and as many women, arms linked, were swaying back and forth and chanting: "Where-was-Moses-when-the-lights-went-out?"

"Down in the cellar eating sauerkraut," said Hammett. He picked up his hat and stick. He said, "I talked with that reporter who did the series on bootlegging last year. He told me Egan Tokzek was a runner for you."

"Tokzek?" said Pronzini in a dazed voice.

"What did he do for you besides run rum?"

"What the hell else was he good for?" he burst out in remembered grievance. "You can't trust them snow-noses for nothing but donkey-work."

"Right you are," said Hammett. He set the Wilton on his silvery hair at a properly rakish angle, then tipped it to the speechless bootlegger. "Thanks for the drink, Dom."

He walked through the wreckage toward the gaping front door, very erect, very proper, no hint of drunkenness in his movements. Behind him the binders funneled down to go through the door like bats leaving a cave. From far off came the clanging of a fire truck.

153

Twenty-three

BOYD MULLIGAN was doing the *Examiner* crossword and waiting for the secretary to get back from lunch when the lean stranger's shadow fell across his newspaper.

"Can I help you?"

"Is Mr. Mulligan about?" The stranger's snap-brim gray Wilton was pulled down to shadow his face.

"I'm Boyd Mulligan."

"It's your uncle I want."

"He won't be in until three o'clock. Give me the message."

The stranger hesitated. He squared broad lean shoulders under his overcoat and leaned closer. "It's from . . ." He leaned closer yet. *"Him."*

"Him?" Mulligan said stupidly, trying to appear wise.

"You know." The eyes darted to the door at the far end of the room. "Is there a private office? Anyone coming by in the street can see me in here, and if they do . . ."

Boyd, thoroughly confused, left his blond-wood swivel and led the way.

Griffith Mulligan had shared the private office with no one since his brother's death a few years before. There were filing cabinets along the left wall, with layers of thick asbestos sandwiched between their sheet steel sides. They were always locked, and Griff Mulligan carried the only key. The secret lives of half the powerful in San Francisco were locked away in these drawers; the secrets of the other half were locked away in Griff Mulligan's shrewd Irish skull.

Boyd turned to face the stranger in the middle of the room. "Is this private enough for you?" he demanded, without bothering to conceal the sneer in his voice. He wished the damned girl would get back; he was starving to death.

The stranger slid his eyes down the blank right-hand wall where the room's only window had been bricked in and plastered over years before.

"This'll do," he said.

154

He put a sinewy open hand against Boyd's face and shoved. Hard.

Boyd windmilled into Griff's chair. The chair tipped over backward. He slammed knees-first into the wall and yowled. He struggled to his feet still too shocked for either fear or anger.

"Are you *crazy?* I'm *Boyd Mulligan!*"

The stranger stood in the center of the room with his legs set wide, leaning toward Boyd as if against a strong wind.

"And I'm Dashiell Hammett," he said.

"Ham . . . Hammett?"

He felt his lower lip tremble. He pushed the lank black hair from his eyes. He wasn't ready for this. He, well, hell, he just. . . .

"Dorothy . . . will be back from lunch any—"

"Twenty-two minutes," said Hammett. "Sit down, punk."

Boyd found himself righting his uncle's chair and lowering himself gingerly into it, keeping a tight grip on the wooden arms. His cheeks burned. Wait until he put out the call on this bastard! He'd have them start by breaking his shins, and then his forearms, and then smashing his kneecaps, and. . . . But dammit, his uncle had said nobody touched Hammett. And what his uncle said. . . .

"I just came to put you on notice, punk," said Hammett. "I'm going to fry the man who killed Vic Atkinson. *And* the men who—"

"Listen, I don't—"

"*And* the men who pointed him in Vic's direction."

Boyd fought his panic. Hammett was just trying to trick him into spilling something. Well, Boyd Mulligan didn't spill. He was tougher and smarter than that.

"I don't know what you're talking about."

"You know, punk." Hammett stepped closer, eyes on fire. "Why do you suppose I took apart Pronzini's last night?"

"But the papers said Chinese gangst—"

"Jesus!" Hammett laughed gratingly. "You *are* just an errand boy, aren't you? Well, tell your uncle that Pronzini spilled his guts. To me. About the Mickey Finn in Vic's drink.

155

About calling your uncle. About who your uncle called. Everything. *Everything*, punk."

Boyd was licking his lips, again and again. His heart seemed to be thundering in his chest. "I . . . he wouldn't . . . Atkinson didn't. . . ."

Hammett crossed the office in long strides. He jerked open the door. He spun abruptly on his heel to look back.

"You ever seen a man who's been hung, punk? He ends up with a neck three feet long."

He was gone. Boyd, stunned, dragged himself from his uncle's swivel chair. He reached the windows of the front office just in time to see Hammett striding down Kearny toward the Hall of Justice.

The Hall of Justice! With shaking hands, he reached for the telephone.

"You had fun last night," accused Jimmy Wright.

Hammett drank bad coffee from the rotund detective's gas ring. Through the window he could see a strip of the Southern Pacific baggage shed roof. Just a week ago, he'd been standing there looking at Vic's pulped features. A week, and nobody tagged for it. But. . . .

"Had some more fun this morning. You *sure* that wireman has the Mulligan Bros. phones covered?"

"I just came from the phone company. They're covered."

Hammett lowered his coffee cup and looked in as if waiting for something to surface. "Who stepped on this bug?" he asked. Laughter brimmed in his voice. He looked very youthful, his eyes sparkled. "I just left Mulligan Bros. Bought breakfast for their secretary the other morning and picked up their routine. When she was out to lunch and Uncle Griff wasn't in yet, I went in and pushed Boydie-boy around a bit."

"How is he?" asked the op in an interested voice.

"He sings soprano. I'm hoping he used the phone after I left."

The op shrugged, and fed him the straight line. "So he calls Uncle Griff. . . ." He liked to watch Hammett work.

156

"When he did, Uncle Griff should have been sitting in Dave's Barber Shop on McAllister and Fillmore, waiting for a Mr. Hambledon to show up with some hot mining stock tips. Dave's Barber Shop isn't a place Uncle Griff ever goes."

"That wouldn't be Mr. Dashiell Hambledon, would it?"

"The very same. Incognito for this important occasion."

In crisp sentences, he outlined what had happened at Pronzini's the night before, to appropriate comment and a lot of chuckles from the op. Finally he stood up and put on his hat.

"How does the interrogation of the police brass look?"

"An Inspector O'Keefe sounds brittle. And I think the lieutenant on the take from Molly is starting to get religion. I've got both of them coming back tonight. I'll be taking them on myself. Want to sit in?"

"Let me call you later." From the door, he asked, "What did the Pinks have to say about Tokzek?"

The op snapped his fingers. "Good you asked. Meinbress didn't know me, so he wanted to check with some of the other boys before he looked in the files for—"

"Meinbress?"

"He took over as Resident Sup. when Geauque went out. I'm supposed to call him this afternoon, and he'll give me whatever they have on him."

When Hammett walked up the hill from a Geary Street car three hours later, Preacher Dan Laverty was leaning against the side of a dusty parked Reo, arms folded on his chest. He was talking with the wispy Frenchwoman who ran the hand laundry in the street-level shop below Hammett's apartment building.

She went back inside with a dissatisfied look on her face when Hammett arrived. The Preacher faced Hammett squarely. He was troubled, his hard cop's eyes worried.

"Ah . . . look, ah, Dash, what do I hear about you being mixed up in this thing last night at Dominic Pronzini's joint?"

"The tong binders?" Hammett shrugged. "I had to put pressure on Pronzini, and they were the only people in town

157

I could think of who wouldn't be scared to go up against him."

"Yeah-h-h. . . ." Laverty was hesitant, oddly unsure of himself. He began, "Dash, I want to . . . ." He stopped and shook his head. He sighed. In a tired voice, he asked, "What made you want to pressure Pronzini anyway? Why do you think he had anything to do with Vic's death?"

Hammett ticked off his points on his fingers.

"Vic called me that night, around one o'clock, from the YMCA on The Embarcadero. He was given directions and the password to Pronzini's joint at the cigar store in the Hotel Commodore. With that, I went after Pronzini. He admitted, to me, that he fed Vic a Mickey. He admitted that he called Griff Mulligan. He admitted that someone came around to take a look at Vic. But he claimed that the last he saw, Vic was alive."

"You believe that?"

"It might be the truth. But I know damned well it was his boys who dumped Vic's body behind the Southern Pacific station."

The sunlight had finally broken the noonday fog to move Laverty's shadow, black and hinged in the middle, around on the sidewalk and up the tan bricks of the apartment building as he shifted position. In a thickened voice, he said, "I'd like to get that devil's hound Pronzini down in the basement of the Hall of Justice for an hour. We'd find out the truth."

"Mulligan Bros. would have him out of there on bond before you could work up a good sweat. And if you took him to a station house instead of the Hall, that White Top cab parked outside their shop on permanent call would deliver the bond before you could get him booked."

Laverty nodded. The brief flash of fire within him had died. He asked, "Where'd you get the chinks?"

"One of the big wineys in Chinatown owed me a favor."

Laverty jerked his head in assent and went back to his black Reo. Seeing the car reminded Hammett. He leaned an elbow on the edge of Laverty's open window. "Dan, you've seen the coroner's report on Egan Tokzek by now. Was the guy cocked up?"

"To the eyeballs. C-and-M crystals. Still had the snuffbox in his watch pocket. Damned lucky for me he was, he emptied a .44 at me without hitting anything but glass."

Hammett watched Laverty's car go down Post Street, then stood unmoving for a full minute after it had disappeared. Egan Tokzek was a dope addict, longtime, habitual, as Pronzini had intimated. And he'd been on the hop the night of his death.

Which didn't make any sense at all, unless. . . . Yeah, unless you turned it around. Considered the fact that he was a rumrunner for Pronzini, and that Pronzini brought most of his Canadian booze into Bolinas. Obscure excitement moved through him, feeding on half-understood. . . .

He crossed quickly to Dorris Auto Repair and called the Townsend Hotel for Jimmy Wright. Dammit, by this time Jimmy should have heard something from Pinkerton's on Tokzek.

"Did you call?" he asked without preamble.

"Yeah. And from the tone of your voice I ain't going to surprise you much to tell you that Heloise Kuhn, your fat dame up in Marin, is Egan Tokzek's sister."

"Good, good," said Hammett rapidly. "Sure. What I thought. I kept trying to remember her from two hundred pounds back. She was a looker, was collared on a Mann Act rap, right?"

"In 1916, right. Pinkerton's made the collar in a white slavery case, and Tokzek drew five years—although it's the sister who sounds like bad medicine. He got out in twenty-one."

"What were they supposed to be doing?"

"Supplying Oriental girls to Colosimo's house in Chitown."

"Wasn't Johnny Torrio running the house then for Big Jim?"

"Torrio. Right."

"And when he retired, the Scarface took over," muttered Hammett to himself. He raised his voice. "Better count me out tonight, Jimmy, on those interrogations. I'm going to be busy."

"You have all the fun," grumbled the op.

159

Hammett laughed and hung up and dropped another nickel and asked for DOuglas 6400. He was lucky enough to catch George Biltmore in.

"Well. Hammett." He sounded slightly uneasy. "What can I do for you?"

"How's my credit after Sunday's performance?"

Biltmore's heavy, relieved laugh boomed out. "With me, A-one. But May wouldn't be too delighted to see you again. Since she obviously can't blame the grieving widow, she's blaming you."

"Yeah, well, I brought the booze. How's that chauffeur of yours in a brawl?"

"Harry?" The laughter boomed again. "He fought in the First Matabele War in ninety-three against the flower of Lobengula's warriors. Lost his eye in the Battle of Imbembese."

None of which meant too much to Hammett; he hadn't been born until a year later. "Think he'd be willing to drive me somewhere tonight?"

"Promise him action, he'll be there."

"Nine thirty ferry in Sausalito," said Hammett. "He can pick me up at the slip. It wouldn't hurt to bring a gun if he's got one handy, although I don't expect shooting."

"You don't need another man, do you?" There was a wistful note in Biltmore's voice.

"Your wife's sore enough at me the way it is."

Twenty-four

IT was the damnedest car Hammett had ever seen, a huge dark-green beast with a chest-high hood. Its owl-eyed headlamps were augmented by a searchlight mounted on a nickel stanchion on the right running board. A second set of folding windshields protected riders in the back seat.

"What the hell is it?" he asked Harry. The solid, compact chauffeur wore dark clothes and a soft knit cap instead of his uniform.

"This is the new Cadillac four-passenger Sport Phaeton, sir," he said in his formal South African accent.

"Make that Dash," said Hammett.

"Very well, Dash. Sir."

"Have it your way."

He had a hunch the South African was grinning.

The motor roared, then dropped to a throaty grumble. The car's interior had glossy burled walnut paneling and seats of pale hand-crushed leather.

Harry said, "If I could know where we're going, sir. . . ."

"To rescue a damsel in distress on the Bolinas Road."

"Sir."

The car slid smoothly away from the curb. A few miles out of Sausalito, they swung left into the Bolinas Road at Dolan's Corner, where their lights briefly showed them a rundown country store. They had the crushed-gravel road totally to themselves at that time of night.

"Whom might the damsel in distress be, sir?"

"A fifteen-year-old Chinese ex-whore named Crystal."

Harry was silent, digesting this.

"We're saving her from a fate worse than death, is it, sir?"

The big car began the climb out of the valley on a road that wound and twisted back upon itself through grove after grove of close-packed eucalyptus trees and then, quite suddenly, redwoods. They kept climbing this shoulder of the mountain that lay between them and the sea. Hammett checked his strap watch.

"We ought to be there by eleven. Time I explained the set-up, Harry."

He did so as the Cadillac cleared the redwoods and rolled across windswept grassy hilltops clumped with genista and greasewood bushes. Far behind, across the black void of the bay, Hammett could see the twinkling lights of the city through the clear air. There was no fog.

"I don't quite understand why you think the missing girl might be held at the farmhouse here in Bolinas."

Hammett explained the way he had been run off on his previous visit.

"The way a bootlegger chases off someone snooping around his barn. We know there's a connection between the girl and the woman, we know the girl was once kidnapped into the white slavery racket and taken to Illinois. We know the Kuhn woman and her brother were arrested for white slavery back in sixteen—picking up naïve Chinese girls through newspaper ads for domestics, and running them back to brothels in Burnham, Illinois. I think that all goes beyond coincidence."

In hairpin turns the road made its descent along the face of the coastal hills toward Stinson Beach. The wind whipped and plucked at them as it poured up over the bluffs from the sea. Hammett was glad of his wool clothing and knitted cap in the open touring car.

"But how would the Kuhn woman get her hands on Crystal at this time?"

"On May twenty-seventh, Crystal apparently saw something in the papers that terrorized her so completely that the next afternoon she disappeared. Nobody's seen her since. She might have come up here to hide, if she'd been told the house was now empty. Anyway, that's what I hope we'll find out."

They had passed Stinson Beach, a crossroads store with a gas pump and a couple of houses, and had swung away from the coast toward the long lance of Pacific known as the Bolinas Lagoon. The Kuhn farm was on the eastern shore of the lagoon.

"What did she see in the papers that frightened her so?"

"Again, I just don't know. But I think it was an article about a man named Egan Tokzek who was killed in a running gun battle with police and had a dead Chinese girl in his car when they got him. Tokzek was the brother of Heloise Kuhn.".

Harry cut the lights and motor, and the sounds of the marshland night closed in on them. Carrunking frogs, saw-

162

ing crickets, and trilling cicadas. The car motor creaked as it cooled. Harry took a gun from the pocket of his black horsehide coat and laid it on the pale leather seat. Hammett picked it up.

"Holy Christ!" he exclaimed, startled. "What kind of howitzer is this?"

"A howdah gun, sir. Originally intended as a personal sidearm when hunting tigers from the back of an elephant. In case the beast leaped up on the elephant's back with you—"

"I can stick my fingers down the bore," said Hammett in awe.

"Yes, sir. It fires a .577 Snider with eighty grains of black powder. Made by Wilkinson, the London sporting goods suppliers. Beyond about two yards it's rather less effective than throwing a rock, sir, but—"

"Yeah. But you'd hate to have it blow its nose at you, even so."

Hammett walked up the grass ruts shoulder to shoulder with the South African. He was damned glad the case had brought him back here. He didn't like the depth of terror this woman and her idiot son had opened in his psyche; he wanted to scab over the wound with a second confrontation.

When the house came into sight, they hunkered down. Harry brought his lips close to Hammett's ear.

"If I might say so, sir, I'm damned good as a red Indian."

Hammett watched his bulky shape melt into the night. Strain as he could, his ear could catch no crackle of leaf or rustle of grass. He waited with the placidity of long hours spent in windy doorways, tailing suspects. He yearned for a cigarette, but otherwise. . . .

To mind, abruptly, vividly, came the time Gloomy Gus Schaefer's jewel gang had been traced to a roadhouse near Vallejo. Hammett had been sent in to learn where the Shapiro jewels, stolen in Minneapolis, had been hidden. He'd waited in the weeds like this for an hour, then tried to climb up the side porch to the second-story window of the room where the thieves were meeting. The drainpipe gave way and

163

dumped him in the underbrush, bruised but unhurt. Shapiro's men had searched for half an hour before. . . .

A strong hand imprisoned his, with his .38, in his pocket. Harry, after a moment, took his own hand away. Red Indian was right.

"Nobody on watch, sir," he said in almost normal tones. "Just that light in the living room. I checked the barn, also. No auto. The back door is locked. . . ."

"And the front porch creaks like hell, I noticed that the other day. Is there a pantry window?"

"Locked, sir."

"That's all right."

When they were pressed up against the side of the house, they heard a high thin ululating whine through the wood. After a moment, Hammett chuckled and motioned the South African on. At the rear of the house he found the pantry window and took a roll of automobile friction tape from his pocket to lay three overlapping strips against the glass where the inside thumb-latch was. He tapped the tape twice with his gun butt, then peeled it away in one piece. He snaked a forefinger through the opening where the adhering glass had come away with the tape. He opened the lock.

"Very handsome," breathed Harry.

"Streets and houses, Harry. *My* kind of hunting."

From another pocket, Hammett pulled a black woolen sock with a knot in it. From this he took a heavy square-cut oblong of brown laundry soap with which he waxed the tracks until the lower half of the window slid up easily and noiselessly.

Gun in hand, he slipped over the sill to the utter blackness of the pantry. Only the pale strip of light under the door was visible. He crouched and laid an eye to the floor. Nothing to trip over between him and the door to the kitchen.

They went toward it and through it.

The dim light came down the hall from the front room. At the far end of the hallway were the stairs to the second floor and a wide archway into the front room. Hammett slid an eye around the doorframe.

It was a barren room with dime-store shades, no drapes or curtains at the windows. The couch spilled horsehair from half a dozen rips. The kerosene pressure lamp that coned light down on the fat woman in the overstuffed chair needed pumping. The chair was so permanently sagged by her weight he could see the bottoms of half a dozen springs resting right on the floor beneath it.

Heloise had her head back and to one side and was snoring. Her mouth was open and her false teeth had slipped enough so one edge of the upper plate was visible.

Against the wall was a floor-model Silvertone radio receiver, the six-tube console model. One of the knobs on the cabinet door had been replaced with an acorn. From the radio came the thin whine Hammett had earlier identified as a dead station.

He stepped back into the hall, pointed at Harry and then into the room, then pointed at himself and up the stairs. Harry nodded. Hammett started up the inner edge of the stair treads, his .38 cocked and ready in his hand.

Nobody.

The bathroom held a claw-footed tub and a surprisingly modern low-tank closet toilet. The three bedrooms held only beds, chairs, and bureaus. The far one stank of Heloise and its bed sagged nearly to the floor.

In the middle room, Hammett was rewarded with several long glossy black hairs on a greasy pillow. He stood cold-faced for several moments, staring down at the circle of light from his flash: There were blond hairs, too. Andy, the idiot son. The bathroom clothes hamper yielded a pair of silk panties that would not have stretched around Heloise's thigh.

He went back downstairs and into the living room.

"The kid took her off somewhere, probably right after I was here last time. Somebody isn't taking any chances."

He didn't bother to lower his voice. Heloise slumbered on, merely stirring in her sleep and making chomping noises. Spit had dribbled from the slack corner of her mouth.

Harry said in an almost apologetic voice, "Better let me

165

have a bash at it, sir. I had a bit of experience at this sort of thing during my younger days in South Africa. Now, if we could just have a bit of dance music on the radio. . . ."

Hammett twiddled the knob. "Ain't She Sweet" suddenly came from the instrument.

"KPO. They go off the air in twelve minutes," he warned.

"That's time enough. Now turn it up sharply, sir."

Hammett turned it up sharply, and backed away as a blaring voice began extolling the virtues of Iswan Ginger Ale. A hoarse shriek that did not come from the radio whirled him about.

Heloise bellowed again and tried to crowd her vast bulk back into the chair. Harry's face was six inches from hers. His left hand was holding up his eyelid so the first thing she had seen upon being jarred from sleep was the moist empty pink socket the lid usually covered.

Harry straightened up. "That's got you awake, then, has it?" he shouted over the radio cheerily. He turned to Hammett with a quieting motion.

Hammett was glad to reduce the volume as Bob Nurok and the Ginger Ale Joys began rendering "Give Me a Ukulele and a Ukulele Baby."

"Where's the chink twist?" demanded Hammett of the fat woman in the language she'd be most likely to respond to.

But Heloise had recovered from the shock of Harry's gaping eye socket. She told Hammett where to go. She told him what to do when he got there.

"On your feet, you disgusting sow," said Harry. "We want a little dance from you."

Heloise began repeating her advice, this time to Harry. He made a smooth movement that brought the pistol into his hand, and blew the arm off the couch across the room. He swung the gun muzzle toward her.

Heloise found a remarkable turn of speed in getting to her feet.

Harry blew a hole in the floor beside her right shoe.

Heloise started to dance in time to the music. She was grotesque. Blobs and billows of flesh jounced and shook in ragtime. Her breaths were groans.

The side seam of her cotton wash dress ripped with the sound of a board breaking. She wore no underwear.

"Where's the chink?" asked Hammett. He was goddamn glad Harry was interrogating her, not him.

"Dance faster," ordered Harry.

But as he said it, he put away his pistol.

Heloise saw her chance. With an elephantine shriek of rage and triumph, she charged.

Harry spun back toward her and drove off a crouch as if he were opening a hole for Red Grange. He heaved up and away with a hoarse bellow as his shoulder sank into her gut.

Heloise stopped in midflight. Her feet flew straight out in front of her on either side of Harry. From midair, she sat down.

She landed on her chair like a flash flood. It burst asunder. Collapsed, it looked like a spread-out pattern for itself. Heloise sprawled in the midst of it making noises like a bathtub emptying.

"Where's the chink?" asked Hammett.

Heloise didn't answer. Harry took out his pistol again and thumbed back the hammer. With the ritual tenderness of a man entering a woman, he pushed the muzzle forward until it touched the end of her nose. Sweat popped out on her forehead. The mean black raisins buried in the folds of flesh beneath her nearly hairless brows crossed slightly.

Very, very softly, Harry said, "Take out your teeth, you unspeakable dung heap."

Her eyes rolled. Her mouth worked to form some sort of word. It might have been, "Please."

Harry waited. The sweat ran down her face. Finally something he saw in her eyes, some capitulation, perhaps, made him relax and straighten.

Very slowly, while she stared at his face as if mesmerized, her right hand went up to remove the full set of dentures. She slipped it from her mouth and sat with it on her half-opened hand in her lap. Her face looked collapsed from the nose down, as if someone had removed part of the essential underlying bone. The teeth gleamed like an uncatalogued fossil.

Harry put out a calloused palm. After a full thirty seconds, her hand laid the teeth on Harry's hand.

The radio had stopped playing. The silence of the room was broken only by the softening hiss of the kerosene lantern.

Harry dropped the plates on the floor. He carefully brought his heel down on them, then twisted and turned the heel. The teeth gnashed themselves to rubble beneath his boot.

Tears spilled over to run down Heloise's satiny skin and into the corners of her shrunken mouth.

"Goddamn you!" she cried mushily. "I was beautiful once!"

"Where's the chink?" said Hammett.

Twenty-five

"BRIGHTON Street," lisped the fat woman on the front seat between them.

The main street of Bolinas, Brighton wound around the point of the peninsula and dead-ended at the ocean.

"Point out the house," said Hammett.

It was a plain white Victorian in midblock; the gas lamp on the corner gave just enough illumination to show them the porch pillars. The yard was overgrown with weeds; the house was still and dark. A black flivver was parked in the driveway beyond a white picket fence that needed paint.

"Right on by," said Hammett, before Harry had a chance

to slow the big car. "Park on the other side of the street facing back this way."

Animation entered the lisping voice. "You won't hurt my baby. . . ."

"He's the one with the shotgun."

"He ain't but seventeen."

"The girl was eleven when you sold her to the cathouse in Illinois."

Heloise did not respond.

Harry stopped the car. He started to get out, but Hammett forestalled him.

"Streets and houses, Harry. My kind of hunting. Remember?"

Harry made a face and nodded. They had planned their strategy after Heloise had given them the layout of the house, but the big South African still felt his role was too passive.

The fat woman quavered. "My boy. Don't hurt my. . . ."

Hammett leaned back into the open car. His irrational fear of the irrational boy with the shotgun lay on his stomach like an undigested meal.

"Your boy!" he said in a low tight vicious voice. "In the south they keep his kind behind the stove."

He walked away feeling slightly nauseated. It had been a destructive night, and it wasn't over yet.

The gate was ajar, the front porch solid and uncreaking underfoot. Only one window was open, that of the second-floor bedroom in which Heloise had said her son was holding the Chinese girl. Hammett's skeleton key worked the simple mortise lock without difficulty. Nothing came out of the inner darkness at him, but his hands were clammy by the time he had been through the downstairs rooms. There was no way to duck a shotgun blast if it came.

He checked his watch, then started up. Harry and the fat woman would be getting out of the car in another thirty seconds.

He stopped with a foot half raised. Above his head, the boy's muffled voice. Door of the room shut. A muffled laugh, remarkable for its idiocy, then an answering female voice. What sounded like a pleading tone.

. Hammett raised his head slowly above the level of the hall floor. Pitch blackness. From behind the unseen door, the girl's voice again. The idiotic laughter. Harry and the fat woman would be coming up the silent street now, Harry's cannon half buried in her side.

The bedsprings started that cadence that can never be mistaken for anything else. Go or not? Go. He went up the final stairs in a quick silent rush.

The tempo was increasing, becoming frenzied. He felt his way down the hallway to that door, traced enough of its surface to know which way it opened. Downstairs, the creak of a floorboard told him that Harry and the fat woman had come in.

The boy started making animal noises. The girl cried out, a wild lost sound. Hammett was flattened against the wall beside the door, his gun in his pocket, his soap-weighted wool sock in one hand and his flashlight in the other.

Three . . . two . . . one . . . *now!*

From downstairs came Heloise's terrific bellow. Another. A cry, a curse inside the room.

The Chinese girl shrieked, the sort of shriek that brought the hairs erect on Hammett's neck.

Scuffling noises downstairs. Harry's cursing. Then the fat woman's yell of warning.

"ANDY! LOOK OUT!"

Bare feet hitting the floor inside the room. Pause to get gun. Running feet. The door was ripped open. . . .

Hammett was already spinning off the wall. His right arm swept the homemade blackjack as his left hand thumbed blinding light into Andy's face. The soap-weighted sock caught the youth between the eyes with such force that his head snapped back and the shotgun squirted from his nerveless fingers unfired.

Hammett's light followed him down, the arm swinging the sock with the tireless rhythm of panic even as Crystal, inside the room, cried, "Look out! He's got a gun!"

Hammett dropped the sock and straightened with the .38

170

in his hand, his light arcing the other bedroom doors. None of them opened. Andy had been a lone jailer.

"Hammett!" yelled Harry from below. "Is . . ."

"He's out."

The Chinese girl hurled herself into the lean detective's arms, crying and clawing at him, tears streaming down her face, her naked body twined around his.

"He was . . . they wouldn't . . . he forced me to . . . ."

"That's all right, it's okay now, that's all right. . . ."

Hammett's voice was soothing. He tried to disentangle himself from her. Her body was hot and lithe, arousing.

"Get some clothes, on, Crystal, we're getting out of here."

He got her back into the room and himself out into the hall. Harry followed his flashlight up the stairs.

"Heloise get away all right?" asked Hammett.

"Should have seen the fat bitch run." Harry was chuckling.

"We can be damned sure she won't go to the police," said Hammett. "But she'll be sure we won't either. She'll be back to get Andy, so you'd better get back to the car just in case she tries to disable it or something."

Hammett turned on the hallway light for the first time, and broke the fallen boy's shotgun to jack out the shells. Andy was breathing regularly, still out cold.

Hammett could hear Crystal's muted sobbing as she moved around the room. Through the closed door, she called, "I will be ready right away."

She came out looking very young and very fragile, her long black hair pulled back and tucked under a rope-stitch wool hockey cap with an incongruous bushy pompom on top. She wore tweed knickers and argyle socks and a leatherette sport jacket with a corduroy collar. The clothes were rumpled and coated with the sort of thick dust that accumulates on the floors of closets.

The girl's huge, famished, tearstained eyes looked at Hammett across the boy's naked body. "Thank you," she said.

The boy stirred and groaned at the sound of her voice. She looked down at him gravely. Her shoes were heavy squaretoed sport brogues of imitation alligator. With all the force at her command, she kicked him in the side of the head.

171

"Now I am ready to go," she said to Hammett.

At the head of the stairs she faltered, so he half led, half carried her down, uncomfortably aware of the slight, beautifully formed body beneath the cheap clothing.

When they reached the car, she thanked Harry with simple dignity and added, "I'm sorry she escaped. I wished to kill her."

"Do you think you'd of been able, dear?" Harry grinned.

A ghost of a smile touched her small mouth. "I could have kicked her."

"You'd have had a big enough target," said Hammett. To Harry, he said, "How'd you make her yell right on cue?"

"Jabbed her in the arse with my knife. Could have put it in six inches without touching bone."

Crystal fell asleep on the drive back to Sausalito. Hammett picked two splinters from the ribbed wool of his sweater, and wondered how he was going to get the whole truth out of her. It had become complicated again.

Dawn was breaking behind the Oakland hills as the four thirty car-ferry churned its way toward the Hyde Street pier. The light made pastels of the harsh gray granite and cruel yellow-stone disciplinary barracks as they passed Alcatraz. Hammett was blear-eyed and yawning. It had been a hell of a night.

Crystal clung to him like a little child as they went down the worn timber gangway to the pier, her head lolling like a puppet's against his arm. The pompom on her cap came just to his shoulder.

"Are the mobsters on to you?" asked Hammett. "I have to know."

A look of terror entered her eyes. She pulled her childishly small fingers from his hand.

"Molly said something about trouble back east."

"Molly? But Molly is hidden where even I do not know—"

"I found her."

They walked a block over to Polk, where an early Number 19 streetcar waited to start its run. One of the beefy Italian conductors collected their fares and went away. The other manipulated the controls to send the heavy car up the Polk Street incline with a rush of power.

Crystal said, her eyes suddenly enormously yearning, "Can I go and stay with Molly?"

"I found her," Hammett repeated.

"Oh." Her voice was very small. "You are right. If they find me again, they will kill me."

"The fat sow and her dim-witted kid?" Hammett shook his head. "They're still running."

"The ones they were holding me for."

They left the car at Sutter Street. Hammett found it pleasant walking hand-in-hand with this girl. Her abrupt gaiety was infectious: He found himself swinging his arm in wide arcs with hers.

"Where is this place you are taking me?"

"A hotel." Then seeing her expression of alarm, he added, "Forget it. You're too skinny."

She giggled. "You're no one to talk."

"I may be thin, but I'm aww-ful wiry. We turn here."

They entered a basement doorway flush with the sidewalk and went down steps to a narrow concrete corridor the length of the building, which led them across enclosed backyards. They went through a door in a sidewall, down more concrete steps, and across a basement floor. Another door put them in the enclosed courtyard behind a three-story building.

"Up we go, sweetheart."

Hammett used a key in the fire door. Very narrow wooden stairs took them winding upward. He used the key again at the first landing, which put them on the building's second floor. Halfway along the hall that paralleled Post Street, Hammett rang the buzzer under a wooden OFFICE sign. The upper half of the Dutch door swung wide. A tousled white thatch was thrust out so snapping black eyes could regard them.

"Got a desperate fugitive for you to hide out, Pop," said Hammett.

Twenty-six

THE room was small but meticulously clean, with a steel-framed bungalow bed and a steam radiator. Above the bed was a framed print of "Spring Song," with the little girl sitting on the bench watching a bluebird sing at the edge of a copse of birch trees. Across from it was a dresser set at an angle between the two windows. The single straight-backed chair was childishly decorated with painted vines and garish flowers.

Crystal entered the room like a cat, daintily sticking her head into the closet and around the frame of the bathroom door. Also like a cat, she made the room her own, bouncing on the bed as a child might do to test its springiness. They had come up a very narrow uncarpeted stairway from the rear of the hotel's top floor, to this single small separate room built right on the tar-and-gravel roof of the hotel.

"I could sleep for a week," she said.

"Ain't much *to* do but sleep, here," said Pop from the door-way.

"Pinkerton's used to put surprise witnesses up here until it was time to testify," Hammett explained. Pop said he would bring milk and doughnuts up from the Eagle Market, and Hammett added, "Coffee, too."

Crystal gestured after the old man. "Shouldn't you . . . I mean, he's pretty decrepit. . . ."

"This lets him feel he's handling the situation." Hammett drew the garish chair closer to the bed and sat down. "And gives us time for a little talk."

"I . . . don't understand." Her eyes slid away from his.

"Fat mama and the idiot boy didn't put the snatch on you at high noon on Market Street."

The girl was looking down at her hands. Her voice was very small. "No, of course not. But. . . ."

"Remember Vic Atkinson?"

"The man with the ten-year-old dog?" She jerked her head and gave an involuntary nervous giggle.

174

"Vic's dead. Murdered."

"Oh! I'm sorry." Her eyes went back to her hands, which clasped and unclasped themselves in her lap. "I . . . I didn't know."

"Everybody keeps talking about a threat from the mob back east. You, the cops, Molly. Vic's murder *could* have been a mob killing, it had the earmarks. Or it could have just been made to look that way. I'm pretty sure *where* he died—in the back room of Dom Pronzini's speakeasy." The name had no apparent effect on her. "If I knew *why*, I'd probably know *who*." He added thoughtfully, "The mob might be trying to get a toehold in the city through Pronzini. . . ."

The girl said nothing.

"What did you see in the newspaper that made you start running?"

The girl's dark almond eyes flashed up briefly at him, then back down to the hands busy in her lap again. She said nothing.

"I need some answers, sister. Was it because of a newspaper article identifying a dead man as Egan Tokzek? The brother of the fat bitch up in Marin?"

The fingers of one hand picked at the other. Her eyes watched. She spoke to her hands, her voice soft and hesitant. "If you are to understand, you must know something that happened four years ago, when I was only eleven. . . ."

"You answered an ad for a domestic and were grabbed by the fat woman and her brother and shipped to a brothel back east," said Hammett in a brutally impatient voice. "I know all of that. What about—"

"But how can you . . ." Her eyes were wide and shocked. "Nobody . . ."

"Tokzek did time for white slavery ten-twelve years ago. He and his sister specialized in Chinese girls then. Why would they have changed by the time you came along?"

The girl's head remained bowed. Hammett leaned forward to raise her face. Tears were welling from her eyes, but she made no attempt to look away.

"I am so ashamed."

Hammett took his hand away. "It happened." He'd

175

learned years before that a matter-of-fact approach worked better than sympathy when witnesses were on the edge of collapse. "Talking about it won't make it happen again."

"I . . . know. All right." She knuckled her eyes in a little-girl gesture. "First I went to an office in Chinatown, the address listed in the ad. The fat woman was there. She interviewed me and sent me to an address on McAllister Street. It was my first trolley ride, I was terrified. Tokzek was there. He kept me in the attic for three days, putting things into the food so I was always . . . always foggy. . . ."

Keeping his voice neutral, Hammett asked, "Who broke you in? Tokzek?"

She nodded.

"He beat you? Maul you around?"

"No. Just . . . just . . ." She overcame the rising note of hysteria in her voice and spoke coldly and clearly. "Just taught me how to be a whore."

"And then they sent you back east."

"In a compartment on the train with a man whose job it was to transport me." Her voice, her gestures, even her eyes had taken on a bitter, smoky edge. "Part of his pay was using me on the trip. I was put in the Harlem Inn in Stickney."

Hammett stood up, lit a cigarette, and sucked acrid smoke into his lungs. Crystal went on in her hard whore's voice, looking straight ahead as if seeing through the wall of the room.

"We used to parade for the johns. I had to wear high-heeled shoes and gingham baby rompers with a big bow in the back. It was two dollars for five minutes. The landlady was called Auntie Adelaide. She used to sit in the hall at the foot of the stairs. When you went upstairs with a john, she'd give you a towel and a metal tag with a number on it. The john would give her two dollars."

Hammett had quit prowling the room to look out a window. Past the edge of the roof he could see the blocky tip of the Russ Building skyscraper.

"Sometimes I can still hear Auntie Adelaide's voice." In a strident Midwest twang, she said, " 'Goddammit, Number Eight, somebody's waiting. *All* right, Number Five, there's a

176

girl out here got to pay the rent.' If the john ran over his five minutes, the upstairs madam would pound on the door and ask for another two dollars. That was Tante Hélène. We called her *tante* because she was a Creole from Louisiana. After another minute she'd come in and thump him on the back. She was nice. She used to wink at me past the john's shoulder." She was silent for a moment; when she spoke again, it was in her usual voice, although now it sounded tired. "I remember Tante Hélène's wink sometimes, too."

"How'd you get out?" The cigarette between his fingers, he noted with surprise, was crushed and twisted. He'd burned the side of his index finger without realizing it.

"I just walked away one Sunday morning. The house commission was fifty percent, they charged ten percent of our net for the towels. Mostly the girls netted seventeen or eighteen dollars a night, but they owed me forty-two because Saturday was the biggest night of the week and I was a big grosser. I thought that if they owed me money they wouldn't be so quick to come looking for me."

"Then why is the mob after you?"

She shook her head back and forth exaggeratedly, again like a child younger than she was. "I can't tell you that. Not anyone. Not ever."

You're going to have to come up with the story, kid, he thought grimly. *You just don't know it yet.* He said solicitously, "How did Heloise Kuhn. . . ."

"How *did* Heloise Kuhn get hold of her?" Goodie was in a new blue *crêpe de Chine* negligee decorated with darker blue flowers made of lace and ribbon. She poured more coffee into Hammett's cup. "Are you *sure* you don't want an egg?"

"People keep sticking food in my face," he complained. He waved out the wooden match he'd used on his cigarette. "She thought the house would be empty, so she went there. And got tagged out."

"I . . . don't understand."

Hammett paused to feather smoke through his nostrils. He drank coffee.

"Working for Molly Farr she picked up gossip about a fat

177

woman living in Marin who'd just retired from the skin-trade and had left town, and she figured it had to be the same woman who'd grabbed her years before."

"Why did she give that address to her parents as her employers' address?"

"It was the only address in Marin she knew, and she'd already told her folks she was working over there. She couldn't really tell them she was maid in a cathouse . . ." He broke off to exclaim, "Hey! It's seven thirty! You'd better get ready for work if—"

"Oh, I . . . ah . . . quit my job." Her blue eyes were troubled. "I've gotten a better one, at a lot more money."

"Hey, that's great. Secretarial?"

"*Personal* secretary." She was momentarily enthusiastic. "I start the first of the week, when the girl I'm . . . replacing, leaves."

"I'll tell you what, sweetheart," said Hammett, "I'll take you out tonight and we'll celebrate. The works! Dinner and—"

"Gee, Sam, I'd love to, but. . . ." She found a tentative smile. "I've . . . got a date already. . . ."

Hammett was surprised at his own reaction. A stab of jealousy. Wasn't this what he'd always wanted? Goodie at arm's length, just for laughs? He made himself lean back in his chair with a wry smile.

"That's good, sweetheart. Have yourself some fun."

Jealousy, for God's sake. Kid's stuff. Not since Baltimore had he. . . . Baltimore. Three-story red brick house with white marble steps. They'd gather on the front stoop at dusk, boys and girls together. Long dresses and long hair for the girls then; girls with short hair were considered loose—perhaps even free-love advocates. Who was that girl who. . . .

Sure. Lil Sheffer lived next door, and her girlfriend was Irma Collison. Irma's kid sister was in school with Hammett, but he had a terrible crush on Irma. Worshiped from afar. . . .

He realized that Goodie was interpreting his long silence as censure. ". . . *you're* never around anymore, Sam."

178

"Yeah," he said. "Sure not."

He didn't see the tear glint in the corner of her eye. He returned to Crystal's story.

"When Molly's got raided, Crystal was arrested along with the girls. She realized that if she showed up at the arraignment, news photographers were liable to be there and might get her picture. So she had to hide somewhere. Then she saw in the newspaper about Egan Tokzek being shot—and with a dead Chinese girl in his car. She was sure that would make Heloise cut and run because if Tokzek had been carrying any papers that showed her address, some smart reporter would make the white-slavery connection. So she went over to Marin on the ferry right after leaving Brass Mouth Epstein's office. She—"

"Why didn't she just go stay with Molly Farr?"

Hammett jerked his shoulders in an almost irritable shrug. "You're not thinking, sweetheart. Look how easy I found Molly. Somebody else could. And if somebody else did, then Crystal's picture would be all over the papers for sure. As it was, of course, she walked right in on Heloise, who shoved her into an upstairs bedroom and put Andy the idiot boy on duty outside the door with a shotgun while she contacted her mob friends back east and offered to sell them Crystal all over again. For keeps, this time. Of course Andy didn't stay outside all the time. . . ."

"How terrible for her!"

In apparent callousness, Hammett said, "Well, it wouldn't have been an exactly unknown experience. After I showed up, she was hustled over to Bolinas, and was there until Harry and I pulled her out last night. A couple of times a day Heloise would come in to tell her that the negotiations were under way, and then were closed, and that the killers were getting on the train, that they'd gotten to Denver, they'd gotten to Salt Lake City, that—"

"Then you showed up," breathed Goodie.

"The White Knight to the rescue." Hammett yawned and stood up. "I'm dead, kid. Almost forgot what I came for. Could you run down to the Post-Jones Pharmacy and pick up

179

whatever you think she might need? Toothbrush, tooth-paste, anything. . . ."

After she had gone, Hammett began pacing the room. He'd taken the little Chinese girl out of the hands of the fat woman and her dim-witted son—she had nothing further to fear from them; but what had he really learned? Despite what he'd told Crystal about them still running, he doubted if they'd even begun. Why should they? They sure as hell knew he and Harry hadn't been cops.

He paused to light a cigarette.

Could they somehow be *made* to take it on the lam? Where would they run, and to whom, if they got the wind up?

He stopped pacing again to chuckle aloud. Hell, he could use that ploy he'd invented for one of his Continental Op stories back in '24, just after Phil Cody had taken over as editor of *Black Mask*. In "The Golden Horseshoe" the Op had caught up with a murderous Englishman named Bohannon and his equally murderous teenage doxy in Tijuana. He had nothing evidentiary on them, so he scared them into admitting their guilt by taking it on the lam.

How had it gone? Yeah. He'd very earnestly urged them to give themselves up to stand trial for the murder of Bohannon's wife.

So why not have the *real* op, Jimmy Wright, do the same thing with Heloise and Andy? He rang up the Townsend. In thirty seconds he was explaining to the fat little detective what he wanted.

"Who am I supposed to be?" demanded Wright.

"A Pinkerton operative looking into the death of the girl found in Tokzek's car. You know Heloise is Tokzek's sister and you know, although you're not sure you can prove it, that she supplied the girl to Tokzek. You want her to come back to San Francisco to face arraignment on kidnapping and white slavery charges." A new thought struck him. "Make it even stronger by reminding her that the hired killers she was bringing out from back east aren't going to be too happy with her when she doesn't have Crystal to give them. Tell her she'll be safer in jail than anywhere else."

"And you think that'll make her and the kid do a bunk?"

"I guarantee it."

"Sounds awfully complicated to me."

"It'll work," Hammett insisted. "It worked before, on a case that you . . . that I was involved in. Just throw a scare into her, and after that it's just a straight tailing job."

The op sighed. "What'll you be doing all this time?"

"Sleeping," said Hammett. And hung up the phone.

Twenty-seven

THE op pulled on the handbrake of the '25 Marmon 8 Sedan he'd rented from a Third Street hire-car outfit. By God, Hammett had been right. The fat woman and her idiot son had stuck around. At least their flivver was parked behind the farmhouse.

Dragonflies hovered on gossamer rainbow wings in the scorching sunlight, but the op wore his overcoat as he trudged stolidly up the creaking porch steps. In the right-hand pocket was a big black Colt .45, just in case Andy the idiot boy mistook him for a gorilla from Chi-town and started waving around that twelve-gauge.

He used the heel of his hand on the screen-door frame. It was warped enough to rattle loudly. By pressing his nose against it he could see the fat woman waddling toward him from the kitchen. Fat? That was like saying that Babe Ruth played baseball.

"This here's privute property, mister."

"And this here's my ID as an operative for the Pinkerton Detective Agency, lady," said Wright in his nastiest tone.

He didn't expect her to fall on her knees and babble out a confession of white slavery, but he'd hoped for more than a

181

crossing of fat-huge arms on her immense bosom and the single monosyllable she dropped at him.

"So?"

"So we're looking into the death of the little Chinese girl your brother raped and murdered. . . ." He went through the pitch that Hammett had worked out, but could see it wasn't taking. He finished up barking, "So you'd better come over to the city with me now, sister. We can do our fighting in court."

She turned her head to yell, "Andy! You, Andy! Git on down here." She turned back to Wright. "You ain't got nuthin', gumshoe. *Nuthin'.* Me 'n' my baby boy hain't been over'n the city in weeks, and cain't you nor nobody else prove no diffrunt."

Andy clattered down the stairs from the second floor. Hammett had done a job on him, all right. His lips were puffed and split, one eye was swollen shut, and there was a nasty bruise on one temple. The fat woman was now standing arms akimbo like Strangler Ed or the Scissors King squaring off for a wrestling card at the State armory.

"You move outta here quick, mister, afore Andy moves ya."

The op hesitated, then with a muttered curse turned away. It rankled, but Hammett had wanted him merely to throw a scare into them and depart. He went back down the steps. The only one who'd got scared was him. The look on that witless kid's face. . . .

He fired up the Marmon, adjusted the spark and smoothed out the mixture. Hell, maybe Heloise *had* been acting, raising his call, riding out his bluff.

Two hundred yards north of the farmhouse lane, the main road took a curve. Here he pulled the Marmon off into the weeds and got out. No place to leave it, close enough to keep the mouth of the lane under surveillance, where it wouldn't have been seen. That meant he'd have to go up through the woods afoot to take his plant on the house.

Sweating and swearing and slipping, he swarmed up the steep earth bank and into the greasewood. And him in city suit and shoes! Nettles stung his face and hands; once he stepped squarely into a red-leafed cluster of poison oak. *Damn* Hammett, anyway. If they didn't run. . . .

Then a new thought made him try to make better time through the baffling underbrush. What if they ran too soon, before he was even in position? He planned to go afoot down the lane behind them if they fled, counting on the Marmon's eight powerful cylinders to soon catch him up. But if they were gone when he got there. . . .

Twenty minutes later he'd worked his way around through the hardwoods to the ridgetop behind the depression that cupped the farmhouse and outbuildings. He still couldn't see the place, but he was pretty sure he'd have heard the flivver being cranked up. He paused, spent and blowing, under a live oak tree. About time to start downhill toward the edge of the cleared land.

A shotgun crumped. He froze, after a moment mopped his tough lumpy face with his handkerchief while listening intently. No repeats. But it had seemed to come from the farm.

Slick leather soles sliding on the dry grass, he went quickly downhill through the trees, hanging on trunks and branches to keep from landing on his backside. Summer-dry blackberry bushes clutched at his suitcoat.

Whump. Another shot.

He broke into a shambling, sliding, stumbling run, cursing and slapping at the mean black-bodied deerflies that seemed to have found him suddenly tasty.

He pulled up, chest heaving and eyes smarting with sweat, at the edge of a copse of birch trees a couple of hundred yards above and to one side of the weathered sagging barn. The Model T was still in the yard, but he could see the top of a black touring car just disappearing down the lane. Goddammit, anyway. But then he saw that a boy had emerged from the woods in front of him. Not Andy. A much smaller kid, eleven or twelve, maybe, just ambling down across the open fallow fields toward the barn.

The op still hesitated, the .45 from his waistband now in

183

hand. What had gone on down there while he'd been stumbling around in the woods? Andy shooting crows? Or had he and Heloise been in the car he'd seen departing? Or were they. . . .

The boy burst from the barn before his scream of terror, delayed and thinned by distance, reached the op's ears. His cap sailed off as he fled down the lane with his head back and his arms working.

Jimmy Wright went out across the uneven weed-furzed furrows, picking his way. He was in no hurry; he was pretty sure what he'd find in the barn. If he were right, all he had to do was clear out before the kid came back with the law, and find a phone to call Hammett.

"*What?* Both of them?" Hammett scratched washboard ribs under his white shirt. "Okay. I'm on my way now. I'll call you at your hotel when I get back."

He rehooked the receiver, stood frowning at it, then picked up the phone again and was connected with the Weller. Pop answered.

"How's the patient?" asked Hammett. He listened. "Fine. Keep her locked in that room unless I'm. . ." He broke off abruptly to listen, exclaimed, "*Telephone?*" and listened some more. He finally said, "Yeah, okay, I should have thought of getting word to her folks myself that she's okay . . ." He interrupted himself. "Listen, make damned sure she doesn't wander around the hotel anymore where someone can see her. All of a sudden it's gotten tricky and I don't know why. Yet."

When he hung up, he became aware of Goodie at his elbow, holding the toilet articles she had gotten for the Chinese girl.

"What is it, Sam? What's happened?"

"Those killers on the train from back east must have gotten in. Somebody gunned down the fat woman and her son a half hour ago."

"Hell, all I know for sure is that somebody didn't like 'em."
The sheriff was nearly as tall as Hammett, heavier in the

way that a bull mastiff is heavier than a greyhound, with direct pale eyes and a mouth made angry by a sullen lower lip. His deputy was an overweight youngster wearing cord trousers and a wide leather belt with a brass buckle.

"Can't even be sure it's them," said the deputy.

They lay side by side on their backs in the barn. The straw around their heads and shoulders was sodden with blood and brain matter. The bodies had no faces left.

"Kid had a broken finger on the left hand, improperly set," said Hammett. "So does the corpse. And you'd raise hell finding that woman's double outside a circus. Once you get comparison prints from—"

"Who'd you say you was?" The sheriff's face was stony.

"Private investigator looking for a wandering daughter from Nevada."

"Thought you was a mighty observant sort of feller. Missing girl, you say." He pointed with the straw he'd been chewing on. "Now tell me this: Wasn't about to mistake her for this one, was you?"

Hammett chuckled appreciatively. "Mrs. Kuhn's brother did time for white slavery before the war. She wasn't convicted, but she was involved, too. Somebody answering my client's daughter's description got off the ferry in mid-May at Sausalito, and had a hire-car drop her at or near the Kuhn house. Once I learned the background, I had to check these people out. But nothing came of it."

The three men paused in the weeds outside the barn's sagging double doors. The flivver that had been parked in the drive of the Bolinas house the night before was now parked near the kitchen door of the farmhouse.

The sheriff's interest in Hammett had been dulled by the detective's offhand lies, but he said, "Maybe your client decided the Kuhn woman had spirited his daughter away even so, and—"

"My client is a fifty-seven-year-old bank president confined to a wheelchair since a hunting accident three years ago."

An old black Chandler with side curtains on the rear windows and a badly dented fender turned in to chug its way toward them up the incline from the road.

"Doc Straub," said the deputy.

A small gray-haired man bounced out of the car with that irrepressible enthusiasm most men who handle bodies professionally seem to develop.

"Gentlemen," he said. He went by them into the barn.

"Who found the bodies?" asked Hammett, apparently idly.

"Jimmy Gibson from the farm a mile down the road. Heard a shotgun here twice, figured it was Andy shootin' crows so he come down to see could he tag along. That Andy'd shoot anything that moved. Only just as Jimmy come out of the trees up the ravine, a big man he didn't know come running out of the barn. He jumps in a big black car and goes tearin' out of here. So Jimmy naturally looked in and saw—"

"Didn't get a plate on the car, I guess."

"Big and black. That's it. If he had to guess, he'd say a Reo."

Doc Straub came out of the barn wiping his hands on his handkerchief. "You figgered they was gonna raise up from the dead or something, Jeremy, you run me out here to see 'em *in situ*?"

"Just going by the book, Chet," said the sheriff in a soothing voice. "What can you tell me about the deaths?"

"Lead poisoning." He gave a short whoop of laughter. "Shotgun. Close range. Better th'ow a canvas over 'em unless you want blowflies layin' eggs in your evidence."

He went by them down the slope toward his Chandler. The deputy went back into the barn with an unhappy look on his face to cover up the bodies.

Hammett and the sheriff started down the slope toward Hammett's hire-car.

"Looks like mob work to me," said the sheriff. "Her brother was a rumrunner for some wop in the city, and with a shotgun being used and all . . ."

"You knew the brother?"

"Hell, knew the whole family. This here's been the Tokzek farm for fifty years. When they was kids, Heloise was a looker. . . ."

186

"Somebody told me Egan was on the hop pretty regular."

"For ten years and more, gettin' worse." The sheriff gave a meaty chuckle. "Y'know, fathered that boy back there. On his own sister." He cast an expectant glance over at Hammett, seemed let down that there was no visible reaction. He said defensively, "More of it than you'd guess, rural families. Like to killed their folks. Heloise took the name of Kuhn to explain the kid, and moved over to the city to have it. Started puttin' on all her weight after it was born." He paused a moment. "Born here, raised here, now she's dead here. Ain't a hell of a lot of sense to any of it, is there?"

"They were executed for not delivering me," said Crystal in a tight, terrified voice.

"I could buy that except for one thing." Hammett leaned back against the garish flowers painted on his chair. His eyes burned and he was yawning with fatigue, but otherwise he felt all right. "If they expected hired killers from back east to be looking for you, why'd they hang around to be found?"

"You do not believe what I have told you?"

He made angry gestures with hands, eyebrows, mouth. "Quit clowning around, Crystal. Too many people are dying. Who's after you, and why?"

"But I cannot tell anyone, ever, because—"

"I've had enough of this."

He was on his feet, hurling his cigarette across the room against the radiator. It fell to the floor in a shower of sparks. As he picked up his hat and coat from the dresser, he ground it into the rug with his heel. Crystal was off the bed to catch his hand in both of hers and try to kiss his fingertips. He jerked his hand away. She started to cry.

"It's a nice act." Hammett sneered.

He watched her wipe her face on her sleeve. "I must tell it in my own way."

"Just so you tell it."

When she had fled Capone's Harlem Inn in Stickney, she had hidden in Chicago's Chinatown for several weeks, until her cash had run out. Then she had gotten a job as a domes-

187

tic in a rooming house on North State Street. She held it for over two years.

"Mrs. Rotariu was very nice. She called me Crystal and let me call her Anna even though I merely worked for her. The house was owned by a famous author named Keller or something—"

"Harry Stephen Keeler?"

"You know of him?" she exclaimed.

"I've read some of his stuff." Hammett's voice was flat, and a tense, wary look had entered his eyes.

Crystal went on with her story. Early in October, 1926, a very pleasant young man calling himself Oscar Lundin had taken the back second-floor room that had been Keeler's studio. Then one of the front rooms overlooking State Street had become vacant, and he had taken it even though it was much smaller and cheaper, with worn-out furniture.

"Just two wooden chairs and a dresser and an old brass-frame bed and a gas ring," said Crystal with her eyes far away. "The day he switched rooms he paid a week's rent on the new one, and then walked out and didn't come back. The next day two men who'd visited him once before moved in."

Two days later Crystal had just started down the back stairway to the alley after she had finished work, about four o'clock, when there was a tremendous racket from the front of the building.

"It sounded like many auto backfires very close together, with a heavier, sort of booming sound, too. Then it stopped and the door of Mr. Lundin's room flew open and the two men ran out."

The man in front was about twenty-five and carried a tommy gun. The second man was heavily built, and dark, and had a shotgun. She was slammed up against the wall by the man with the tommy gun. The second man ran by her, then a dozen steps below her stopped and said, "Hey!"

"That was when I saw his face clearly for the first time." Her hands were twisting in her lap like warring animals. "Twice I had seen him out at the Harlem Inn. He . . ." Her cheeks began to burn. "Both times he . . . used me. He did not pay like the others."

188

"And he recognized you on the stairs."

"Yes. He pointed the shotgun at me and pulled the triggers, first one and then the other. I heard two clicks. He cursed and turned around and ran after the first man. They climbed out the ground-floor window into the alley."

She had run to her cheap Chinatown rooming house, got her money from under the mattress, and caught the first train leaving Chicago. It was going to Minneapolis so that was where she went. She stayed there until one icy night a car tried to run her down. She went to Detroit. The restaurant where she worked as a waitress was bombed when she should have been there, but had been off sick. She finally returned to San Francisco where the mob had few connections, and went to work for Molly as a maid.

"And you never knew what happened in the rooming house. Was it right across State Street from Holy Name Cathedral?"

Crystal shrugged. "There was a church there. I do not know what it was called."

"Sure not. But you recognized the man on the stairs. Was it the man who owned the Harlem Inn? The one they call Big Al?"

She said, barely above a whisper, "Yes."

"The Scarface himself," said Hammett. "No wonder they keep trying to kill you! You saw him thirty seconds after Hymie Weiss was rubbed out in front of his headquarters at 738 North State Street. You can finger Al Capone for murder!"

Twenty-eight

HAMMETT lit his fifth cigarette of the day and flopped open the newspaper that Moms had slammed down on the counter in front of him. His hand stopped moving with his first cup of coffee halfway to his mouth.

BOOTLEGGER SHOT—GUNNED
ON STREET WHILE LEAVING
SPEAKEASY

Gunfire rocked the foot of Mission Street last night. Dominic Pronzini, 32, owner of the Côte d'Or Club (popularly known as Dom's Dump), died in the 3 A.M. blasts by an unknown assassin.

He was skipping down the story when his eyes were caught by a boldface box announcement.

LATE DEVELOPMENT
Mayor Brendan McKenna has called a meeting of press reporters at 10 o'clock this morning for what his office termed "an important announcement."

"They're trying to bring their gang warfare to San Francisco," thundered McKenna in his marvelous orator's voice. "Well, gentlemen, I'm here to tell you it isn't going to succeed!"

The red-carpeted reception room was jammed with reporters crowding the mayor's huge cherry-wood desk. Hammett hung back on the fringes. He'd tried to get Jimmy Wright at the Townsend Hotel and had failed; it was a good bet he'd be here to listen to the mayor.

"Are you stating as a fact, Mr. Mayor," demanded a reporter from the *Examiner,* "that Dominic Pronzini's death was a gangland slaying?"

"Both the district attorney and I feel this is the case." McKenna began dramatically marking off his points with his fingers. "Dominic Pronzini was murdered with a shotgun. The shotgun is a classical gangland weapon. Less than twenty-four hours ago, a woman and her son were murdered up in Marin County with a shotgun. Less than two weeks ago, a rumrunner in Dominic Pronzini's employ, named Egan Tokzek, was slain in a gun battle with police. That woman mur-

190

dered in Marin was"— he paused to tighten the suspense
—"Egan Tokzek's *sister*, gentlemen."

The newsmen began frantically scribbling in their note-
books. Hammett felt his sleeve tugged. He and the fat little
op, Jimmy Wright, worked their way from the crowd toward
the door. Behind them, McKenna was overriding the reporters' questions.

Hammett closed the door on the oratory. He and Wright
had the hallway to themselves.

"Your little plot didn't come off too well," said the op.

"It worked in my story."

"Yeah." He looked thoughtfully at Hammett. "Only this
ain't a story."

But Hammett had realized there was an ill-concealed excitement in the stocky detective which owed nothing to the
botched events on the other side of the Golden Gate.

"You've got something else for me?"

"Boyd Mulligan made some calls after you left his office."

"Gimme," said Hammett.

Owen Lynch was dressed in a conservative three-button
silk-stripe worsted with a white neckband shirt and a fresh
dressy Norfolk collar. The links of his gold watch chain glittered across his vest.

"I gather you don't think much of Bren's theory concerning the killings."

"It stinks. Better get him in here, so I only have to say it
once," said Hammett.

He smoked quietly in his chair after Lynch departed, his
face keeping his secrets.

McKenna came through the door first, his jaw rather belligerent and his breath rich with brandy. Only his eyes betrayed the anxiety apparent in the worried face of Lynch behind him.

"Hammett," said the mayor coolly.

The detective stood up.

The mayor said, "I understand you disagree with me
about the mobs trying to move into our city."

191

"I don't. The facts do. When I talked with Molly Farr last Sunday, I was convinced that—"

"Molly Farr! But she . . . the DA is looking all over for . . ."

"He's looking. I found." Hammett stopped at an ashtray to stub out his cigarette butt. He rousted his pockets for the pack, and stuck a new one, unlit, in his mouth. "I'm not saying just where because I know my investigators aren't going to get any cooperation at all from the police department, only as much cooperation from the DA as the reform committee can pressure him into giving, and exactly as much backing from *this* office as it cares to give. Therefore—"

"I told you we were with you all the way on this investigation."

Hammett jerked a thumb at the mayor. "Did you tell him?"

He went on before either man could speak.

"Those highbinders who busted up Pronzini's place were my boys—which shoots hell out of part of your gangster scenario, Mr. Mayor." Hammett's grin was tight, almost unpleasant. "They scared Pronzini enough so he spilled some things. Enough so I now believe Vic died in Pronzini's back room, and that the man who killed him went there through the Mulligans. So I threw a scare into Boyd—"

"What good would that do?" asked Lynch.

"Jimmy Wright's boys now have a tap on the Mulligan phone. Griff would be smart enough to expect this, but not Boyd. I wanted to see who he called for help when his uncle wasn't around. In light of the fact that Pronzini was rubbed last night, that phone call gets damned important."

He paused to light a cigarette. The pause grew. McKenna tossed off his brandy in a single convulsive gesture. Hammett handed to Lynch the transcript carbon Jimmy Wright had given him.

June 5, 1:04 P.M.—Out—Mulligan Bros. Boyd Mulligan.
WOMAN : Hello?
BOYD : Hello? Is your husband there?

WOMAN : No. I'm sorry. . . .
BOYD : At work?
WOMAN : Yes. Is there any message?
BOYD : No. No message. I'll catch him there.
June 5, 1:09 P.M.—Out—Mulligan Bros. Boyd Mulligan.
MAN: Detective Bureau.
BOYD : (voice muffled): Is the Preacher there?
MAN : Huh?
BOYD (voice clearer): The Preacher. Is he there?
MAN: Oh. Wait a sec. I'll see.
LAVERTY : Hello?
BOYD : Boyd Mulligan, Preacher. I want to see you.
LAVERTY: There's only one place I want to see you,
Mulligan. Looking out from behind bars. . . .
BOYD : I know all about the way Parelli really died.
LAVERTY (after a long pause): Griff told me that'd never be used. He said he didn't blame me for . . .
BOYD : It won't be used, Preacher. If you help me.
LAVERTY (after a long pause): All right. West Broadway by the Presidio wall. Twenty minutes.

Lynch folded the paper with exaggerated care, making
sure all the creases were sharp and square.

Hammett asked, "Who was Parelli?"

Lynch looked up, his face dazed. "A cheap hood found
beaten to death in Jessie Street a few years ago. Pistol-
whipped. A young girl claimed he'd been molesting her, trying to drag her into his apartment building when another
man stopped him. He ran. The second man caught him and
systematically beat him to death. First she said she would
never forget the second man's face, then said she *had* forgotten it. Then she left town."

"Yeah," said Hammett softly. "If Mulligan got her to
change her story and then got her to leave . . ."

"Dan's alway's had that black Irish temper. If it got away
from him then the way it did with that Egan Tokzek—"

"I think he came around to tell me about it a couple of days
ago," said Hammett. "After his talk with Boyd Mulligan. He
was waiting outside my apartment building to talk to me,

193

only he couldn't bring himself to say it. He knew I'd brought in the hatchet men to wreck Pronzini's joint, and he knew why I did it. Only Mulligan could have told him those things. I think Mulligan wanted him to pry out of me how much I really knew, and I think he wouldn't play along. But you can see why I have to know where he was the night Vic was killed, *and* where he was last night when Pronzini got it."

"You can't think that Preacher would—"

Hammett jerked his shoulders irritably at Lynch.

"I'm not saying I think he did anything, I'm saying I have to find out. If he had something to do with Vic's death, then he might have killed Pronzini to protect himself. Or if the Mulligans *do* have their claws into him, he might have killed Pronzini because they forced him into it."

McKenna spoke for the first time since reading the transcript. "But what about the woman and her son up in Marin? What sort of threat could *they* pose to Dan Laverty?"

"I don't know. But there's a lot I don't know. Why was he out south of the park the night Tokzek was killed? Why did he chase—"

"That I can tell you, at least." Lynch massaged his eyelids with blunt fingers. "Dan got a phone call, at home, telling him that in a few minutes a stolen car would be—"

"There!" exclaimed McKenna triumphantly. "That proves—"

"Nothing at all, Bren," said his secretary in a tired voice. "It's only what Dan told me himself. There's no corroboration."

"Merciful God in heaven!" burst out McKenna. He was at the sideboard again, his features pinched and drawn.

Lynch's eyes were losing their dazed look, as if his mind had begun to function once more concerning the political realities.

"You're willing to let us handle this for the moment?"

"I told Jimmy Wright to put a tail on Laverty."

McKenna began, "That isn't necessary—"

"I think it is. But I'm willing to lay back apart from that. For the moment. But if I don't get the answers I need—

194

straight answers, and quick—I'm going to the grand jury with
what I've got so *they* can ask the questions."

Twenty-nine

AT this time on a sunny day, Hammett was pretty sure
where he'd find Pop Daneri, and he did. The old man was
basking in the sun like a turtle on the minuscule open landing that overlooked the Weller Hotel's enclosed court. The
door was open behind him so he could hear the sound of the
buzzer if anyone came in off Post Street.

"Was she able to identify anyone?"

Hammett took the old man's arm, not gently. "Who?"

"The Chinese girl. Identify the pictures of the Chicago—"

"Oh, goddammit anyway!" exclaimed Hammett.

There was sudden anguish in the old man's voice. "He
was . . . from the Treasury Department of the United
States government. He . . ." His voice faltered. "He had
a . . . a badge and everything. Said you'd given him the address. He took her away with him . . ."

"How long ago?"

"Three o'clock this morning. I was still up. He rang the
bell, came up, showed me that badge . . ." The old man said
softly, "He was a ringer, wasn't he, Sam?"

Hammett merely nodded, frowning in thought. Nearly
nine hours before. An impossibly cold trail. He could mobi-
lize the men under Jimmy Wright's command, but as for the
police. . . .

Hell, any one of them—particularly Dan Laverty—could
have been the one who came and got her. The only cop he
really trusted was Jack Manion. . . .

The old man's face had changed. His eyes had gone dull,

as if something opaque had been drawn across them. He doubled up his fist and struck himself in the face with it.

"Cut it out," growled Hammett.

The old man hit himself again. His brass shell-casing ring gashed his cheek. Blood trickled down his face.

"Stupid!" cried the old man. "Worthless! The oldest trick in the book and—"

"Cut it out, Pop," said Hammett again. "You were taken by experts, they'd know how you feel about the government, how you'd respect a man from the Treasury Department. What bothers me is how they knew where she . . ." He broke off. Comprehension flooded his face, tightening the lean features. "The goddamn phone call!" he burst out softly.

He looked over at the old man. Pop had a handkerchief pressed against the purple-lipped cut on his cheek.

"Were you in the room with her when she called her parents?"

"In the next room. But, Sam—"

"Could you hear what she was saying? Did she tell them anything about where she was?"

"Couldn't hear words, just her voice."

"English or Chinese? The cadence and tenor would be different, even through a wall."

The old eyes, more alive now, sought backward through memory. "English."

"Yeah," he said softly. "Could you identify the guy who took her again?"

"*Big* man," said Pop. "Tall, bulky, hat and overcoat . . ." Chagrin entered the eyes. "Now I remember, kept his scarf up around the bottom half of his face, casuallike . . ."

"Silk scarf? Wool?"

"Silk."

Hammett squeezed the old man's thin upper arm. "Okay, Pop, keep safe. *He* doesn't know you can't identify him."

Late afternoon sunlight slanted through the dusty windows of Hammett's apartment to lay a cool pale oblong on the rug. Summer fog, rolling silent and gray through the Golden Gate and across the western rim of the city, soon would blot it out.

Jimmy Wright was annihilating a Fatima in Hammett's ancient Coxwell. His round tough sleepy face was placid, almost stupid with thought.

Hammett was on his feet as usual, prowling from hallway to window, throwing questions and remarks and comments as he did. He hadn't shaved and his shirt was open to show the top two buttons of his balbriggan undershirt. A lock of hair hung down across his forehead. His eyes were bloodshot. From the kitchen came the plock-plock-plock of his Challenge electric percolator.

"All right, what have we got on the snatch itself?"

"Post Street at three in the morning is what we got. Nobody saw him in or them out. Nobody saw any cars at the curb with the motor running. Nobody saw—"

"The cop on the beat?"

"Five blocks away rattling doorknobs. He says. More likely drinking coffee in the Pig'n Whistle."

"This afternoon I did what I should have done as soon as Pop told me about it. Checked up on her phone call."

He paused beside the op's chair to stab his cigarette into the ashtray, then fished for another in his pocket.

"Jack Manion checked with the girlfriend at the chemist's shop in Spofford Alley. No phone call from Crystal. He checked with the folks. No phone call. They didn't even know she'd been found and was in a safe place." He gave a sudden angry burst of laughter. "Safe place!"

"But then that means—"

"That she called a friend we don't know about, who sold her out to whoever the hell was looking for her. Or that she herself called whoever the hell—"

The doorbell rang.

Hammett poked his head into the hall to yell, "It's unlocked." He used the interruption to light the cigarette he'd gotten out.

Goodie came in. She wore a new silk satin Charmeuse

197

frock that looked expensive. Pearl drops glowed at her ear-lobes, and her golden hair was freshly marceled.

"There's a telephone call for you, Mr. . . . um . . . Wright."

Hammett waited until the stocky detective had disappeared, then said to Goodie, "Long time no see, sweetheart."

She made an abrupt gesture with one hand.

"Your coffee's done."

He could hear the sounds of her unscrewing the electric cord from the wall socket, the rattle as she got spoons and cups, the grunt of the icebox door as she looked for milk. She called from the kitchen in a voice falsely light and gay.

"I've been busy."

"Sure." Hammett watched her set the tray with two steaming cups and other paraphernalia on the davenport table next to his typewriter. When she handed one to him and carried the other over to Jimmy Wright's chair, he added, "You're not having any?"

"I've . . . got a date. . . ."

The fat little op bustled back into the room. He did not sit down, nor did he take any notice of the coffee.

"And there's something else that don't make sense. Our people finally got hold of the police report on the Pronzini kill. He was gunned down at three A.M."

"That's solid?" demanded Hammett in a surprised voice.

"Eyewitnesses, three of them. They didn't get a description of the killer or a license number on the car, they were too busy trying to fit into the same six feet of gutter. But they're sure of the time. Three A. M."

Hammett tugged at his mustache, then caught the look on Goodie's face and shrugged slightly. She had been turning from one to the other, frowning, not understanding.

"At three A.M.," said Hammett, "Crystal was snatched from the Weller Hotel."

"Oh, Sam, no! How terrible for her."

"If we count out the eastern mobsters, the only suspect we've got for the snatch and the Pronzini kill is Dan Laverty, the Chief of Detectives. Since the simplest way is usually the easiest way, we've been trying to fit him for both the killing and the kidnapping. But if they happened at exactly the same time. . . ."

Goodie was still quite a way behind him. Her voice was shocked. "Sam, a *policeman?*"

"I told you a long time ago that everybody's for sale in this burg." He turned to Jimmy Wright. "What's Laverty been doing since we put the tail on him?"

"Down at the Hall, doing his job. Hasn't seen anybody he shouldn't have. No phone calls when he's been out and around. Which ain't saying much, since we can't tap into his phone at the Hall."

"Tell the boys to stick tight."

"Will do. If anything develops, you'll be where?"

"Here. I'm waiting for a phone call from Lynch. He's supposed to be working on it from the other end."

The op nodded and put on his hat and left.

"You don't seem terribly worried about that girl, Sam," said Goodie.

"I think she called whoever came and got her. I think she arranged for him to spring her out of the hotel with that phony badge. It's the only thing that makes sense."

"Then she's not *really* in danger at all?"

"Oh, she's in danger, right enough. She just doesn't realize how much. She's playing some sort of game, and she thinks she can handle whoever it is."

"I don't see how you can believe that, Sam!" she exclaimed. "You say you count out the eastern mobsters, but if Al Capone himself is after her for—"

"Sometime when I've got a week, I'll tell you all the holes in *that* story."

Goodie's eyes softened. She put a hand on his arm.

"Sam, if you have to stay here for a phone call, I'll stay and make us something to eat and . . ."

"What about your date?"

"I could break it."

He almost said yes. But he still hadn't told her about Josie and the two girls. Tell her now. Let her know how futile it is.

199

Hurt her now so you hurt her less later. Can't. He said, "I wouldn't want you to do that, kid."

As if to punctuate the sentence, an auto horn sounded twice in the street below. Color rushed into Goodie's face. She checked her wristwatch. Hammett hadn't seen it before. He knew jewelry from his years at Al Samuels' store: This looked like the Elgin eighteen-karat white-gold bracelet watch that retailed for seventy dollars.

"Yes!" exclaimed Goodie. "I . . ." She flew to the window. She looked out. "Yes," she said again. She turned to Hammett. "Are you sure . . ." She stopped, said, "That poor girl," and put her hands on Hammett's forearms and went up on tiptoe to kiss him on the mouth. There was yearning and desperation and passion in the kiss. He put his arms around her. He responded. Goodie tore free and ran to the hall doorway and out.

He stood in the middle of the floor for nearly a minute, face set, then moved to the window to stand looking down into the street.

Goodie went across Post to the massive Hispano-Suiza Cabriolet gleaming on the far side. A uniformed chauffeur, very correct in visored cap and gleaming boots and the beige uniform with flared breeches, got out to hold the door of the enclosed rear compartment for her. Hammett had last spoken with the chauffeur about jabbing a knife into the backside of a fat woman in Bolinas.

The electric lamps came on along Post Street. Hammett paced his apartment. At some point he heated a can of Campbell's tomato soup and turned out a tin of Booth's Crescent sardines. As he ate, he glanced through his partially revised manuscript of "Black Lives." Goodie's phone didn't ring. He got interested in the manuscript.

He piled his dishes on the drainboard and moved over to the Coxwell with the manuscript. Soon he was frowning in concentration. He had written Harry Bloch at Knopf that some revision was wanted but that he wasn't sure he could, or would, do it. Now he was sure.

Of course. Now some of the changes jumped right out at him. Get specific. Make a question about an address into a specific reference to Golden Gate Avenue. And forget that line about Homicide men messing around in the op's job. Wordy. Just wonder who'd been killed. Good. Clean and crisp.

An hour later Goodie's phone rang, unheard and unheeded.

It was that damned ending. The ending of Part I of the novel had to be strong. Words again. Too damn many of them. Hey! Just end it where he said of his work that it got done. The last three paragraphs could go. He lined them out. Good. End it with the simple declarative. That livened the dull spot at the end of the first quarter.

That still left problems of course: too many murders, too much of a gap between the first two quarters of the story and the rest of it—but at least he'd made a *start* at revisions along the right lines. . . .

He leaned back and rubbed his eyes. Goodie's phone was ringing. He went to answer it.

"I tried to get you earlier, but there was no answer." Owen Lynch's heavy, considered tones. "I spoke at length with Dan about—"

"Where was he the night Vic got chilled?"

"Home in bed. Asleep."

"Sure. With his wife beside him. Double bed?"

Lynch said in a rather stiff voice, "I don't know."

"Jesus!" Hammett exclaimed. "Sensibilities! Okay. No way to prove he wasn't. I don't really think he did it. I think it happened with Tokzek about the way he told it, too. Which means that somebody set Tokzek up for a fall. Somebody who knew that Laverty, when he saw the Chinese girl, would go berserk. Knew, because he did it once before with a cheap hood named Parelli."

"If you're right, it could only be the Mulligans," said Lynch. "He swears he was home in bed when Pronzini died, too." His voice was exhausted. "I asked him for his badge, just until all this is cleared up. He cried when he laid it on my desk. If you're wrong, Hammett, and it turns out to be the eastern mobs moving in . . ."

"Yeah."

Lynch shook the lethargy from his voice. "Any news on the Chinese girl?"

"Lots of negatives. Not anybody from the Treasury Department. No known hoods in by train from back east, nobody out with a Chinese girl under one arm. Our eyewitness on the snatch can't identify the guy."

Hammett went back to his own apartment, leaving both doors open in case Jimmy Wright called with news about Crystal.

The ringing of Goodie's phone woke him a final time at four fifteen in the morning. He was sprawled in the Coxwell chair, icy cold from the mist blowing in through the open windows. His neck was stiff as hell and his shoulder was sore. He groped around in the half-light for his shoes, the wisps of his dream still fogging his mind.

Ten years old, living on North Stricker opposite the orphan asylum the old man always threatened him with when he was bad. But he's been good, and he and his dad are duck hunting in the salt marshes along Chesapeake Bay, he with a four-ten single-shot too big for him.

"Coming, goddamn you," he muttered at the phone. Four fifteen. Why in hell didn't Goodie answer it? Oh.

Waking up cold and stiff. Swing your legs over the edge of the bed in the hunting shack, stretch and yawn and scratch your backside through the trap in the union suit. Plank floor numbing cold-blue feet as you grope for your socks with a cautious toe. Out in the living room, pull on stiff canvas pants by the intense white light of the hissing kerosene lamp. The big potbelly iron stove starting to glow red.

He shambled down the hall, still yawning and massaging his neck. Cold air blowing a gale through the open door.

Cold salt-marsh air as you come out of the cabin into just enough predawn light to see the path through the rushes and elephant ears in front of the shack. Cold wind straight from the north, hint of snow in it to keep the ducks moving nervously around and coming upwind into your guns.

Into Goodie's open front door.

The op shocked him fully awake. "Better get out here, Dash. We've found Crystal."

In the pause, Hammett thought again: Goodie wasn't home. Something ending, as Crystal had ended.

Because the op was saying, "At least we've found what was left of her."

Thirty

WIND-DRIVEN fog lanced through Hammett's topcoat as he swung off the trolley on Presidio Avenue. He stood staring through ornate wrought-iron gates: The fog hid the rolling green acres of Laurel Hill cemetery. A shiver as much mental as physical ran through him. He crossed the street. A thick shape materialized.

"Why do these bastards always have such a flair for the dramatic?" demanded the fat little detective. He was sucking on a Fatima.

"Dumping her in the cemetery?"

The tone of Hammett's voice jerked the op's head around, but the stocky detective said only, "Yeah," and then, "This way."

They followed the gravel drive used by the hearses, then cut off on an earth path. Jimmy Wright used a hand torch against the fog. Hammett stumbled and cursed behind him, hands thrust deep into his coat pockets.

"Trolley conductors," said Wright over his shoulder.

"They were ahead of schedule, so they stopped to have a smoke. Otherwise they'd never have heard her, and she probably wouldn't have been found until the weekend."

"You mean she was *killed* here, not just dumped here?"

"Yeah. Kept screaming for almost five minutes, according to the witnesses. They were just about here when they heard the shot."

Moisture dripped from Hammett's hat-brim and his mustache bristled with it.

"Just the one shot?"

Their feet crushed tough aromatic wild flowers massed across the path. Jimmy Wright slipped and cursed.

"He used both barrels at once. Shotgun. I figure him for a big man to take the recoil."

The path angled between two black wet cypresses grown scraggly as winter dogs from lack of care. This part of the graveyard was full of weed-grown, unmonumented plots.

"What time was all this?"

"Little over an hour ago." The op flashed his light on his wrist briefly to confirm it.

"And Laverty was—"

"I'm damned if I know for sure, Dash. One of my men put him to bed last night, but there's an alley runs the length of the block he lives on, he could have back-doored my man through the night. I left word that when my operative calls in, he should go pound on Laverty's door and see if he's home. But that ain't going to prove anything either."

They had come up on the moving lights carried by a couple of patrolmen searching for clues. Two Homicide dicks were standing off to one side with their hands in their pockets and their hats tipped back on their heads. Hammett didn't know either one of them.

Both he and Wright were sopping to the knees. Palpable fog-forms seeped between the old graves and ornate crumbling tombstones like dawn-harried wraiths. Directly beside a chesthigh marble gravestone bearing the dates 1831–1893 was a white marble obelisk knocked down by the 1906 quake. Flanking it were two shattered cylinders of dark marble.

204

The dead Chinese girl was sprawled facedown across the obelisk. One arm was folded under the body so the childishly small hand formed a cup. Blood from the shattered head had arteried the curved marble to run into the cup. The other arm was outflung. Hammett recognized the tweed knickers and argyle socks and leatherette sport jacket. The legs were apart enough so he could see the crotch of the knickers was stained.

Hammett squatted over the body. He touched his fingers to the crotch of the knickers, and sniffed them. Urine. Bladder voided in death. Raped? No way to tell yet. He realized with an abrupt touch of nausea that the girl's limbs unnaturally fit themselves to the contours of the unyielding stone beneath her. He put a hand on the body.

"Hey!" One of the Homicide dicks took his hands out of his pockets. "The medical boys ain't seen her yet."

"Seeing her isn't going to make her any less dead," said Jimmy Wright.

Hammett removed his hand and wrapped his forearms around his knees and remained squatting with his chin on a kneecap, his face brooding. Without looking up, he said, "Worked over with a baseball bat. No wonder she was screaming."

He shifted the body enough to get a look at the face hidden by the shimmering ebony hair.

He sighed and stood up and wiped his hand idly on his topcoat, then rested it on the upright gravestone. The marble was icy to his fingers. The Homicide cops had gotten still and intense when he had looked at where the girl's face had been. It was gone right to the hairline, leaving only splintered bone and red meat.

"Instant leprosy," he said with studied indifference. The dicks lost their expectant look when he didn't throw up or even turn pale. He said: "Her name was Crystal Tam or Lillian Fong, depending on when you knew her. She has parents named Fong in Chinatown who'll need notifying."

When Hammett and Jimmy Wright reached the place where the path split the two cypresses, both men stopped and looked back. The girl was a rag doll, hurled carelessly against the fallen marble monuments. A gray dripping dawn had harried the fog up enough to show, beyond the cemetery fence, the gentle slope of Lone Mountain and the simple white cross that topped it. The cross was nearly invisible against the leaden morning sky.

"A lousy way to die," said the op.

"Tell me one that isn't."

He needed a drink. He needed a lot of drinks. Vic Atkinson. Crystal Tam. And Hammett at home playing author, instead of being out in the streets where he belonged as a detective. He'd thought he had it pretty well figured out until her death. But now. . . .

Jesus! Unless the. . . . But that was unutterably evil. If. . . .

He needed a *lot* of drinks.

"You lousy bastard," said Hammett distinctly.

"Sam, please—"

He tipped up the bottle, then let his arm drop limply. The bottom of the half-empty quart thudded on the carpet.

Goodie tried again. "Sam, you mustn't blame yourself for—"

He looked up at her, heavy-lidded. He tried to laugh. His lips wouldn't work right. They were blue, as if with cold.

"Mustn't blame 'self. Then who?"

"If she herself called up the man who did it—"

"Shouldda known she'd call 'im." His eyelids drooped; he popped them open to stare owlishly at her. "Caught you at it, okay?"

"Sam, you're not making any sense. I'll get you some coffee."

"No coffee. Hootch. Know where 'at comes from? The Hoochinoo Indians in Alaska who distill liquor just like 'shine. Was in a hospital once with a guy f'om Alaska. Whitey. . . ."

When she returned two minutes later with the steaming black coffee, Hammett was snoring. She shook him awake and got him to his feet, where he performed a rubber-legged adagio dance with her until he fell face-forward across the bed and pulled her down on top of him in a swirl of silken thighs. He started to snore.

She stood looking down at him, pity and anger and infatuation playing across her face.

"Oh, Sam!" she wailed softly. "Why?"

He turned his head enough to open an eye at her. "Why? She read 'bout dead Chinese girl in Tokzek's car, that's why. Read that, knew she had 'im. Tell lie to Molly, go safe hideout, make contact. *Had* 'im. Only he got her, instead."

"Sam, shouldn't you get some sleep?"

"Shleep. Remember, dead Chinese girl in car is key. Key to whole thing. Raped. Get it?"

He started to snore again.

Voices beside the bed were talking around him as if he didn't exist. Around him and over him and through him, as parents did when you were little. As if you couldn't hear or understand or reason because you were little.

Or drunk.

Or sick.

Starchy white uniforms. Smell of ether and disinfectant, this won't hurt much, just an ouch Jesus Christ what're you doing, good-looking redhead from Butte, Montana, marry that girl sometime. Josie. Ah, shit. Josie. Screwed it up, all up.

Talking around him and over him and through him with the doctor.

Next day, doctor's office. Desert heat shimmering through the open window, baking out the impurities.

—I got only one year to live, Doc?

—ahem. Never sure with consumption, Sergeant Hammett, but the indications—

—then I'm leaving the hospital.

—but without proper care . . . as the disease advances through the lungs. . . .

—I don't mind dying, Doc. I just mind dying here.

207

He opened his eyes and stared at the ceiling above the bed. The streetlight outside the window cast curtain-patterns across the plaster. The Chinese girl was dead. Vic Atkinson was dead. Unspeakable evil?

"Where's that bottle?"

"Sam, please. . . ."

"Gimme the bottle, goddammit, I know what I'm doing."

Jimmy Wright's voice sneered, "Give him his goddamn bottle. Sucking on it is what he's good for."

Hammett struggled to a sitting position. He looked at the square-bodied little detective. The op looked back. Goodie shoved the bottle into Hammett's hand.

The op said, "How long's he been like this?"

"Since this afternoon. He was the same way after Vic Atkinson was killed."

Beat the drum slowly and play the pipes lowly. Play the dead march as they carry him along. He set the bottle to his lips.

"Yeah, he's a sweetheart," said the op.

Hammett removed the bottle. "Fuck you, Jimmy Wright," he said distinctly.

"That solves something?"

He'd show them. Both of them. As he used to show Josie when she was always at him. He drank in long swallows.

His belly tried to reject it, vomit it back up, but he stopped only when he started to strangle, even as the girl cried out in anguish, "Oh my God, Sam, you'll kill yourself!"

"Don't worry 'bout me, sister." He giggled. "You got old goat with lotsa money, I got wife an' two kids to worry 'bout me. Josie. Josie's a *woman* . . . ."

He stopped because Goodie was staring at him with wide terrified eyes. She turned to Jimmy Wright.

"Is . . . is that true? A wife? A . . . a wife and *children?*" Wright was silent.

Her face turned white. "But . . . *Sam.* Last night I . . . didn't. Because I . . . you . . . I thought. . . ."

She ran blindly from the room, hitting the doorway in-

208

stead of the wall only by instinct; her eyes were squeezed tight shut.

The fat little detective shook his head. "I hope you know what you're doing, Dash."

"Gotta do it sometime."

"Your timing's shitty. And your manners. What's this about the dead Chinese girl in Tokzek's car being the key to all this?"

"Beaten *an'* raped." Hammett felt deliciously sleepy. Good night's sleep would fix him up.

"I don't follow you."

"Try 'is one, then. Crys'al never worked in North State Street roomin' house. English too good. Kep' couple years. Bright. Listened an' learned. Chicago, maybe, sure. But. . . ."

He fell straight backward from his sitting position on the edge of the bed. His head hit the wall a resounding thump. The bottle hit the floor with a like thump as his hand let it go. Bottle empty. He lay still, eyes shut, as if he'd passed out again.

Drunk on the outside. Outside only. Wish my *head* was empty, like the bottle. *Hope you know what you're doing, Dash.*

He knew. Dying. Dying of rotgut and a head that wasn't empty and a gone marriage and a lot of fictions he'd never write.

Head full of jumbled ideas, thoughts, intuitions, fears.

Full of facts, too. Facts about the ambush of Hymie Weiss in 1926, for instance. Capone had been seen countless places during the two days Crystal had him holed up in that rooming house. So . . . her story had been a lie. Why? What had she been covering?

No way to find out now.

Crystal. Thought you could handle him. Thought he. . . .

He. Didn't know who *he* was. Not for sure. Few clues. Silk scarf instead of wool. Dan Laverty doing what Dan Laverty probably had done, pushed on by. . . . *God,* the man's control!

209

Tomorrow. Soon enough, tomorrow, to decide whether he believed that the evil which was unthinkable *was*, did exist.

Tomorrow. Nobody left to die tonight anyway. Was there?

When he woke again, it was icy and black; one of those predawn hours when sick people die in their beds. Dark. Cold. *God* the cold! But some guardian angel was working the cool delightful neck of a bottle between his teeth.

He sucked thirstily at it. No whiskey came out. His furry tongue tasted metal.

Someone had shoved the muzzle of a revolver so far into his mouth that it touched the back of his throat, making him want to retch.

Then the voice came from the darkness above him. It was not unexpected. And somehow, though it had nothing to do with the owner of the voice, he knew—*knew*—that he was right and that all the whiskey in the world couldn't drown that knowledge.

Then the voice grated, "Okay, wise guy, let's move. You're all out of time."

Thirty-one

GOODIE paused to look around her suddenly bare little apartment. She was dog-tired. But she was packed. Finally, at three in the morning.

Without warning, she burst into tears. She put her face in her hands. So bleak, so depressing, stripped of everything that had made the apartment uniquely her own. She wiped away the tears with the heel of her hand, like a little girl, smearing the dust on her nose. She'd made the call to Bilt-more hours ago, when she'd fled Sam's apartment. Her mind was made up. If only he'd *told* her! A wife and children. Now, one more phone call. . . .

Oh, *damn* anyway!

She went through to the tiny cramped bathroom.

By the medicine-chest mirror she fitted on her close-bobbed golden head the Copenhagen blue sport tam she'd bought that day. The girl at H. Liebes had said that Clara Bow wore just such a ribbed velveteen cap in her latest Paramount picture.

She could afford to buy things like that now. With the new job as Mr. Biltmore's secretary starting on Monday. And the watch he'd given her, the new negligee and the dresses and the fancy dinners and. . . .

She turned quickly away from the mirror. She tore the tam from her head and went back to the kitchen. She sat down and finished her coffee and lit a cigarette. Her hands were shaking and her feet were cold.

The clothes and the job and the dinners meant the same thing as the phone call she was about to make. Harry the chauffeur was waiting for it. He would come and pick her up. Biltmore had promised to stay at the Bohemian Club for a few days, until she was used to his town apartment, until she was ready to . . . ready to be. . . .

If only Sam had . . . no! *Josie is a* woman. . . . She hated the very *name* Josie, she. . . .

She looked around the stripped apartment again. The carefully packed bag held everything she owned. Well, next week she could throw out all those awful cheap working-girl frocks. She'd have what every small-town girl who came to the big city dreamed of! A lovely apartment, and servants, and . . . and. . . .

She started to cry again. As she did, there was an echoing thump as something heavy fell against the outside of her apartment door. She stifled a scream, stood wet-faced and stiff-legged in the center of the little apartment, heart pounding wildly. Who was it? Some drunk, trying to. . . .

Sam!

She crossed quickly to the door and without hesitation

211

twisted the knob and pulled it open. Sam awaking, coming out of his apartment still drunk and shambling, falling. . . .

His door was open, but he was not lying unconscious in the hall. Should she go in, see if. . . .

She whirled when the elevator rattled behind her down the long hall. Two men were just entering the cage. One was heavyset, his hat jammed down on his head to hide his features. The other was Hammett. Hatless, coatless, wearing the same white collarless shirt he'd been wearing when he'd passed out. His face was haggard, and he almost fell as the other men shoved him into the elevator.

"Sam!" she cried.

But the door was already closed. Neither man had heard her.

Hammett's arms had been pulled back and his wrists handcuffed behind his back. Was the other man a policeman? Only policemen used handcuffs, didn't they? But then she remembered Sam saying that it might have been a policeman who killed Atkinson and that man who ran the speakeasy and kidnapped. . . .

She ran back through her apartment to the kitchen window overlooking Post Street. Hammett and his captor were just crossing to a black Reo.

The fat little sleepy-faced man! He would know what to do. But . . . his *name?* She rummaged desperately through her mind. No name surfaced. She'd taken a phone call for him, had gone into Hammett's apartment, had said. . . .

Wright! Jimmy Wright!

The sound of the Reo's starter jerked her eyes back to the window. The engine caught, popped, smoothed as the man behind the wheel adjusted the mixture. The car pulled away, out Post Street. No way to see the license plate.

Jimmy Wright. But how to reach him? He was in a hotel somewhere, that she knew, but she'd never heard the name of it, or the phone number, or. . . . *Think, girl, think.* Like Sam and the dead Atkinson he'd been a Pinkerton operative before. . . .

She was sobbing again before the idea hit her. She ran to

212

the phone, sniffling, to leaf through the gray-covered directory while waiting for the operator. "Give me FRanklin three-four-one-oh, the Weller Hotel," she said in a breathless voice. "And for God's sake, hurry!"

Hammett's teeth were chattering so hard that he put his chin on his chest in a vain attempt to stop them. Cold air whistled through the gaps in the canvas top. The Reo panted up the rise beyond Van Ness Avenue, going very fast through the silent deserted midnight streets.

Preacher Laverty turned craggy features toward him.

"Cold?"

"Ye-ye-yeah."

"I hope you freeze to death, you bastard."

He returned to his driving. Hammett wasn't *sure* where they were going. Then he thought bitterly, to hell. That's where. He shot a quick glance over at the big cop.

"Going to kick my balls off, too, Preacher?"

He looked over at Hammett. His big hands convulsed around the steering wheel. "I'd like to."

They entered the rich broad streets of Pacific Heights: thirty-room stone mansions and rich green yards trimmed with exotic plantings nurtured and pampered by Japanese gardeners.

"Poor old Dan Laverty, fall guy to the end."

"You would see it that way." Laverty's eyes were wolfish. "To you, anyone who doesn't help spread the corruption. . . ."

"So that's how he did it," muttered Hammett.

He was sure now. He'd caught up with the subtle mind it had bothered him that the Mulligans didn't possess. He felt a momentary sense of peace, even knowing that in minutes or hours he would be dead. It was possible that Laverty didn't realize he was driving Hammett to his death.

Could he make Laverty see what was being done? Doubtful. He'd be battling a lifetime of friendship. A true long shot. Like his stumbling against Goodie's door. Even if she'd heard it, why should she know what it meant?

213

He found a grin. "How did he get you to do his killing for him, Preacher?"

No answer.

He probed again. "Let me guess what he told you. Pronzini killed Atkinson and was going to kill again if he wasn't stopped. So it was really just an execution. Okay. But what about the woman? And a *seventeen-year-old* kid? Retarded, at that?"

"What are you talking about?"

The shock in the voice, the pale cop's eyes, was unmistakable. But then how. . . . Sure. He said: "I bet he called you up, asked to use your car yesterday morning, didn't he? His was broken down. Right?"

He saw the confirmation in Laverty's ill-concealed reaction. So simple! So direct! The man was a genius! And so foolproof. It explained everything, justified everything. And if things went wrong, there was Laverty to take the rap.

The big detective parked at the corner of Pacific and Presidio.

Hammett was numb and beyond feeling in his arms and legs. Wouldn't be able to run even if he got the chance. But at least the icy air had cleared most of the liquor fumes from his mind. He was glad of that. He wanted to see it coming.

"Must be right about here that Tokzek stole that Morris-Crowley."

The corner of his eye caught Laverty's momentary hesitation. He tried to widen the breach in the big cop's defenses.

"Odd that he'd need to steal a car right *here*." He jerked his head at the fine old brown shingle houses that had survived the quake and fire so well. "Didn't you ever wonder whether the tipster who called knew you, and knew how you'd react to seeing that dead little girl in the car? And knew Tokzek, knew he'd be sniffing dope and so paranoid it would be impossible to take him alive?"

"Just . . . shut the hell up."

Hammett slid out of the car awkwardly, and almost fell when his legs took his weight. He stopped on tingling feet in the middle of the deserted street. On the north side of the block were five brown-wood shingle houses, simple of design and timelessly elegant in that simplicity, backed up on the low stone wall that bounded the southern rim of the Presidio.

In one of those houses he would die.

He looked straight up. There was no fog, so he could see a few stars. The last stars he'd ever see. Dead at thirty-four. Well, what the hell? At least he'd beat Christ.

"Come on. Let's go."

Laverty shoved him roughly ahead, up a narrow walk between two of the houses to a plain narrow door.

"Didn't it bother you that Tokzek was hooked on the nose candy?"

Laverty didn't answer. Inside the doorway was a landing, with steps leading both up and down. They went down. At the foot of the stairs was an open area of concrete floor. They stopped in front of one of the doors opening off it. Good. Every second alone with Laverty, to work on him. . . .

"We wait here."

"Sure. But tell me, Preacher, have you ever known a snow nose who was interested in even *normal* sex with anyone? Let along being so sex-crazed he'd beat and rape a little girl to death?"

For a moment, he thought he'd done it. Laverty wavered as the question sank in. Because every cop knew the answer to that one. They saw it so often. Habitual use of most drugs depressed the sex drive to, often, impotence. If. . . .

But then Laverty shook his head.

"That's . . . got nothing to do with this, anyway."

Hammett took his final despairing shot. "How did he convince you that I'd sold out, Preacher? You've been a cop all your life, cops want evidence. . . ."

"I've got evidence. I've questioned Joey Lonergan."

Joey Lonergan! Vividly into his mind shot the scene at Lonergan's Garage, Jimmy Wright posing as the little eastern killer, Garlic, and Hammett telling Lonergan they were the spearhead of the mob back east, moving in. . . .

"He told me all about it," said Laverty. "You and your tor-pedo friend from back east knocking him around and *telling* him you were taking over the town."

"It was a con, Preacher," said Hammett wearily. "To get in-formation."

"How about Boyd Mulligan pressuring me to get informa-tion about you, find out what you were up to and what you knew? Was that a con, too? He knew you were trying to move in on his operation. . . ."

"Get hold of Jimmy Wright and—"

But the time to get hold of Jimmy Wright was gone. A door straight ahead opened and the bulky brown-haired man with the strong, calm face came through it. He nodded to Laverty.

"I see you were able to bring our traitorous friend along without any trouble, then," said Owen Lynch.

Thirty-two

IF only he'd had more time. Time to work on Laverty, make him see that they both had been used. . . .

"Dan, remember that Tokzek was a hophead. Remem-ber—"

Lynch's fist drove the words back into his teeth.

"You goddamn Judas! I can hardly stand the sight of you!" He looked past Hammett, over at Laverty. "You'd better leave him for me now, Dan. Go home, use the alley door the way you came out. You've been there all night. I'll make sure this garbage has the message loud and clear for his masters back in Chicago."

Hammett spat out blood to speak. His voice was thick. "Why don't you have me down at the Hall being booked, Lynch, if I'm guilty of something?"

216

"You know damned well why, Judas."

Laverty, moving slowly toward the stairs with a troubled face, paused. "Maybe he's right, Owen. Maybe he *should* be booked instead of just run out. He arranged for Pronzini to murder his friend—a charge of conspiracy. . . ."

"We can't do that, Dan, much as I'd like to." Lynch's voice, his eyes, carried sincerity. "What would it do to Bren politically if it came out that the man he picked to spearhead the cleanup of our police corruption was actually employed by the eastern mobs—who were out to move into the power vacuum? And if Bren goes down, it means the department stays corrupt. The department we both love so much."

Hammett was silent. If he tried to speak, Lynch would stop him anyway. All he'd have to show for it would be a smashed face. He watched his last hope turn and start up the stairs.

"Better leave me the handcuff key, Dan."

"Oh. Sure." Laverty tossed down the key. He looked like walking death.

"Don't let it bother you, Dan," said his friend. "I didn't mean for you actually to shoot Pronzini, but at least it allowed us to unmask this vermin in time." He grabbed Hammett by the upper arm. "All right, you. Inside."

Lynch waited until the door at the head of the stairs had slammed behind the departing policeman before he actually opened the door. When he thrust Hammett ahead of him, the lean detective knew why he had waited. This was nothing for straitlaced Dan Laverty to see. It was the damnedest thing Hammett had ever seen, that was sure. A . . . what?

A bower of carnality.

Huge ornate four-poster, dominating everything. Silken coverlets. Oriental carpets three and four deep on the floor. Rich folds of damask draping the walls. An ornate brass oil lamp that probably heated incense: The faint scent of musk still lingered on the air.

Pictures. Aubrey Beardsleys with their richly embellished decadence. Illustrated scenes from De Sade.

And mirrors. No matter what you were doing on that big four-poster bed, you'd be able to watch yourself doing it.

217

"The room tells it all, doesn't it, Lynch?"

But Lynch seemed untroubled by conscience. He jerked Hammett roughly toward two waist-level brass rings that hung from brackets embedded in the concrete behind a break in the damask. He rammed Hammett face-first against the wall, and kept a shoulder in the small of his back while working.

"I'm taking off one of the cuffs for a moment. I'd love it if you tried something. You've caused me a great deal of trouble."

Hammett was quiescent. A curious lethargy had seized him. He just wanted it to be over. The open cuff was threaded through the ring so the chain between the bracelets was now through the ring. The steel bit deeply into Hammett's wrist as the cuff was resnapped.

Lynch stepped back. The gleam in his eye was close to madness. What Hammett couldn't understand was what had pushed him to the edge, after all the years of seemingly rigid control.

"I suppose I should say that I'm sorry about what's going to happen to you."

"But you aren't." Hammett found his voice was steady. "You're going to enjoy it."

"Yes. I must admit I am."

"Quite a lot, up until now, makes a sort of sense. Using the fact that Molly was in trouble as a way to break with the Mulligans and let them go down in the reform committee probe. I finally figured out there had to be someone like you behind them, someone with a subtle mind pulling the strings. The Mulligans were just too crude. But why did you *want* them to go down? You could have run this town for years yet from behind their—"

"It was the only way I could be sure Bren would be elected governor. He'll make a great one. And also, Boyd Mulligan is a fool. He doesn't know who I am, but he knows there *is* someone behind his uncle. If Griff should die. . . ." He shrugged. "This way I'm safe."

"And God knows it will have made you rich enough, over

218

the years." Hammett stood up straighter. His hands were so numb that he couldn't feel the steel shackles cut into his flesh any longer. "And I can understand why Vic had to die. He saw you at Pronzini's and knew what your being there meant."

"Yes."

"And Tokzek because with that dead girl in his car he'd have crumbled as soon as police got to him. And Pronzini because you didn't know how much he knew and how much he'd told me. But where does it stop? Now it's me. . . ."

"You were going to the grand jury. If Dan got up and told them the story I've given him, they'd see through it instantly. As you did."

"As Laverty himself's going to someday. When he admits to himself that Tokzek didn't rape and kill that little girl."

As he spoke, Hammett glanced over at the door by which they had entered. Ajar! Had Lynch left it that way? He couldn't remember. Or had Laverty. . . .

"He's going to realize that kind of murder takes a particular sort of sickness, and then he's going to realize *who* it was, and he's going to come looking. So that makes him expendable too, doesn't it?"

Lynch's eyes gleamed. Hammett wondered again what had sent him out of control.

Lynch said, "I've done all I can for Dan. If he becomes expendable . . . well. . . ."

"Don't you mean all you can *to* him? How many years, Lynch? With Heloise and her brother periodically supplying you with girls and making sure they disappeared back east into the whorehouse pipeline once you were through with them? Maybe you didn't even violate the first ones. But then the raping started. And the beatings. And the beatings got more violent, and finally one of them died. It was inevitable, couldn't you see that?" He answered himself. "Of course not. You thought it would go on forever."

"I had no one. . . ." Lynch was speaking to himself, his eyes glassy. "No one. My wife, gone. No children. Whores sicken me."

219

"But not virgin girls you've turned into whores?"

"I had no one. But now . . ."

"Now you can go on with the double life. And when the pressures get too great, you càn have another little Chinese girl brought down the back way. Down here where nobody can hear her when she starts screaming—"

"Oh, stop it," snapped Lynch impatiently. "It's over now. Finished. I'm fulfilled. I don't need any of that any longer. Once you're dead. . . ."

Hammett shook off that premonition of the evil that should have been unthinkable, and said, "*Is* my death going to end it, Lynch? What if another one survives everything that's done to her in the whorehouses and cribs of Chicago, and comes back the way that Crystal did? And calls you up, as Crystal did on that Monday? Calls you with demands you have to meet? What then?"

"You don't know what you're talking about."

"I know you were horrified when you found out the Mulligans didn't know where Crystal was. Is that why Heloise died, Lynch? Because Crystal had ended up back with her? After you borrowed the Preacher's car to go over there, so if anything went wrong he'd take the fall for it?"

Lynch laughed. His laughter was unforced.

"Well, that's enough, Hammett. I thought I would hate killing Vic Atkinson. Only I didn't."

"I know," said Hammett. "I saw his head."

"So I think I'll use the bat on you, too."

"As you did in the cemetery. Keeping her alive and screaming while you smashed—"

The door slammed open and Dan Laverty stumbled into the room. He stared about wildly at the bizarre carnal trappings, his face dazed, crumpled, drawn in and down as if he had suffered a stroke while listening outside the door.

"Owen," he said, and even his voice was tortured. "Owen. He . . . I had to come back, had to listen . . . *had* to. . . ."

"Dan, you don't understand—"

"I was a straight cop. I . . . I *murdered* for you! You . . . the little girl in the car. . . ."

He left the doorway to start hesitantly toward his friend.

Lynch was backing away. "And Vic Atkinson? And the girl in the cemetery? *You?* That filth? That sickness?"

Lynch had backed into the wall beside the ornate bed. He was reflected in a dozen different ways in a dozen different mirrors. He looked from side to side. Laverty was in front of him, crowding him. Hammett could see only Laverty's massive back, but a mirror gave the policeman's expression: puzzled, almost frightened.

The black Irish rage. How to trigger in him the. . . .

Lynch did it for Hammett. He broke. He came off the wall in a leap, trying to reach the other, interior door leading up to the main floors of the house. Laverty was on him like a gorilla. Of their own volition those huge hands closed about his windpipe, spun him about, slammed him up against the wall again.

"Owen!" cried Laverty in an anguished voice. "Don't run from me. *Talk* to me. Make me understand."

With a convulsive movement, Lynch tried to tear free. The thick back and shoulders hunched and tensed to pour their strength into the fingers. Past that back and shoulders, Hammett could see Lynch's bulging scarlet face.

Lynch swung a fist without effect. He tried to ram his locked hands up between the iron arms.

Laverty's right knee pumped, twice, up between Lynch's spraddled legs. The horror of it was that Laverty himself cried out each time, as if he were taking rather than giving the rupturing blows.

The knee pistoned twice again. It moved of its own volition.

The shoulders hunched further, writhed with effort. A muted pop. Another. A muted tearing noise. The calloused fingers were sunk almost out of sight in the corded neck. Laverty's body began to shake and buffet with its own sustained and total effort. There was a sharp snapping sound.

Lynch's heavy handsome head dipped sideways against the clutching fingers. The fingers began unburying themselves from the ravaged throat. They opened. Moved away. Only their purple shadows remained embedded there.

Laverty turned slowly away. The blind look was dying

221

from his eyes. Behind him, the body slid down the wall like a collapsing puppet. It ended in a heap on the floor. Laverty didn't look back.

"Forty years I knew him. Forty years I loved him. He was closer than any brother could have been. Do you understand that? Do you?"

"I understand."

"You wanted me to come back and hear. You."

With a sleepwalker's movements he took out the long-barreled police positive with which he had shattered Egan Tokzek's spine. He thumbed back the hammer.

His mad eyes glared into Hammett's.

"You," he said.

He rammed the muzzle of the revolver, upside down, into his own mouth and blew the top of his head up against the ceiling.

Hammett sagged against the shackles. He squeezed his eyes tight shut so only the pink nothingness of the lids moved against his pupils. But when he opened his eyes again, nothing had changed. Nobody had gone away. And it was still there. The blackness he had first glimpsed in the cemetery, the blackness he had fought by telling himself it was the result of eight years as a detective, eight callous years of brutality and cynicism. And of the years since, writing about that brutality and cynicism.

But it was no good.

Too many indications, too many clues for a good detective to ignore. And goddammit, he'd been a good detective.

Like, why had Crystal suddenly begun dutiful visits to the parents she had previously ignored? Could it have had something to do with Heloise finding it more difficult—and dangerous—to procure girls who wouldn't be missed?

And why had Crystal told Hammett that Tokzek broke her in, four years ago, when the man already had been a hopeless junkie, incapable of even normal sex, let alone the determined sexual effort necessary to rape and condition a child?

And how had she known who Lynch was and where he could be reached on that Monday she had disappeared?

222

And why had she called Lynch to come and remove her from the Weller Hotel, where she was safe?

And finally, why had the fat woman and her son died, unless to protect—and perhaps delight—someone? And why with their faces blown away in Marin, unless to insure that no one would question a Chinese girl's face being blown away in San Francisco?

He was not even surprised when the interior door across the room swung open. He merely said, "Hello, Crystal."

Thirty-three

"HOW did you know?" cried the Chinese girl in great delight. With a joyous laugh she stepped over the policeman's exploded head as if it were a section of curb. "How did you figure it out?"

For one of the few times in his life, Hammett was speechless. He was looking at evil: sprightly, beautiful, and totally corrupt. She was dressed in a spun jersey bloomer dress, hand-embroidered around the collar and cuffs, with sweet little pearl buckles on each side of the front pleats. It was the outfit a girl of nine or ten might wear, with bloomers of lustrous sateen just peeking out from beneath the hem of the childishly short skirt.

Crystal pirouetted slowly in front of him, then curtsied like a child completing her number at the school recital.

"Do you like it?"

Her lispy little-girl voice literally raised the hairs on the back of Hammett's neck. The voice, the slight body in the child's dress, even the curtsy—these all *belonged* to a little girl. But beneath the bodice were a woman's breasts, beneath the sateen bloomers a woman's hips. And the naked pale legs were a woman's, beautifully rounded.

223

The face, framed in its gleaming mane of ebony hair, was a child's face. But it was made up as a woman's—and had a look of innocent depravity that was terrifying.

Crystal batted her eyes and stuck out her tongue at him.

"Mean Mr. Hammett doesn't like little Crystal's dress!"

She darted to Lynch's body, and swooped over it to take the handcuff keys from his pocket. In the process, she gave Hammett a flashing look at the tautened shiny bloomers. She looked back at him with childish delight as she did.

"*Daddy* liked my dress." She straightened. "Daddy liked to take my dress off me. I was Daddy's *little girl*." She kicked the dead man in the temple. She smiled sweetly at Hammett. "Daddy wasn't a very nice man."

"Daddy's little girl isn't a very nice little girl." It was the first thing he had said since she entered the room. He felt only that same odd, debilitating lassitude he had felt ever since Lynch had chained him there.

"Well, she's had a lot of lessons, hasn't she?" The lisp was gone.

"Not from me."

"No. Not from you." She sat down on the edge of the bed, her hands clasped between her thighs, just as she had sat on her bed at the Weller a couple of lifetimes ago. He recognized it as a habitual pose. "How *did* you guess? What did I do wrong?"

Hammett yawned, hugely and involuntarily. He could almost welcome death, he thought. Then at least he could quit talking. He had talked the night and two lives away. Three, counting his own.

"So many things, Crystal. It wasn't luck. Just logic."

Her pout was genuine. "Tell me. I thought I was awfully good."

"At the acting, yes. I've never seen anyone better. It was almost too good. The first time I saw you, at Molly's, you were playing the dumb little chink. Every time I saw you, it was a different role. Once I realized you'd gone into hiding deliberately, for your own purposes and not because you were in fear of your life, I was ready for that whole Capone scenario—"

The girl made a slight deprecatory gesture. "I'd told Molly I was scared of mobsters from back east, just to keep her from asking questions, but I'd never bothered to make up a story. When I saw I was going to have to give you one, I thought the Hymie Weiss killing would work fine. I didn't know you'd remember so much about it."

"Yeah. And once I knew you *hadn't* spent your three years back east dodging Capone, I had to wonder what you *were* doing."

"I could have just been at the Harlem Inn in Stickney."

"I believed that part of your story," said Hammett.

Her eyes had a quizzical expression. "You're a funny kind of detective. It's too bad you have to . . ." She broke off.

"And you're a funny kind of ex-whore."

His hands in the tight handcuffs had gone numb, but he knew it would do no good to ask her to remove them. Lynch's death hadn't altered his peril any.

"So here were three years of your life unaccounted for, and here you were with a command of English, when you forgot yourself, like a college graduate. Molly mentioned that you would have been terrific dressed up as a little girl, driving the older johns wild—deflowering young virgins is a common sexual fantasy. You said yourself that they dressed you that way at the Harlem Inn. So I thought about the possibility that some rich old man in Chicago had taken you out of the cathouse and . . ." He raised his shoulders in as much of a shrug as the cuffs permitted him.

The girl's eyes were momentarily far away, as they'd been when she'd told him of her introduction to whoredom.

"He was seventy years old, and important enough in Chicago that he could just tell Capone he wanted me, rather than ask. He kept me in a house on the West Side. After the first year, he trusted me to serve as hostess when he entertained. I watched and listened and learned." It was her turn to shrug. "Then he died of a heart attack at home with his wife. I just packed up and left."

"And came out here to go after Lynch. But why him? Was he the one who really—"

"Yes." She spat the word, her tilted eyes narrowed and

225

alive with hatred. "He liked them ten years old, eleven. First, he'd take down the bloomers and give them a spanking. Then—"

"But it got away from him."

"Even four years ago I knew it would. He broke one of my ribs. When they locked me in a train compartment with a man who didn't care whether I had a broken rib or not, I stayed alive by telling myself that one day the one who'd had me first would kill one of the girls, and when he did I would be ready for him."

A blood-curdling depth of hatred, Hammett thought. He said: "So you came back and went to work for Molly . . ."

"I didn't know the man's name, of course. So I needed the fat woman. After three months at Molly's I picked up word about her. Once I had her name and where she lived, it wasn't hard to make her do whatever I wanted. She was a stupid woman. Greedy and stupid. First I frightened her by threatening to expose her for furnishing occasional girls to Lynch, then I offered her money . . ."

"And then, nine months ago, you started visiting your parents again. That's the part I can't handle, Crystal. Using your visits to your parents as a way to scout out the occasional girls Lynch wanted. Without him knowing you were involved, of course. But . . . little girls . . ."

She shrugged. "There are many who are never missed, they are forever being smuggled in from Hong Kong. Manion's last slave raids were less than three years ago."

"But you knew what you were condemning them to—"

Her eyes flashed.

"Let them take their chances as I did!" She stood up. She strutted in front of him, forcing his awareness of her body. The taunting calculation was back in her eyes and voice. For the first time, Hammett wondered uneasily just *how* she intended to kill him. "What else did I do wrong?"

"You yelled a warning to me about Andy's shotgun—after it was too late for the warning to help me. You rubbed your clothes on the closet floor to make it seem they hadn't been worn for days, but you got splinters in them, which got into my sweater and started me wondering. So when Heloise and

Andy died in gangland-style and I knew no gangsters were involved . . ."

She looked at her watch. "It is as well you must die."

He was damned if he was going to give her any satisfaction.

"Their deaths made your mobster scenario real to everyone. Except me, unfortunately."

She clapped her hands in delight. "You think *that* is the main reason they had to die?"

"I *hoped* it was. I hoped the slaughter of the Chinese girl in the cemetery was Lynch's evil, not yours."

"Evil!" she spat. She thrust her face close to his. "What is evil? Show it to me! I live and then, after a time, I die. Neither has meaning, except to me. So what is evil?"

Hammett said evenly, his voice back under control, "All right, you wanted to be officially dead. You needed someone to die in your place. You found a final Chinese girl, lured or forced her to the cemetery . . ." He paused, truly curious. "If you were there when she was killed—maybe were even doing the screaming to make sure she'd be found right away—how'd you keep Lynch from turning the shotgun on you instead of her?"

"I had no fears of Lynch. When I telephoned him for the first time on that Monday I disappeared, and told him who I was and what I wanted, I also told him I had everything written down concerning each girl Heloise had furnished him, including the one who'd been in Tokzek's car. When I called him from the Weller, I told him to kill Heloise and her son, and how to do it. I also told him to take me from the hotel. Of course, after that . . ."

She ran her hands slowly and voluptuously down her body, pausing to cup and massage her breasts. She laughed.

"After that and before the girl in the cemetery, I had him for a night. I gave him total fulfillment of every fantasy he'd ever had. He was mine, then." She looked over at the dead man and giggled. "Mine. Begging, like a dog begs for scraps. It was so easy to make him do . . . *everything* I wanted him to."

Hammett shivered. He believed her. He finally knew what

227

had tipped Lynch over the edge. Crystal, the totally corrupt and endlessly inventive, had transfigured him. She'd be able to do it to any man she wanted. Hammett included.

"This morning, poor Daddy, out of guilt, was going to commit suicide. He didn't know that yet. That was to be the final price." She gave her joyous laugh. "But how much better that he should have been choked to death by his lifelong friend! So that the marks on his throat will fit Laverty's fingers! And then that Laverty should kill himself with his own gun, which will bear only his fingerprints! So you see, you are . . . unnecessary." She looked at her watch again and giggled. "So in an hour, perhaps two hours . . . perhaps five minutes. . . ."

He met her mocking gaze steadily. He asked a single question. "How?"

"A fire in the wiring? Gas that seeps in? An explosion? Oh, but you'll enjoy yourself so much more, wondering . . ." She came close. She wet her lips and let them get pouty. The lisp was back in her voice. "Wondering just how *evil* little Crystal can be to the big detective mans."

In that moment, Hammett's only regret was that he would be unable to take her with him. She saw it in his eyes: no terror. Not even fear. Only rage. Realizing that his eyes betrayed him, he shut them. She drew a finger along the line of his jaw. The lisp was gone.

"Good-bye, Hammett," she said in a soft voice.

Kill him how?

And with the thought, he had such an intense need for a cigarette that he actually opened his mouth to cry after her. Then he got control of himself and remained silent.

How? And how long?

Dawn couldn't be far away, but nobody would wonder about him until long after noon. By then. . . .

Christ, his final dawn.

How? And when?

He sniffed the air automatically, got angry all over again, as if she were still there to witness his weakness. Fire? Or leaking gas? Or. . . .

It had to be soon. Before an arriving cook or housekeeper found him alive. He caught himself flaring his nostrils again. Stop it, goddamn you, Hammett. Go out right. If only he had a screwing cigarette.

His mind constructed the whole sequence: getting it out, thrusting it between the teeth, getting out the match, striking it, bringing it to the tip, sucking in that first harsh-soothing smoke that. . . .

Death.

Had he ever really—*really*—considered death before? He'd known it intimately, but now all of a sudden he didn't any longer. Now he just spewed meaningless words about it on paper. He had to start all over again, refamiliarize himself with it. Death. Cessation of consciousness. Sleep, to never wake. He hated it.

Of course. You hated death because you were involved with life. Life was. And dammit, life *would* be, when you weren't. That's why you hated death. Its unfairness.

Never again, the exquisite moment of sliding into a woman.

And never again the joy of a page dragged up dripping from your guts. Never again realizing that there were ten pages of fresh manuscript stacked beside the typewriter that hadn't been there before.

Never again the special, little-understood joys of manhunting. The blood-sport of beating the man who was trying to beat you. Most special when the stakes were high, when what you were trying to take from him was something he valued deeply, often his liberty and sometimes his life.

Cessation. Waste, of everything: sensed, learned, read, remembered. All wasted.

You should never regret the *was*. But you could regret the never-was. And the never-to-be.

Jesus, for a cigarette.

Regret. Because the tomorrow had come. The tomorrow that was the today and the yesterday and the forever and the never. The last, the only, the never-again.

Because he'd become an amateur. He'd played with his typewriter while he'd become a nonprofessional. No longer a real manhunter. He'd known, when he'd crouched over that devastated body in the cemetery, that Crystal was still alive. He'd *known* it. The old detective instincts. But he'd rejected what they told him. Played the writer's game of walking around evil, drank himself insensate. Because the writer hadn't wanted to know what the manhunter had known intuitively about the evil in one slight fifteen-year-old girl.

Hammett cursed aloud. He'd treated Crystal as a literary creation rather than as a real person. He had *pretended* to be the op, or Sam Spade, instead of *being* them. He'd become a writer playing at being a manhunter. A typing desk was safer than a street corner. The tiger in his mind had sheathed its claws. He'd become able to risk less. Death had stopped looking over his shoulder.

And so he had died.

The door across the room opened. Jimmy Wright strolled in, a Fatima in his mouth and a fedora on his head. For a terrible moment, Hammett thought he *had* died. Jimmy Wright had his hands in his overcoat pockets because each pocket contained a naked .45 with the safety off. So he could fire through the pocket without having to draw.

Because Jimmy Wright *was* a manhunter. The fat little op would never be anything else. Drunk or sober, nobody would ever get the drop on him the way that they'd gotten the drop on Hammett. The way the girl . . .

The girl! Crystal!

"Jimmy, get to hell out of here! The house might go up any second—"

"Been through the house, Dash." He stepped across Laverty's body with the same casual disregard Crystal had shown. He crouched beside Hammett to unlock the cuffs. "Quite a dump. Fancy. Big for a guy living alone. Give you fantasies after a bit. This room'd give you nightmares. Somebody's been busy down here."

"Laverty," said Hammett. He leaned weakly against the wall, waiting for the agony as the blood started getting back into his white, pudgy, useless hands. "He killed Lynch with his bare hands, and then shot himself."

Wright grunted, standing in the middle of the room with his hands on his hips, staring up at the mess drying on the ceiling.

"Why?"

"End of a dream. Christ that hurts!" He had begun gingerly shaking his hands. But he loved the pain because it told him he really was alive, that Jimmy Wright was real, that Crystal. . . . He said delicately, "Anyone else in the house?"

The op shook his head. "Cook's day off, maybe. I'd better call O'Gar. We'll need the meatwagon here."

"Sure. Listen, Jimmy, how did you . . ." He waved an arm weakly.

"Goodie was up packi . . . was still up, when you managed to thump her door as Laverty took you out. Figured out that Pop Daneri would know where to reach me. I went over to her apartment and sat around twiddling my thumbs until the call came."

The call. A horrible suspicion dawned in Hammett's mind. He sat down on the edge of the bed and began flopping his aching hands against his thighs to hurry the wake-up process.

"Call?"

"A woman. Called Goodie's, asked for me, said you were shackled in the basement here with a couple of stiffs. Said the front door would be open and the keys to your handcuffs would be on the telephone stand in the front hall. What's so funny?"

Because Hammett had begun to rock with helpless laughter. Tears streamed down his face.

. . . you'll enjoy yourself so much more, wondering . . . just how evil little Crystal can be. . . .

"She sounded Oriental, must have been the maid or something."

Or something. In this single contemptuous gesture she had shown Hammett just how thoroughly he'd been beaten. Sam Spade? Even Sam couldn't have done much with her. *No* manhunter, real or fictional, could.

Because Hammett couldn't touch her. He knew all, could prove nothing. She was above it, beyond it, she'd won. She'd

231

had them all killed, methodically and maliciously, but had killed none of them herself.

Anyone—*anyone*—who could prove anything against her was dead.

Hammett could tell his story until he was a little old man with a bent back and a long beard, and no DA in the land would take him seriously. A fifteen-year-old whorehouse maid did *what?*

He stood up.

"I'd better call Goodie. She'll be worried."

"She's gone," said the op. He didn't try to soften it. "As soon as the call came that you were here safe . . ." He shrugged. "She was already packed."

Hammett rested his forearm against one of the bedposts and pressed his forehead against it. So. He'd driven her to it. Stupid drunken bastard. Once Biltmore possessed her, there'd be no turning back for her. No more small town and houseful of well-loved kids and. . . .

"Said to tell you she'd gone back to the porch-swing cowboys. Said you'd know what she meant."

He felt a soaring of spirit. For every evil, a good. For every Crystal, a Goodie. He found he was grinning broadly.

Sure, goddammit, who ever said you were going to get it all? A piece of it was the best any self-respecting manhunter *ever* expected, anyway. And in the meantime. . . .

Hell, in the meantime he was on salary.

He jabbed a finger into the op's hard, ample gut.

"Okay, Jimmy, use the phone upstairs to call the rest of the boys. Lynch was behind the Mulligans. It won't get made public, but it's going to come out where it counts, so I want a raid on the bailbond office right now. Legal. Court order. Before Mulligan finds out his boss is dead and sends his tame cops in after the stuff. There's enough dynamite in those files to blow up this goddamn town, and we're going to light the fuse!"

Thirty-four

IT was Wednesday, August 29. Eighty-nine days since Molly Farr had jumped bail to start it all.

Hammett had spent the morning, as usual, passing details of the investigation to the grand jury in closed session. It wasn't over yet, but it was drawing to a close.

The Mulligans already were under indictment on multiple felony counts of bribery, conspiracy to commit bribery, and conspiracy to commit extortion.

Gardner Shuman had resigned as police commissioner, and one of the city supervisors had committed suicide.

Fifty-seven policemen ranking from patrolman to captain had resigned quietly; fifteen more had been removed by dismissal and five had been indicted for perjury and extortion.

According to the tabloids, Laverty had killed himself while depressed over ill health, and Lynch had been murdered by an unknown assailant he had surprised rifling his home.

The probable hobo who had rolled and accidentally killed Victor Atkinson was still at large.

Famed ex-Pinkerton detective Jimmy Wright had been conducting a sweeping investigation of graft and corruption in San Francisco under the personal direction of Mayor Brendan Brian McKenna. The name of Dashiell Hammett had not appeared in the newspapers at all.

The bookies were still thriving. And the taxi houses. And the speakies. Rinaldo Pronzini had taken over his son's club, which, thanks to its notoriety, was flourishing.

Hammett paused outside the hearing room to check his watch. Jimmy Wright, on his way in, stopped beside him. "Just had another photo-session with His Honor, Dash. Without his wife to point him in the right direction and tell him to smile . . ."

"Yeah, but nobody's going to stop him. He's cleaning up San Francisco, he's Irish, he's handsome, he's a hell of an orator, his wife has aged beautifully, and his best friend died

233

defending the sanctity of the American home. Given all that, they'd make him governor if he was a hydrocephalic."

"Listen, Dash, I've closed the deal with Vic's widow for the agency. That partnership offer is still . . ."

"We can kick it around next week, Jimmy, okay?"

Ever since Jimmy Wright had walked into that basement charnel house to free him, Hammett had been immersed in the corruption that had spewed from the asbestos-lined filing cabinets hauled from Mulligan Bros. Bailbonds. He was tired, worn out, sick of it. He was barely aware, as he went down the echoing marble-floored corridor, of the rushing attorneys, the nervous accused, the testifying cops and witnesses, the spectators and hangers-on congregated around the doorways of courts just convening for the afternoon sessions.

Then he passed a knot of reporters, and some of their remarks caught his ear.

". . . Brady promised the circus of the century, then he doesn't even show up for the hearing. . . ."

". . . veil, can't even be sure it *is* Molly Farr. . . ."

". . . Brass Mouth showed up. . . ."

". . . anything for money. . . ."

Molly Farr! Brass Mouth Epstein! Of course. Today must be the eighty-ninth day since she had jumped bail. It would be forfeit today if she didn't show up for arraignment. Brass Mouth had *said* he'd have her in court. And had bet Hammett five bucks he'd get her off.

Hammet caught a passing reporter's arm.

"Whose court?"

"Judge Kelly."

Hammett paused in front of Room 306. He looked in through the round glass window. Yep. There was Brass Mouth. Beside him a shapeless veiled female form; apparently Molly Farr come for her arraignment on three counts of Contributing to the Delinquency of a Minor.

But no crowds. It should have been bedlam, after all the newspaper space Molly's flight had generated. No reporters.

No Evelyn Brewster and her husband, there to savor the supreme moment of triumph.

And the most amazing fact, no District Attorney Matt Brady. The people were represented by Assistant District Attorney Michael Bender, on his first court appearance. Why, for God's sake, Hammett wondered, as he slipped inside to take a seat on a rear bench in the nearly deserted chamber. Brady, as soon as he convicted Molly, could just about walk into the mayor's office and sit down behind the desk.

Brass Mouth Epstein was just sitting down. He was impossibly dandy in a dark-blue double-breasted suit with a viciously subdued silver silk stripe. At his breast burst a white display handkerchief, on his chest glittered gold studs, on his soft rolled cuffs, gold links.

Now Bender was on *his* feet: a slender Irish lad with mobile features and blue eyes and a shock of gleaming black hair. He gestured at the demurely triple-veiled woman Epstein was defending.

"I agree that's a human being sitting next to distinguished counsel, but how's anyone supposed to know whether it's Molly Farr or not?"

"I *am* Molly Farr, you black Irish—"

Hammett recognized her voice even as Epstein cut her off. "You hired me to do the talking." To the bench, he said, "This *is* Molly Farr, Your Honor."

"I continue to oppose restoration of bail," said Bender.

Epstein was on his feet to yell, "In all my years practicing law, this is the first time I've known the district attorney to oppose release of bail when the defendant has returned to surrender voluntarily. Why is he trying to crucify this unfortunate lady?"

"Your Honor—"

But Epstein now was in full tongue. He shot his cuffs, he danced like a welterweight on the Friday night card at the Winterland Rink on Steiner Street.

"I could stand on the steps of the Hall of Justice and throw a handful of buckshot, Your Honor, and hit so many houses of prostitution that the district attorney would be kept busy for a year. So why is he picking on Molly?"

"I object!" yelped Bender. "I object, I object, I obj—"

"Objection sustained." Kelly said to Epstein, "Counselor,

235

you are not giving your closing argument to a jury. I would like to get down to the matter before this court. How do you plead your client to the charges?"

"We plead guilty to one misdemeanor count of Contributing, and not guilty to two felony counts of Contributing."

The judge, shaken, looked from one attorney to the other. He said, "Misdemeanor?" He fixed on Bender. "Mr. District Attorney—"

"So stipulated, Your Honor." Bender was nearly inaudible.

"Counsel will approach the bench."

Hammett swallowed the laughter that bubbled up inside him. Epstein had muzzled the wolves snapping at his client's heels. Hammett owed him five bucks. With a single misdemeanor charge against her, Molly might get off with. . . .

Epstein's voice, still angry, rose. ". . . not acceptable to Your Honor, then I will plead my client innocent of all charges. It will not only cost this county a great deal of money, but certain people will be called upon to—"

"No!" cried Bender in alarm. "No, the misdemeanor charge is sufficient to establish. . . ."

His voice became inaudible. The attorneys retreated from the bench. Molly was called forward. Was she willing to waive her right to plead innocent? Was she willing to accept the sentence of the court to the single charge of misdemeanor Contributing? Epstein dug an elbow into her ribs.

"I am, Your Honor."

"Then the court must agree, Mr. Bender, with the defense contention that, although the defendant has pleaded guilty, she might very well have been acquitted of all charges in open court. Therefore, I find the defendant guilty of one count of misdemeanor Contributing, I assess defendant five hundred dollars, and I remand her to the women's section of County Jail Number Two in San Mateo County for one year; the latter portion of this punishment to be suspended upon condition that the fine is paid and that the defendant discontinue her present occupation." He leaned forward to regard Molly from behind his massive hardwood desk. "Have you any other means of employment in mind, young lady?"

"I do, Your Honor. I am going abroad as paid companion to a wealthy heiress."

"Counselor?"

"That is correct, Your Honor," said Epstein. "I have just finished representing the heiress in the matter of her estate, and she has expressed her eagerness to have Miss Farr accompany her in this capacity."

Judge Kelly slapped his gavel down. "Court is adjourned."

"All rise."

Hammett pushed past the spectator barrier as Kelly retired to his chambers.

"Congratulations, Molly."

"Hammett!"

Epstein watched sourly as the tall blonde, now freed of her triple veil, threw her arms around the lean detective and kissed him passionately on the mouth.

"I get her off, he gets kissed!"

"We were in love with each other one afternoon," said Molly.

Hammett handed the attorney a five-dollar bill. "Brass Mouth, you made the DA crumble up and blow away, just like you said you would. But I'm damned if I know how you did it."

"Because I understand Evelyn Brewster—also like I told you." He rammed a repeated forefinger into Hammett's spare gut for emphasis. "This morning at seven A.M., a crew of my process servers simultaneously delivered subpoenas to Mr. and Mrs. Dalton W. Brewster, Mr. and Mrs. Edmund N. Calloway, and Mr. and Mrs. C. Gerald Gordon, informing them that they, as well as their teenage sons, were to appear for the defense in the case of The People v. Molly Farr."

"Jesus Christ!" breathed Hammett as the beautiful implications sank in. "Everyone in town would know their kids had been the ones caught in Molly's cathouse—"

"Parlor house," said the ex-madam.

"No wonder Brady didn't show up in person. I'll bet he had a hell of a morning assuring all the ladies he'd let the whole case die this afternoon." His laughter was bitter. He could hear Evelyn Brewster's words again. *We are here from a*

moral commitment . . . no matter who is hurt or what hardships
fall upon their families. . . .

"So much for civic duty." Hammett chuckled.

Hammett stepped off the Sacramento cable and crossed
the intersection to the three-story brownstone corner apartment house, 1155 Leavenworth. In his mailbox was a single
envelope.

He trudged up to the third floor with deliberate slowness,
slipping a forefinger under the flap of Goodie's letter. It bore
a Crockett postmark and her parents' return address.

Goodie. He missed her. Missed her so much that he'd
finally moved out of 891 Post Street, trying to convince himself that he was doing it because too many policemen knew
where he lived and might try to take him out of the investigation.

He'd meant to get up to Crockett to see her, but he'd been
so damned busy. As for writing to her . . . well. . . .

He stopped, key hand outthrust in front of his door, as he
finished reading.

She was getting married in two months. Son of the fore-
man at the sugar refinery. She hoped that Hammett would
always feel she was his friend and she hoped that when she
and Fairfax were married, Hammett would come to visit with
them and. . . .

He opened the door with a flat brass key, went through the
foyer and into the living room.

A petite impeccably groomed woman rose from the chair
she had turned to the front window. She was superbly clad in
a City of Paris frock of beige satin with rich brown trim at the
hips, throat, and pockets; brown leather pumps with gun-
metal silk ornamentation; and in her left hand soft brown
leather gloves. On her breast glowed a deep-blue sapphire
brooch. Her hat was a Dobbs cloche of Army blue felt.

"Hello, Hammett," she said in a demure voice.

Only then, impaled by the huge dark eyes that dominated
the face, did he realize he was looking at Crystal Tam. The
transformation had been complete, from the inside out. She

238

was into another role. Superbly, of course. Probably because for her there were only roles.

"I'm sorry," he said, "for a moment I thought the manager had let a lady into the apartment."

Crystal laughed her tinkling laugh and sat down on the front edge of the chair, alert and erect as befit a smart young society matron.

"Do you really hate me so much? After all, I let you live, did I not? With nothing more than a small scare?" She giggled. "I realized it was important that you be alive to testify, if it ever became necessary, that little Crystal killed no one, no one at all."

"I could lie about what happened."

"But you would not." Her clear laughter rippled again. She stood up. "That is why I am invulnerable. You are the only man of absolute integrity I have ever met."

"Then we're even. You're the only woman of absolute evil I've ever—"

"We are back to that? Evil?" She shrugged. "Of course. Only the man to whom evil is a concern would see me in that way. Any other man. . . ."

She completed her sentence by arching the beautifully shaped body in its exquisite frock into a blatantly sexual pose. Hammett found himself physically stirred, as always, by her. Her knowing laughter taunted him.

"Poor Hammett! The frustrated manhunter. . . ."

He sat down on the edge of the bed and leaned back against the wall with his hands locked behind his head.

"Just about finished with the manhunting, Crystal."

"You will always be a manhunter."

"Nope."

She walked over to stand in front of him, legs slightly apart, hips thrust slightly forward, her hands on them. She put her head to one side while looking down at him solemnly. The eyes were huge in the delicately boned face.

"Then your integrity can sleep," she said softly.

"It doesn't work that way, sweetheart."

She spun away with a burst of her innocent, joyous laughter. She leaned back against the edge of the table, and her body arched again in its explicit **sexual** offering as if she were an exotic tropical bird creating a complicated mating ritual. "I can offer you sensual experiences, physical sensations, that you do not know exist. Possess **me** to know total fulfillment—"

"Like Daddy Lynch?"

"Daddy Lynch was pathetic."

"Most men are, with their pants down."

Her pose shifted and she was once more the young matron, matter-of-factly drawing on her gloves. Her eyes were flat and unreadable as they watched her busy fingers. "Did you really believe I was making a genuine offer?"

"I believe you were getting a hell of a kick out of whatever you were doing."

"I came to tell you about the final condition I imposed on Daddy Lynch."

And Hammett knew what it was, could hear again the scene in Judge Kelly's courtroom that afternoon.

"I'll be damned. *You're* the heiress. Lynch made you his legal heir!"

She was above time, beyond morality. Neither he nor anyone else would ever touch her, arouse in her normal human feeling. Nothing but death would reach her.

"The estate was just settled," he went on. "Rushed through by your attorney, Phineas Epstein, I'll bet."

"Molly told me he was the best," she said demurely.

"And now you're a wealthy young heiress, ready to travel. With a paid companion, of course, as is proper for young ladies traveling alone."

"Don't you find me irresistible?" she asked in a bubbly voice.

Hammett didn't say. "Does poor old Molly Farr know what she's letting herself in for?"

"I will tell her a story." She shrugged. "Molly is sentimental."

"Yeah. The whore with the heart of gold."

"Perhaps I will make her my lover," Crystal said thought-

240

fully. A cold finger touched Hammett's spine. "We will go to the East. The exotic East with its exotic perversions. You know what my wealth will buy me, Hammett? The knowledge that no one will ever again touch my body unless I want him to."

"Not until the embalmer gets you, anyway," he agreed. He glanced down to hook a cigarette from the pack in his pocket. "If they use embalmers in the exotic East. . . ."

He looked up. She was gone. He lit a cigarette and squinted through the smoke. The door stood open.

"Don't ever get her mad at you, Molly me darling," he muttered. To the empty room, he added, aloud, "I wonder what in Christ's name she's going to be like by the time she turns sixteen?"

Hammett realized he had never shut the door. As he did, someone knocked on it. He found a boy Crystal's age who hadn't yet outgrown his pimples and would never outgrow his freckles.

"Yeah?"

"I'm from the Crocker-Langley San Francisco Directory, sir. We're gathering statistics for the 1929 directory. Your landlady said you had recently moved in. . . ."

"Hammett. First name, Dashiell."

"How do you spell those, sir?"

"H-A-M-M-E-T-T. D-A-S-H-I-E-L-L."

The young census-taker, writing laboriously, left the second *l* off Dashiell, but Hammett didn't bother to correct him. He wouldn't be around San Francisco much longer. Write to his sister, Reba, suggest that they share an apartment in New York for a while. The ideas of somewhere else, and of family, seemed to appeal at the moment.

"And could I have your occupation, sir?"

"Writer." Then he added, *"W-R-I-T-E-R."*

He shut the door. He leaned against it for a moment, then burst out laughing and went back into the living room.

Writer. He'd snatched enough hours to finish the revision of *The Dain Curse* in the past couple of months, but *The Mal-*

tese Falcon would have to wait for final revision until after the investigation was completed. Maybe even until after he'd left San Francisco.

But meanwhile he thought he had an idea for a new book. A corrupt city, unnamed—hell, not San Francisco, he'd had a bellyful of this burg for a while, but—why not Baltimore? The Baltimore of his childhood? Corruption and politics and murder and friendship and love. Not a detective novel. Hell no. He'd had a bellyful of that, too.

A political hanger-on. There'd be a girl, of course. Not a Crystal, not an Oriental—he'd never be able to write Crystal. But still, a woman who would use other people just as she pleased. Bent on vengeance, for some reason he could work out. . . .

And in extracting her vengeance, use everybody. Except the hero. Nobody would be able to use . . . Ned? Sure. Ned. Base him physically on Fingers LeGrand. Maybe even his character a little bit, too.

But nobody could use him unless he wanted them to. Cynical, hard-drinking, always loyal, and never corruptible. . . .

Sure, the thought, beginning to pace the length of the living room from window to door and back again, sure. That was going to work. That was going to work just swell.

Author's Note

I. HAMMETT

In such novels as *The Maltese Falcon* and *The Glass Key*, Samuel Dashiell Hammett (1894–1961) elevated the hard-boiled detective story he found in the pulps from a minor form of popular entertainment into literature. How he did this puzzled as knowledgeable a critic as Howard Haycraft, and still seems to puzzle students of the detective novel today.

Which in turn puzzles me.

Because Hammett did not start out, like the other *Black Mask* contributors, as a writer learning about private detection. He was a private detective learning about writing. He had spent eight years as a field operative with the Pinkerton Detective Agency. Thus, as a writer, he retained his man-hunter's subconscious attitudes.

I wanted to write a novel about Hammett the detective because this experience *was* so seminal to his art. But it is not Hammett the detective who fascinates readers; it is Hammett the detective-turned-writer. My novel, therefore, had to probe the central tension existing between his two worlds.

Writing—even writing hard-boiled stories of mayhem and murder—demands insights and compassions (and allowed self-delusions) that are destructive to the manhunter. Begin seeing your antagonist as a fellow human sufferer, rather than the enemy, and you lose that hard edge that lets you survive emotionally—and in rare instances, physically—as an investigator.

Because 1928 seemed to offer excellent possibilities to

probe this essential tension fictionally, I chose it as the year in which to set my novel.

II. HAMMETT IN SAN FRANCISCO

A good year for Hammett, 1928. He was living in San Francisco; his personal life was stabilized; his health was relatively good; he was in essential control of his drinking; and for my purposes, his detective days were not impossibly far behind.

And an exciting year for Hammett the writer. *Red Harvest,* appearing in serial form in *Black Mask,* was due as an Alfred A. Knopf novel the following February. *The Dain Curse* was scheduled for *Black Mask* serialization, and was the subject of editorial discussion with Knopf concerning revision for book publication. *The Maltese Falcon* was already finished in rough (as forthcoming Hammett studies will confirm).

A secondary reason for choosing 1928 was sentimental. Hammett lived that year at 891 Post Street; and it is in this apartment house that he places Samuel Spade's apartment in *The Maltese Falcon.* Many addresses have been advanced as the one where Spade dwelled. But if one keeps in mind the fact that Hammett *did* live on Post at the corner of Hyde, and then approaches the novel's references to the apartment with a San Francisco map in hand, he will be driven to accept this location as the correct one.

I began work on the novel with the usual belief that little more will ever be known of Hammett's San Francisco years than is summarized in William F. Nolan's indispensable study, *Dashiell Hammett: A Casebook* (McNally & Loftin, 1969). Pinkerton's employment records of the era no longer exist; he seldom spoke of these years, not even to friends; the wife who shared some of them is dead, the daughters fathered during them were infants when the family disintegrated. The solitary San Francisco years were spent in drinking too much and writing all night, and those with whom he worked at Samuels' Jewelers have been scattered by time. Albert S. Samuels himself, to whom *The Dain Curse* was dedicated, is dead.

But I'm a detective myself, and I went after Hammett as a detective, not as a writer. I treated him as a man I'd been hired to track down, and used the manhunter's, not the scholar's, techniques and sources.

Starting points were three facts from Nolan: Hammett came to San Francisco early in 1921; he worked for the local Pinkerton office; he quit after finding stolen gold cached aboard a steamer from Australia.

Results of this preliminary investigation:

Five cases upon which he worked as a local Pinkerton op have been isolated. He probably resigned from the agency on Thursday, December 1, 1921. Shortly thereafter he went to work as a publicist for Samuels' Jewelers (on Market near Fifth at that time, not at the present location of Market near Powell). He and Josephine (*née* Dolan) were living at 620 Eddy Street until sometime in 1923, when she and their infant daughter left San Francisco for the first time.

Until their return, Hammett inhabited cheap rooming houses while trying to eke out a writer's existence. One of these was 20 Monroe Street—directly across Bush from the mouth of Burritt Street, the dead-end alley where Sam Spade's partner, Miles Archer, was to be gunned down a few years later.

By 1925 Hammett and the family were back together at 620 Eddy Street. He had begun selling his fiction regularly, but ad-writing for Samuels' was still necessary. By 1927 he and Josephine and their (now) two daughters had moved to a larger apartment at 1309 Hyde; but that same year saw their final schism.

We pick Hammett up in my novel in 1928, living alone at 891 Post and writing full-time. For the purposes of my story he leaves here for 1155 Leavenworth, his ultimate San Francisco address, at the end of that summer. This dating is fictional; he was living at 891 Post as late as March 30th of the following year (1929).

The above are hard facts.

Working detectives and working novelists seldom have the luxury of a scholar's certitude, but the following points have been established to *my* satisfaction:

Hammett was a heavy drinker and a chain smoker; he did not drive automobiles (was unlicensed in California); he felt no need of a telephone; he dressed well and at times flamboyantly, but always with the panache to carry it off; he gambled heavily, perhaps compulsively, on horses, cards, dice, prizefights, and probably women. He was a man of many acquaintances and (by choice) no friends. He was, however, witty and charming and gregarious. This pleasant surface masked the very private man.

For example: When I ran to earth (under another name and in another town) the Peggy O'Toole who served as partial inspiration for Bridget O'Shaughnessy, she did not know of her own partially masked appearance in *The Maltese Falcon* until I told her of it.

She has never read the book.

Finally, you will find in this novel a great many details about Hammett that, as a detective, I would include as raw, unverified data in an agency report. As a novelist, I leave to you the judgments as to whether any particular item is fact or fantasy. An example: A woman named Goodie had an apartment at 891 Post Street in 1928. But was this apartment next door to Hammett's? Was she a cute little blonde? Is she *my* Goodie? Have fun.

Serious Hammett scholars, by the way, may feel that I play games with my reconstruction of how the prizefight scene in Chapter IX ("A Black Knife") of *Red Harvest* came to be written. My explanation is fictional, of course, but the timing fits: the four *Red Harvest* novelettes appeared in *Black Mask* from November, 1927, through February, 1928, and Hammett would have had time before the first two weeks of November, 1928 (when he got the *Red Harvest* galley proofs from his publisher) to write and insert the boxing scene. *Red Harvest* was published by Alfred A. Knopf in book form on February 1, 1929.

It is a common literary device to illuminate a character's present by his past. Throughout, you will find Hammett recalling his youth and past life. Many of these facts appear here for the first time, so the question must inevitably arise: Are they indeed fact? Or invention?

Anything from Hammett's early life that is presented as hard fact *is* hard fact. Thus, Hammett's father did get sick when he was one year into high school, and so he quit Polytechnic Grammar School to work as a messenger boy for the B & O Railroad to help swell the family coffers. He did work at the Charles and Baltimore streets office. But it is invention that Hammett, cutting across the yard because he was late for work one morning (that he was often late is well established), stumbled over the body of a brakeman killed by a switching engine.

Facts: Hammett's father took the children to the Philadelphia city dump; there was a billy goat at the dump. But though *I* once knew a billy goat who would douse live cigarette butts in the bizarre fashion mentioned in the novel, I rather doubt that Hammett did.

Facts: A girl named Lillian Sheffer lived next door to the Hammett house at 212 North Stricker in Baltimore; she had a girlfriend named Irma Collison; Irma's little sister was about Hammett's age and a friend of his. But Hammett's mute childhood crush on Irma is my own invention.

Thus, the facts are indeed true; the way they are specifically related to my own story is often fictional.

Some of this material can be traced to Nolan's study, cited above.

But the vast majority of it is the result of remarkable original scholarship by Professor William Godshalk of the University of Cincinnati. He simply handed over to me all of his original Hammett research. This novel would not have its present depth of background without Professor Godshalk's stunning generosity. He has in progress (to be published by

Twayne Press) a critical biography of Hammett that should prove to be *the* major academic source for years to come.

IV. SAN FRANCISCO

How do you go about re-creating a city as it existed several years before you were born? Since I am a writer, not a scholar, my method was to set up criteria and work within their bounds. Because of the 1906 earthquake and fire that razed the city, San Francisco has a disproportionate number of her "old" buildings (erected during her rebirth rather than during her original nascency) still standing and in good repair. Thus I was able to set almost all of the novel's action in places that existed in 1928 and exist today.

I spent many hours with newspapers, magazines, and books in conventional research of the era and the city. The picture of the white slavery traffic and of whorehouse life in Capone's Chicago, to cite two examples among many, are reflections of this sort of research. Nuances of everyday language often came from my mother's (once my Uncle Russ') treasured and tattered collection of *Captain Billy's Whiz-Bangs*. Such parts of the San Francisco *mise-en-scène* as the Prescott Court speakeasy, Coffee Dan's, Yee Chum's (today Yee Jun's, best greasy spoon in Chinatown), the fan-tan parlor, the nameless Italian café, the use of White Top cabs almost exclusively by those outside the law—these, as well as many other backdrops, came from written or verbal reminiscences.

In all of this, my main concerns were to create a believable Hammett and a believable city.

One of the facts of San Francisco life since the pre-World War I days of Abe "The Boodling Boss" Reuf has been a high degree of skillfully localized political corruption. It was true in the twenties; it is true today. *The Maltese Falcon* gives a flawless picture of it. So I decided to build my plot around that curious child of the twenties' weak law enforcement, the reform committee.

To this I grafted elements of that marvelous San Francisco brouhaha stirred up in the late thirties when a newspaper-pressured DA hired Los Angeles private eye Edwin Atherton to investigate graft and corruption in the police department, *and Atherton did!* Horror! Consternation!

Connoisseurs of that vintage San Francisco will doubtless identify the real-life counterparts (moved back a decade in time) of Victor Atkinson, Brass Mouth Epstein, Molly Farr, Dr. Gardner Shuman, and Griffith and Boyd Mulligan.

The rest of the officials and politicos and cops and assorted good guys and bad hats who are based on real people are right out of the city's Roaring Twenties. Lovers of *that* era might feel a twinge of nostalgia at Brendan Brian McKenna, Owen Lynch, Dan Laverty, George E. Biltmore, his wife May and Chauffeur Harry and little white dog Bingo, and many others. You will look in vain for models for Crystal Tam and Heloise Kuhn. They are only mine. Sergeant Jack Manion of the Chinatown Squad appears under his own name. And District Attorney Matthew Brady, although he never appears in person, permeates the novel just as he permeated San Francisco life of the twenties. (For a brilliant, thinly veiled portrait—as "District Attorney Bryan"—see Chapter XV, "Every Crackpot" of *The Maltese Falcon.*)

Finally is Jimmy Wright. Anyone who doesn't know the person upon whom *he* is based has a lot of reading to do before he can claim familiarity with the work of the remarkable man and remarkable writer whose enigmas sparked my need to write this novel.

V. Acknowledgments

On a book such as this, a great many people must be conned by the writer's enthusiasm into doing much of his work for him. If I have forgotten anyone, please—*mea culpa.*

My agent, Henry Morrison, who started the whole thing during a San Francisco visit with the innocent remark, "I wonder what would happen if somebody wrote a detective novel using Dashiell Hammett as the protagonist. . . ."

My dear friend and peerless editor, Jeanne Bernkopf, who pointed the way when I faltered, walked beside me to the end, and taught me a great deal about the craft of the novel in the process.

Bill Godshalk, whose massive contributions are detailed elsewhere.

Clyde C. Taylor, my editor at Putnam's, who labored far above the dictates of mere duty on behalf of the book.

Gladys Hansen, without whom the San Francisco Public Library's Special Collections would crumble to dust, who always seemed willing to suffer this fool gladly as he stumbled through her demesne.

Dave Belch, the library's publicist, who harried the original Atherton Report the length and breadth of the state's library system for me.

Dori and Richard Gould, co-founders of Comstock Books, who opened their stockroom to me and whose enthusiasm, delight, and excitement with the project never failed to amaze me. Dori also gave unstintingly of her precious time to offer detailed editorial comment most valuable to me. A very special lady.

My editor at Random House, Lee Wright, who opened closed doors (and files) for me, even though her house was not doing the book. The height of professionalism in a great editor, the height of friendship in a grand lady.

My brother, Rog, who found two absolutely indispensable source books for me: the 1927 Sears catalogue and the 1929 World Almanac.

As always, Dean and Shirley Dickensheet with their scholars' wisdom, their friends' enthusiasm, and their collectors' library.

My mom and dad, who were young and in love in the twenties and who enriched my life immeasurably over the years with their memories of that era.

Herb Caen, because he understands San Francisco so well, and has written so often and so evocatively of what Hammett should mean to all of us who love this city.

Bill Targ, who furnished eleventh-hour Hammett information nowhere else available.

Finally, for their investment of time, worry, substance, and scholarship: Bill Blackbeard, founder of the San Francisco Academy of Comic Art; Bill Clark, world's leading authority on *Black Mask;* Brooke Whiting, Curator of Rare Books for the UCLA Library; C. M. Ingham of Pacific Telephone; John H. Brooke (formerly) of Yellow Cab; Albert S. Samuels, Sr. (deceased) and his son, Albert S. Samuels, Jr; and fellow writers Jack Leavitt, Art Kaye, Curt Gentry, William F. Nolan, and Bill Pronzini (who lent me his name and his bootlegging great-uncle).

And of course, Susan, who persevered through the years when my writer's income would seldom buy the groceries, and who gave those years so much of their point and meaning.

San Francisco   JOE GORES
October 1974

THE PERENNIAL LIBRARY MYSTERY SERIES

Delano Ames

FOR OLD CRIME'S SAKE (*available 12/82*)	P 629, $2.84
MURDER, MAESTRO, PLEASE (*available 12/82*)	P 630, $2.84

E. C. Bentley

TRENT'S LAST CASE	P 440, $2.50
TRENT'S OWN CASE	P 516, $2.25

Gavin Black

A DRAGON FOR CHRISTMAS	P 473, $1.95
THE EYES AROUND ME	P 485, $1.95
YOU WANT TO DIE, JOHNNY?	P 472, $1.95

Nicholas Blake

THE CORPSE IN THE SNOWMAN	P 427, $1.95
THE DREADFUL HOLLOW	P 493, $1.95
END OF CHAPTER	P 397, $1.95
HEAD OF A TRAVELER	P 398, $2.25
MINUTE FOR MURDER	P 419, $1.95
THE MORNING AFTER DEATH	P 520, $1.95
A PENKNIFE IN MY HEART	P 521, $2.25
THE PRIVATE WOUND	P 531, $2.25
A QUESTION OF PROOF	P 494, $1.95
THE SAD VARIETY	P 495, $2.25
THERE'S TROUBLE BREWING	P 569, $3.37
THOU SHELL OF DEATH	P 428, $1.95
THE WIDOW'S CRUISE	P 399, $2.25
THE WORM OF DEATH	P 400, $2.25

Andrew Garve

THE ASHES OF LODA	P 430, $1.50
THE CUCKOO LINE AFFAIR	P 451, $1.95
A HERO FOR LEANDA	P 429, $1.50
MURDER THROUGH THE LOOKING GLASS	P 449, $1.95
NO TEARS FOR HILDA	P 441, $1.95
THE RIDDLE OF SAMSON	P 450, $1.95

Michael Gilbert

BLOOD AND JUDGMENT	P 446, $1.95
THE BODY OF A GIRL	P 459, $1.95
THE DANGER WITHIN	P 448, $1.95
FEAR TO TREAD	P 458, $1.95

Joe Gores

HAMMETT	P 631, $2.84

C. W. Grafton

BEYOND A REASONABLE DOUBT	P 519, $1.95

Edward Grierson

THE SECOND MAN	P 528, $2.25

Cyril Hare

DEATH IS NO SPORTSMAN	P 555, $2.40
DEATH WALKS THE WOODS	P 556, $2.40
AN ENGLISH MURDER	P 455, $2.50
TENANT FOR DEATH	P 570, $2.84
TRAGEDY AT LAW	P 522, $2.25
UNTIMELY DEATH	P 514, $2.25
THE WIND BLOWS DEATH	P 589, $2.84
WITH A BARE BODKIN	P 523, $2.25

Mary Kelly

THE SPOILT KILL   P 565, $2.40

Lange Lewis

THE BIRTHDAY MURDER   P 518, $1.95

Allan MacKinnon

HOUSE OF DARKNESS   P 582, $2.84

Arthur Maling

LUCKY DEVIL   P 482, $1.95

RIPOFF   P 483, $1.95

SCHROEDER'S GAME   P 484, $1.95

Austin Ripley

MINUTE MYSTERIES   P 387, $2.50

Thomas Sterling

THE EVIL OF THE DAY   P 529, $2.50

Julian Symons

THE BELTING INHERITANCE   P 468, $1.95

BLAND BEGINNING   P 469, $1.95

BOGUE'S FORTUNE   P 481, $1.95

THE BROKEN PENNY   P 480, $1.95

THE COLOR OF MURDER   P 461, $1.95

Dorothy Stockbridge Tillet
(John Stephen Strange)

THE MAN WHO KILLED FORTESCUE P 536, $2.25

If you enjoyed this book you'll want to know about
THE PERENNIAL LIBRARY MYSTERY SERIES

Buy them at your local bookstore or use this coupon for ordering:

Qty	P number	Price
_____	_____	_____
_____	_____	_____
_____	_____	_____
_____	_____	_____
_____	_____	_____
_____	_____	_____
_____	_____	_____
_____	_____	_____
_____	_____	_____
_____	_____	_____
_____	_____	_____
_____	_____	_____
_____	_____	_____
_____	_____	_____

postage and handling charge $1.00
_____ book(s) @ $0.25   _____

TOTAL [   ]

Prices contained in this coupon are Harper & Row invoice prices only.
They are subject to change without notice, and in no way reflect the prices at
which these books may be sold by other suppliers.

**HARPER & ROW, Mail Order Dept. #PMS, 10 East 53rd St., New
York, N.Y. 10022.**
Please send me the books I have checked above. I am enclosing $_____
which includes a postage and handling charge of $1.00 for the first book and
25¢ for each additional book. Send check or money order. No cash or
C.O.D.s please

Name_____

Address_____

City_____ State_____ Zip_____

Please allow 4 weeks for delivery. USA only. This offer expires 8/31/83
Please add applicable sales tax.